SUSPECTS

A NORTHWEST MURDER MYSTERY

D1533030

TED HAYNES

This is a work of fiction. Names, characters, and events are either fictitious or are used fictitiously. Upriver Ranch is an imaginary community that incorporates features of Crosswater, Vandevert Ranch, and Sunriver.

LCCN 2016960860
ISBN 978-0-9646506-4-0

Book Design by Mayfly Design
Cover photo by Margaret Buchanan

The Robleda Company, Publishers
1259 El Camino Real, Ste. 2720
Menlo Park, CA 94025
www.robledabooks.com

Available to bookstores through Ingram.

Let us forget with generosity those who cannot love us

PABLO NERUDA

Contents

CHAPTER 1

Running Into Trouble

(Dan)

On the morning Ken Winterpol was assaulted I was thinking about his wife. I had some advice to give her. Not legal advice, personal advice. Candy Winterpol was thirty-one to my twenty-eight. She had seen more of the ups and downs of life than I had. But Candy was an artist, not always practical, and I thought I could help her see her own best interest. What I should have been thinking about, and did finally concentrate on, was running. Head up, chest out, breathe easy, and land evenly on each foot.

It was frigid early morning in June. I could see my breath. On the eastern flank of the Cascade Mountains there is frost at least one time every month of the year. There had been a hard frost that night. But I was out running anyway and at least one soul, even hardier than I, was out kayaking somewhere on the Deschutes River. I saw their gray pickup parked at the launch site by the bridge. Probably training for a kayak race. My own training was for an off-road triathlon in early September—swimming, bicycling, and running. No kayaking.

My training run finished at the entrance to Upriver Ranch, the resort community where the Winterpols had a home down the road from where my parents now lived. I jogged past still-sleeping houses to the Winterpol driveway, back to thinking about Candy and what I had to tell her. The stone walkway around to the back of the house, where I planned to knock on the kitchen door, was still slick from frost. On the back deck that faced the golf course off the kitchen I saw a man, face down. In shorts and t-shirt no less. Brown hair, a big frame, and more than thirty pounds overweight. It was Ken Winterpol, I thought, and he's had a heart attack.

I approached the man slowly, trying to remember what little first-aid training I'd had years ago. The door from the deck into the kitchen was open and I shouted into the house.

"Candy, come quickly. Ken's had a heart attack."

It took a minute but Candy, tall and lean in a white bathrobe came to the doorway. "What happened?" she said, seeming more puzzled than worried.

"I don't know," I said. "I just got here and saw him. We've got to call 911."

"Get him inside," said Candy. "It's cold out there."

Rolling him gently onto his back, I put my arms under his armpits, and lifted the top half of his body. "Can you pick up his feet?" I asked. Candy surveyed the outdoors and came out on the porch to lift Ken's legs. We barely got his butt over the doorsill as we shuffled him in. I instinctively wanted to sit him down, like a witness in court, and ask him what happened. I dragged him over to the kitchen table, slid a chair out with my foot and settled him.

Candy bent over him, and looked in his eyes. "Ken," she said, "where does it hurt?" He mumbled to her, attempted to rise, and fell forward into her and onto the floor. There was red on Candy's robe now and, when I looked closely, Ken's brown hair was matted with blood. There was blood on the front of my sweatshirt too, from when I had picked him up.

I knelt beside him on the tile floor, pressing two fingers into his fat neck beside his windpipe. He didn't react to my finger pressure but the pulse was there and fast, as though he were pedaling a bicycle in a race. I stood up, spotted a phone on a wall, and stepped over to it. I told the 911 dispatcher who I was and where I was and that Ken Winterpol had collapsed, possibly from a heart attack, and had apparently hit his head. We needed help.

"No, he doesn't appear to be conscious," I told the dispatcher. "Yes, he's breathing. ... I don't know how he was injured. Maybe he slipped. It's icy here. Or maybe a stroke. Maybe a heart attack but

2

his pulse is steady, maybe a hundred and ten beats per minute.... Candy Winterpol, Mr. Winterpol's wife. And me. That's it. How soon will you be here? ... Okay, I'll wait out front. Just get here quickly. ... Well, I can't wait out front and stay on the phone at the same time. If you call this number Mrs. Winterpol will answer it. ... Goodbye."

Candy pulled out another kitchen chair and sat on it, staring off into space. I knew she was dazed but I didn't know what to do for her any more than I knew what to do for Ken.

"Have you got a blanket?" I asked. She wasn't listening. "Candy!" I said, louder, "Can you get a blanket to keep him warm?" She awoke and hustled out of the kitchen, returning quickly with a heavy green throw rug. I put it over him and pushed the sides in close to his body. He didn't feel cold. I didn't think he could have been outside very long.

When I heard the siren I went out to the street and waved the ambulance down. I led the two EMTs through the front door, through the living room, and into the kitchen. Candy sat in her kitchen chair and I stood by the refrigerator, trying to stay out of the way. The medics checked his airway and put an oxygen mask over his nose and mouth. They were talking to Ken but they weren't getting any answers.

"How did he hurt his head?" asked the shorter of the two.

"I don't know," I said. "I found him lying on the deck. He might have fallen. Is he having a heart attack? Or a stroke or something?"

"Trauma," said the man. The other man put a needle in Ken's arm and started a drip from a pouch that he held up in the air.

"Is he going to live?" asked Candy.

"Can't say," said the short man. "Probably, if we get him to the hospital right away. I'm going to get the stretcher." As he went out through the living room I heard him say, "Hello Carl," to someone coming the other way. A stocky man with blondish hair walked into the kitchen with a serious look on his face. He wore a light zippered jacket with a logo on it. He was in his early fifties, about the same age as Ken.

"Hello," he said, looking at each of us in turn. "I'm Detective Carl Breuninger with the Deschutes County Sheriff's Department."

Then, with a note of sympathy in his voice, "How is the injured man?"

"He can't talk," said Candy.

"Head trauma," said the remaining EMT. "He's unconscious but he's breathing."

"And how was he injured?" asked the detective with apparent concern, looking at Candy, as though someone getting hurt was a rare event for him and his worry for Ken was spontaneous and sincere.

"I don't know," said Candy. "Please just help him."

"Are you his wife?"

"Yes," she said.

The detective turned to me, with a bit more authority and a little less sympathy. "And you are...?"

"Dan Martinez, friend of the Winterpols and a neighbor," I said.

"And the man who was injured is?"

"Ken Winterpol," I said. "He and his wife, Candy Winterpol"— and here I nodded toward Candy—"are the owners of the house."

Breuninger focused on Candy, standing in front of her so she couldn't see me. "Can you help me understand what happened here? Were you with him when Mr. Winterpol was injured?"

Candy looked at the floor. "No," she said weakly.

"What can you tell me about how this happened?" he asked. As he waited for Candy to answer a thought that had been idling in the back of my brain suddenly revved up its engine. Why had the sheriff's department responded to a 911 call that was only a plea for medical help? What did Detective Breuninger know that I didn't know? And beyond that, what if Ken hadn't fallen? What if someone had hit him? Tried to kill him? And what if Ken died from this? And how did it look to Breuninger—Candy and I, the only people around when he arrived, with blood on our clothes. For that matter, had Candy had an argument with Ken and hit him? Unlikely, but a possibility.

"Mrs. Winterpol wishes to invoke her right to remain silent," I said. "And I invoke mine as well."

"Oh there's no need for any of that," said Breuninger in a

friendly and reassuring tone. "We're all trying to understand just what happened." The "we" seemed to encompass the EMTs, Candy, and myself. And, surely, the man's logic had its appeal. I too was trying very hard to understand what happened.

"Nonetheless," I said, "Until we know what's going on we invoke our right to remain silent."

"Are you a lawyer?" asked Breuninger, sounding impatient.

"Yes, I am," I said, "business, not criminal. Mrs. Winterpol and I also invoke our right to counsel and we'll find criminal attorneys to represent us if necessary."

"Look," said Breuninger, "as far as we know this isn't a criminal matter. The man fell and hurt himself. We've got a lot of work to do. Let's not make this any harder than it is. We don't have to go all Perry Mason."

"You're absolutely right," I said in an agreeable tone. We were both officers of the law after all. "But it's possible someone attacked Mr. Winterpol and Mrs. Winterpol needs to protect herself. So do I, since I am here. We are not answering any more questions. And Mrs. Winterpol doesn't give you permission to search the house."

"This is crazy," said Breuninger. "Who said anything about searching the house?"

"Or the cars in the garage," I said. I was flailing, trying to draw on what I remembered from law school and what I had seen on TV. Still I wanted to slow Breuninger down until I got a criminal attorney on our team.

Candy was sitting in the kitchen chair, shaking slightly, and looking past us into the backyard. "I think you both need to look outside," she whispered.

We turned around to see a deputy holding something up above the fountain on the far side of the lawn. The fountain was set in an artificial hill and was meant to look like a stream splashing down a mountainside. The deputy lifted the object higher and said something to someone else out of sight. What he was holding looked to me like a fireplace poker, presumably from the outdoor fireplace on the back deck.

The wheels were turning in Breuninger's head and in mine.

Finding a possible weapon in such an odd place made it more likely that Ken was, indeed, attacked. And it strengthened my resolve that Candy and I needed all the legal protection we could get.

Breuninger looked at me. "Have you considered that Mrs. Winterpol herself may be in danger? If someone attacked her husband they may still want to harm her."

"My husband has enemies," Candy said. "I do not." I held up a finger in front of my mouth to remind her about staying silent.

The EMTs rolled Ken onto the stretcher, strapped him in, raised the stretcher up onto its legs, and wheeled Ken out the door. That was the last we saw of him.

"Can I give you a ride to the hospital, Candy?" I asked.

"I'll be in worse shape than Ken if I have to sit around a hospital," said Candy. "Have them call me when he wakes up. Then I'll go."

"Then I'd advise you to come to the sheriff's office, Mrs. Winterpol," said Breuninger, "for your own protection. Furthermore, you're a material witness. You need to stay where I can reach you. You can't leave town or disappear."

"Right now," I said, "Mrs. Winterpol is going to stay at my parents' house for a while. If you have paper and a pen I'll give you the phone number and the address, five houses away." Breuninger pulled a small pad of paper out of his jacket pocket and handed it to me. "I am writing my Oregon State Bar number here as well," I said. "For the time being I am Mrs. Winterpol's attorney. We'll find her a defense attorney today, if possible, and then we'll be in touch."

Breuninger took the pad back and looked at it. He didn't like any of this.

"You agree to keep track of her and produce her if we need to talk with her?"

"Yes," I said. I was willing to bet that Candy would stay put.

"And she won't leave the area?"

"Right." I didn't know the boundaries of this commitment but the criminal attorney, once we had one, could tell me.

"I need to put some clothes on and get a few things," said Candy.

"Deputy Newton will go with you." He nodded to a female officer who'd arrived after Breuninger.

6

"Come ahead," said Candy. I wished she hadn't said that. If Deputy Newton saw anything suspicious then all bets were off on searching the house.

"This is not permission to search," I said. "The deputy needs to keep her eyes on the business at hand."

"She will," said Breuninger and he nodded at Deputy Newton. The two women went upstairs and left Breuninger and me standing in the living room, cautious of saying anything to each other. Part of my caution, I realized, was that I still couldn't figure out why the detective was there in the first place. I thought there must be something about the Winterpol household that caught the detective's interest.

"Was Ken Winterpol up to something shady?" I asked. "Is that why you're here? I mean, up until the poker in the fountain, this looked more like an accident than a crime."

Breuninger didn't answer me. He gazed out the picture window at the fake stream on the far side of the lawn as though musing to himself. "An attractive woman like Mrs. Winterpol," he said, "married to an older man, you have to wonder if she might have a young buck somewhere." He was deflecting my question by steering our conversation in a direction I didn't want to go.

"That comment is unnecessary," I said. "You have no reason to think she is anything but a model wife. She's got a good life with Mr. Winterpol. Or she had a good life until this morning. Why on earth would she risk it?"

"You may be right," said Breuninger, "yet people always surprise me."

Another deputy whispered in his ear and then Breuninger turned back to me.

"There's press outside. Do you want a ride to your house?"

"Yes, thank you," I said. That was pretty decent of him, I thought.

"We'll lock up the house," said Breuninger. "Make sure Mrs. Winterpol takes a key with her. I'll call you when we're done here."

When Candy came down, she and I went out through the garage and got in the back seat of an unmarked car. There was no screen between us and the front seat. Deputy Newton drove us to my parents' house.

CHAPTER 2

The Color Red

(Candy)

Now that Ken is dead, I will sell the house in Lake Oswego and keep the one at Upriver Ranch. We designed the Upriver house together and had it built in this newish community fifteen miles south of Bend, the city where I grew up. My painting studio, on the second floor, faces north into a forest of pine trees. Deer and elk wander past the window. To my left I can see Mount Bachelor, the mountain where I learned to ski.

Ken and I both got what we wanted when we married. He got a beautiful younger woman whose paintings appealed to the classier people in Portland. Encouraging this girl from the sticks made the rich and well-connected people feel virtuous. Ken was from Burns, even further out in the wilderness than Bend, and he made his money buying and selling real estate. He was too aggressive to suit my patrons but they had to invite him to their parties if they wanted me to come. He was smart and he would have been accepted eventually if he had lived long enough.

I love the colors in Upriver. The pines are green. The mountains are black and brown, capped with snow most of the year. The little river that runs by the house is dark green with silver ripples. The mounds of willows by the water are light green in the summer, orange and brown in the fall. The aspen trees turn bright yellow in October. Most days the sky is brilliant blue.

We need more red. There isn't enough. The sunrises and sunsets are spectacular but you can't paint them. They have been painted and photographed to death. And part of their appeal is they don't last. The colors change as you watch them. In the early morning, before the sun breaks the horizon, I like to believe the only eyes in the world looking at the clouds lit up from beneath, the only eyes that will ever see this particular instant of this particular sunrise, are mine.

Where there is red is in the bark of old ponderosas. For its first hundred years, a ponderosa's trunk is brown and gray like most trees. Then the red appears in vertical bands, each band offset from the others. Later the stripes expand into plates that are wider in the middle than at the top and the bottom. I made my art recognizable by painting those tree trunks, making the plates more and more abstract, more diamond shaped, like the back of a snake or jewels encrusting a bracelet. I varied the reds and even wandered away from them. The painting that fetched the highest price in my early days was a ponderosa with blue bark and high branches that looked like clouds. Then I began to combine natural landscapes with abstract patterns, diamonds and squares mostly, that blended together so it was hard to say where the natural world ended and the abstract world began.

I want to sell Ken's company as soon as possible. I don't want to sit on the board. I don't want to hear about the company's problems. The lawyers say they can't tell me what the company is worth. Dan Martinez, the boy I've known from childhood, whom the law firm is paying to help with Ken's will, says it could take a year or more to sort everything out. Ken never told anyone what he was doing and Dan says the books are "a tangled web."

Actually the law firm, Oxton, Rath, and Flynn, is paying Dan to hold my hand. I know that. Dan's not reading papers trying to sift through Ken's estate. He's just handling me. The firm is in Portland, not Bend, and I've talked only to the lady who is managing Ken's estate by phone. I don't get along with lawyers, though I do like Dan, and I know lawyers view me as difficult. Dan is a good buffer. The lawyers can't tell me what to do, he says, though it often seems that's exactly what they are doing.

Dan was behind me in high school, so he is twenty-eight now. We had little in common back then but I took painting lessons from his father. I owe my life to Mr. Martinez. He never said I had talent.

He only complimented me on the work I actually produced—the way I mastered some technique, or chose a good combination of colors, or showed some object in a perfect light. We'd paint side by side in the studio at his house. I think he was mostly doodling because he would apply paint to his own canvas to show me something. It took me a while to realize he was ruining whatever he might have been working on just to illustrate something for me. Sometimes he would wipe off what he'd shown me and sometimes he would try to integrate it into his painting. But I always got the message that I was his priority. That was not a message I got at home. My parents had their own problems. I won't go into that. I'm done with them and I live my own life.

My parents paid Mr. Martinez five dollars for each ninety-minute lesson, an amount I didn't realize for a long time was ridiculously low. I went on Tuesday and Thursday afternoons and sometimes on Saturdays. The girls at school teased me that I was in love with Mr. Martinez. In a way, I was. But I didn't like how demanding he was.

Men's eyes follow me all the time. But Mr. Martinez never departed from his role as my teacher. Art was my refuge from not fitting in at school and my problems at home. When I reached puberty my father started to come after me. Lucky for me he was timid. Somehow Mr. Martinez got me to confess, vaguely, what was wrong. He said I should tell my father to stay away from me or I would tell my mother. And that if that didn't work, I should tell my father I would go to the police. I was a kid and I couldn't imagine going to the police. They would always believe my father instead of me. Mr. Martinez told me to say it to my father anyway and my father left me alone after that, at least he didn't touch me. I thought if the threat of telling the police didn't work I would tell Dad I would murder him in his bed when he was sleeping. And I fantasized about doing it. I told myself kids could get away with things like that because people would feel sorry for them. I haven't seen my father since I got out of art school.

I was disappointed that Mr. Martinez wasn't home when the deputy dropped Dan and me off at the Martinez house. But Mrs.

Martinez was there. Like everyone else, I loved Mrs. Martinez. She was shorter than I was and rounder. Her parents, Norwegians named Pedersen, had come to Bend from Minnesota to work for the big lumber companies in the 1930s. Mrs. Martinez started working as a bank teller in her twenties and by the time she retired she headed up all three branches in Bend. Every company and charity wanted her to be on a board or a committee. She was friendly but steady, without a drop of drama. She made me feel welcome every time I came for my lessons with her husband. Better than being kind, she made me think I had a rightful place in her house, that I belonged there. Much as I appreciated her, I would never be like her.

I had been to the Martinez house in Bend many times but this was my first time inside the house in Upriver. Though I exchanged hellos with Mr. and Mrs. Martinez when I saw them around Upriver—I called them Leon and Elizabeth now—we didn't get together. They were living the life of a retired couple and I was either buried in my studio at home or off to Portland.

The exterior of the Martinez house was Pacific Northwest architecture, rustic on a large scale, but the interior was almost European, all plaster walls and bold use of color. That was Leon's touch. I recognized some of the paintings on the walls from the house in Bend.

Leon and Elizabeth had moved from Bend to Upriver for privacy as much as for the open space. They knew so many people in Bend—Leon's former students and Elizabeth's customers at the bank—that they couldn't go shopping or anywhere in town without someone stopping them for fifteen minutes. Also, Elizabeth liked to play golf and she could always find a game at Upriver.

Ken had wanted to play golf too and he worked hard at it. I played with him sometimes but I didn't really enjoy it and the only part I was good at was lining up putts. My artist's eyes could read the greens and see how the ball was going to roll. It came to me as a natural talent and Ken was envious. He just couldn't see it. What he really wanted was to become a member of Waverly Country Club in Portland. He said it would take him years to befriend the right people. But some of those people bought my art and I was part of Ken's plan.

Ken and I met at the opening of my first show. He was heavyset with a square face. His eyes had a dangerous, almost animal, look to them—brown flecked with bits of gold. The suit he wore that night was expensive but the tie didn't go with it. Ken had come to the gallery to buy a painting to hang in the lobby of one of his buildings. He brought a tape measure that he pulled out of his pocket from time to time and held up to some of my larger pieces.

At an art show everyone looks at everyone else, who they are with, and what they are wearing. They talk to each other about where they went on their latest trip or what their friends have been up to. Why not? The drinks and hors d'oeuvres are free. It's a party. Everyone there is either cool or rich or both. The guests talk to the featured artist only briefly or not at all. The gallery owner, or someone the owner appoints, has to stand by the artist all night and make whatever conversation they can so the artist doesn't get depressed. No one looks at the paintings. They don't really know what to say about them. They are afraid of offending the artist or the gallery owner or looking stupid in front of their friends. Some of the people, hopefully, will come back later and have a real look, maybe buy something. The whole point of the opening, really, is name recognition and the press release. After the show is announced in the newspaper, when people run across the name of the gallery or the artist they will say, "Oh, I recognize that name. I've heard of that."

Anyhow, when Ken saw that this attractive girl was the artist he came over to tell me what he needed for his lobby. He sounded like a man going to a hardware store and telling the clerk what kind of bracket he wanted. I asked what colors the walls, the floor, and the furniture were. He couldn't remember. I was so anxious to get a sale I volunteered to go to his building and tell him which painting I thought would be best. At least that got him to put away his measuring tape. I met him at his building and recommended a big horizontal of a blue/green lake with increasingly geometric ripples. After he bought it he asked me out to dinner once or twice a week. A month later he asked me to marry him and I said yes. We hired the architect for the house in Upriver before we even had the ceremony.

Ken took a chance on me but I was a good bet. My art was selling to the top of Portland society. The gallery said they hadn't had a show that successful in five years. People were flying in from Seattle and San Francisco to see it. I was invited to rich people's houses all over town. I brought my fiancé, who soon became my husband. I showed him how to dress but he already knew how to talk better than I did. All I had to do was look pretty and act like the mysterious artist.

Of course there was sex. I didn't mind. Ken liked control. But the way to control me was to please me. He was intelligent about it. I could overcome his fleshy body twenty years older than mine. And I could excite him. We went to a big party at someone's house and I gave him a blow job in the powder room. He loved it. Sex beat washing clothes and cleaning house. We hired people for that.

I wanted to ski all winter and I persuaded Ken to take it up. You had to have money to ski and that weeded out a lot of people Ken didn't want to bother with. He was great at talking about skiing at parties—the latest in skis and boots, who the best instructors were, and what the pros and cons were of all the best ski areas in the West which, of course, we had to visit. And he loved meeting important people on the chair lifts where there was nothing to do but talk to the stranger next to you. He wore the most fashionable ski clothes, selected by me, both on and off the slopes. And he learned to ski well enough to sometimes follow me down a black diamond. But a day was wasted if all the people he met were young ski bums with no money and shabby clothes who could ski circles around him. Ken always bulled his way down the slopes. I had been a graceful skier since I was a child. My long, lean body made skiing look easy. We were a mismatched pair.

After skiing we would sit around the lodge and see who was worth talking to. He didn't mind when people thought I was his daughter. They were embarrassed when I said I was his wife and it flattered him to have power and money to attract a woman like me.

Anyway, Elizabeth Martinez asked me if I'd had breakfast and I said no. She sat me down in the kitchen, blue and white and more Scandinavian than the rest of the house, and brought me coffee and whole wheat toast with jam. I don't usually eat breakfast but I had half a piece of toast to please Elizabeth.

Dan told me not to say anything about Ken or the sheriff and told his mother not to ask. Then he left us to get on the phone and find an attorney for me. Elizabeth and I could see the humor in Dan's telling us very seriously what we could and could not talk about. We both remembered him as a small boy.

"So," Elizabeth asked me, "how's the painting going?" But we didn't talk about my painting. Elizabeth talked about how happy she and Leon were to be retired and how happy they were to have Dan staying with them. Elizabeth said she was worried when his law firm laid Dan off. They liked him very much, she said, but they lost a big client and had to lay a lot of the associates off. He decided to take the time to train for a triathlon, an off-road triathlon, something he always wanted to do. Maybe Oxton, Rath and whatever would hire him back or he'd find another law firm to work for. But Elizabeth was sure Dan would find some work he liked to do. "When he meets a girl he wants to marry he'll decide he wants to make some money."

"Do you think I need a lawyer?" I asked Elizabeth. "I didn't hurt Ken and I don't see how anyone could think that I did. Getting a lawyer seems like making a fuss out of something that will never happen. And having a lawyer just makes me look guilty."

"Better safe than sorry," said Elizabeth. "We shouldn't talk about what happened. But I can tell you something from my experience with the law at the bank. The way everything looks right now is not the way it is going to look a month from now. You don't know what the sheriff and the district attorney are going to think. You need to be careful."

"We're in luck," said Dan when he came back into the kitchen. "My old law firm in Portland knows a criminal attorney in Bend they have a lot of faith in. His name is Tod Morgan and he'll be here in about forty minutes.

"In the meantime, I need to talk with you about some things," said Dan. "Is that all right?" We walked into the living room and Elizabeth disappeared upstairs.

"Can I look out the window while we're talking?" I asked. I sat in the big chair facing out over the lawn, over a stretch of wild grass that became the rough for the golf course, and beyond the golf course Mount Bachelor with snow still covering the top.

"I don't think the sheriff believes you tried to kill Ken," said Dan. "But he will be under pressure to make an arrest and the district attorney will want to prosecute someone. Even if they don't arrest you they may ask you questions you don't want to answer and get into things you don't want to tell them. When Tod gets here we'll all talk together a little bit and then I'll have you talk to him alone. He'll be your attorney and you'll have attorney-client privilege with him. So you should answer all his questions fully and completely. He won't judge you on anything. He's seen all kinds of good people get into all kinds of situations."

"Will you still be around if I need to ask you something?"

"Yes. I've got some work to do here and I'll be here if you need me."

"Okay."

"I don't want to talk with you about what happened this morning. The less I know the better."

"You were there," I said, a little exasperated. "You saw everything I saw."

"Still, the fewer people you talk to the better off you'll be. Just tell Tod."

"Should I tell Tod the truth? Should I tell him you were there and we moved Ken into the kitchen?"

"Yes," said Dan.

"What if Tod decides the best defense for me is to point to you and suggest you must have hit him?" Dan did not seem fazed by my question.

"Let's hope it doesn't come to that. But it's critical that Tod is prepared for whatever Breuninger might figure out or guess at."

Tod Morgan showed up. He was in his mid-thirties, short and wiry with already thinning hair. His face was tense and his eyes focused hard on both of us. I thought some of that focus was an act to impress clients. But at least he was capable of putting on the act.

15

"Very good to meet you all," Morgan said. We shook hands. "Can we get my fee out of the way before we talk? I'll need five thousand to start."

"That's a pretty hefty retainer," said Dan. "If they don't pursue Candy you may never have to do anything beyond showing up today."

"Do you want me to pick up the phone when you call?"

"Yes," said Dan.

"Then it's five thousand. If this goes no further then I'll refund everything except my time today."

"I'll write you a check," said Dan, "and Candy can pay me back later." He fished a checkbook out of his pants pocket and found a pen in a drawer in a front hall table. "I'll want a receipt."

"And here is my contract for services." Dan looked it over for a full minute while we all waited. Then he told me I should sign it and I did.

"Mrs. Winterpol and I should talk alone now," said Morgan. "Can we use the living room?" In other words, Dan was dismissed. I didn't like being alone with this man whom I had just met and who was going to ask me more about my private life than I wanted to answer. I sat in the big chair and braced myself to do what was apparently necessary.

"Why do you need an attorney, Mrs. Winterpol?"

"I'm not sure I really do but Dan and his mother say I should have one. My husband is injured and it looks like he was attacked this morning at our house. He is at St. Charles and I guess he might die. I didn't hit him but people might think I did. I'm a young wife with a rich older husband. Nobody was in the house but Ken and me."

"Have you ever been charged with any crime before?"

"No."

"What happened this morning?" I took Morgan through the whole thing—Dan at the back door, moving Ken, Ken falling out of the chair, the 911 call, what Breuninger asked me and what I told him, as well as I could remember. I told Morgan about the poker in the fountain. Then I asked him a question.

"If I tell you something no one else will ever know, will you have to tell the detective about it?"

"No," said Morgan. "In a civil case I might have to. In a criminal case I don't." So I told him about Ken whispering to me when he sat in the kitchen chair and before he fell on the floor. "He said, 'Where's my gun? Where's my gun?'"

"Did Mr. Winterpol have a gun in the house?"

"He had hunting rifles and shotguns locked in a cabinet and he had a pistol in his desk."

"Did you see the pistol this morning?"

"No."

"So far as you know, the pistol is still in his desk?"

"I don't know. I don't go in there."

"But he didn't tell you he had moved it somewhere else?"

"No."

"What kind of pistol was it?"

"It was a revolver, dull gray with a black handle."

Morgan then asked me about our relationship. I said it was fine.

"Mrs. Winterpol," said Morgan, "if the district attorney wants to prosecute you he will have Detective Breuninger investigate your marriage. If it was contentious, or if anyone can report any serious arguments between you, then the DA will use it and I will need to know about it. We don't need to go into depth today but if you've told anyone you were unhappy with your marriage or anyone has seen you argue, you should tell me."

I said I thought people we knew would say it was an odd marriage but one that seemed to work. Ken's sister, Linda, would probably say that Ken was happy in his marriage. "I haven't seen my own family in years," I said. "We didn't even invite them to the wedding. That's it."

"Did you say anything in an email or post anything on a social-networking site that could suggest trouble between you two?"

"I don't use email. I hired a company to handle Facebook and Twitter and all that stuff to promote my art. I don't even know what they say."

"Any affairs or romances?" he asked. Morgan cleverly didn't specify who might be having the affair and I answered as though he were only asking about Ken.

"No affairs that I know about," I said, "or suspect."

"Okay," said Morgan, "that's it for questions but there's one more thing I want to do today. I brought a camera and I want to take pictures of your arms."

I glared at the man. "No!"

"Mrs. Winterpol, we don't know where this case is going to go. If we get in trouble we may want to claim self-defense. If there are bruises on your arms, and we take pictures today before they fade any further, they will do a lot to make that case."

"Will you keep the pictures under lock and key and only use them if you absolutely have to?"

"Yes," said Morgan.

"And after this is over you will destroy them?"

"If they are not introduced into evidence I will destroy them."

I agreed reluctantly. Just the arms. Not my face or anything else in the photos. I took my blouse off and he took some pictures from the sides. He better not have gotten my face because it had a scowl on it that would have lit a fire.

Then he asked, "Did Mr. Winterpol threaten you this morning or at some earlier time?"

"I'm not going any further with this," I said.

"Let's hope you are not charged and we don't have to delve any further into what happened between you and Ken," said Morgan. "But you and I may need to meet with Detective Breuninger," he said as I put my blouse back on, "and answer some questions for him, to the extent I advise you to do so. I'll keep him away from your relationship with your husband."

"But there are two things you have to do for me," he said. "First, don't talk about this with anyone, not even Dan. If you need to talk to someone, even just to vent, talk to me. And secondly, I want you to get a new cell phone with a new number. Take the one you have and lock it in a safe deposit box. Don't destroy it or throw it out. That way the sheriff will have to get a warrant to get his hands on it." I could see all this was going to be a pain. You let lawyers in your life and they take over.

We found Elizabeth in the kitchen. Dan came quickly from the back of the house. All Morgan said was, "I'll tell Breuninger I'm Mrs. Winterpol's attorney and he should call me if he wants to talk with her."

"Do you want to see the Winterpol house?" Dan asked. "Breuninger called and said he's done with it. I told him he didn't have Candy's permission to search it but he searched it anyway."

"Crime scene," said Morgan, "but it's good that you objected. It might make a difference if anything turns up. And yes, I might as well take a quick look while I'm here."

"Candy, do you want to go back?" Dan asked.

"Yes," I said emphatically. The three of us, Morgan, Dan, and I, walked over to my house with me in the lead. I went around to the back, marched over the porch, and let us in with a key.

We went through the story again briefly, with me pointing to where I first saw Dan in the doorway, to where we sat Ken in the chair and to where he fell. There were still smudges of blood on the floor. I wanted to get through the events quickly and I'm sure I sounded impatient. Then I said I was going upstairs and I went to my studio. I don't know what Dan and Morgan looked at or talked about downstairs but after about five minutes Dan yelled up at me. "Is it okay if we come up?"

"Come ahead," I shouted. They saw the master bedroom with the bed still unmade, and they looked in the two guest rooms. Then they came into the studio and watched me paint for a minute.

"Who is that?" Morgan asked. The painting I was working on was the rough outline of someone's head with swaths of different colors inside and outside the outline. I'm sure they couldn't tell it was Ken.

"It's just a face," I said.

"I'll be going," said Morgan. "It's good I got a feel for the house."

Dan stood behind me for five minutes saying nothing. I did not turn away from the easel.

"Candy," he finally said, "there are some questions I need to ask you. Then I'll go away."

"Shoot," I said.

"Does Ken have a will and do you know where it is?"

"We wrote our wills together," I told him. "I don't know where they are. Ken's will says his sister gets fifty thousand and I get everything else—the house in Lake Oswego, this house, and his real estate company."

"Do you know who the executor is?" asked Dan.

"I am."

"You're going to need an attorney to help you sort out the will and file a tax return."

"Can that be you?" I asked.

"I'm not an expert on wills and estates. We can use the law firm I worked for in Portland if that's all right with you. It's Oxton, Rath, and Flynn. They're one of the biggest and they have a good reputation. The wills and estate person is Patsy Weil. She's easy to work with. I think you'll like her."

"Good," said Candy. "Can I still talk to you about it?"

"Very likely," he said. "I'll have to clear that with Oxton. Are you all right here for now?"

"Yes," she said. "I need paint, not people."

"If you need anything you call me or Mom," said Dan, and he wrote their numbers on the corner of a pad of drawing paper. "I'll call you later." Then he left.

I painted for about half an hour. I was adding a thin strip of purple to the side of Ken's face when I began to cry. I couldn't say why I was crying. I couldn't put it into words. I simply sat facing the painting. Then I began to paint again, to paint as rapidly and as surely as I ever had. The man I painted was powerful but injured. His jaw was strong but a sickly black tinged with green. He was braving pain of some kind, and the wound would sap his power only slowly. Yet, in the midst of all his power, he knew he was doomed. I wanted to cut a vein and paint with my own blood. I would have, except that beautiful red color would not last.

The wireless phone in the studio rang so many times that afternoon that I took it into the bedroom and put in under a pillow. Then I shut both the bedroom door and the studio door.

CHAPTER 3

Playing Defense

(Dan)

When the hospital couldn't reach Candy they called me. Ken had died from a traumatic brain injury. I went back over to Candy's house to tell her. She didn't answer the door so I let myself in and called upstairs to let her know I was coming.

"How did you get in the house?" she asked when I opened the studio door.

"I had your keys in my pocket when I left here earlier. Here they are back." I put them on the table where her paints were.

"Don't ever come into my house like that again," she said.

"I'm sorry," I said. "I won't. But I thought you needed to know that Ken died at one fifteen this afternoon."

Candy sat staring at the painting on her easel for a full minute, not moving.

"Last night he was alive as ever," said Candy. "Without even thinking about it I assumed we'd be together for years. I'm sure Ken assumed the same thing. That's all changed. How I fit in the world has changed. I don't know who I'm supposed to be right now."

"How about if I stay downstairs in case you need some company?"

"No thank you." Candy went back to her painting. The person in her picture looked to be in turmoil, mental or physical I couldn't tell. I bid Candy goodbye and left her keys next to some tubes of paint on the table beside her.

That afternoon, before I went into Bend for my swimming workout, I sat on my parents' deck with a legal pad and a pencil, trying to estimate the risk of Candy being charged with her husband's murder. *Motive? Opportunity? Means?* I scribbled these words across the top of the pad in front of me and drew boxes around each of them. She had them all. Or at least it would look that way to a district attorney and a grand jury.

Here she was, the attractive young wife with her art career taking off, married to a much older man who had money. Maybe she truly loved Ken. But one could easily wonder if her life would be freer, fuller, and happier if she had the money and not the man.

Who had a better opportunity to kill Ken than Candy? The two were in the house alone all night and into the morning. She could choose her moment. Of course, there was another person in the area about the time Ken was hit. That person was me. Candy was not the only person I needed to look out for.

And the means. Maybe. What did I know about how hard you have to swing a fireplace poker to kill someone? Could Candy swing it that hard? Well, Candy knew how to swing a golf club and I didn't think she was a weakling. She stood five foot ten. So yes, if she focused on what she was doing she could land one heck of blow with a poker—hard enough I imagined—to kill her husband.

I'd gotten Candy a good attorney in Tod Morgan. Should I do more, do whatever I could to protect her? I had to. Candy and I went way back, thought I couldn't say we'd been friends growing up. We went to the same schools in Bend and I saw her almost every day. In high school she started coming to our house for art lessons from my father. They would sit in his little studio and paint side by side. Dad said she had extraordinary talent and he made her his special project. To a single child like me she seemed like a suddenly imposed older sister who had no time for me, one I resented for all the attention she got from my parents. My mother said I should be kind to her because her family was poor and her home life was awful. My parents encouraged Candy to finish high school and go to art school. My father helped get her a scholarship. My parents had invested a lot in Candy and I didn't want to see all their love and effort go to waste.

My own relationship with Candy was more complicated. When my school friends said Candy was hot it was a revelation to me.

Candy was not a movie star or a model or a rock singer. How could she be hot? With careful observation, though, I came to see that they were right. She had thick auburn hair that fell over creamy skin and a curvaceous body. In the summer, seeing Candy in a bathing suit flummoxed me. A mighty force pulled me toward her. Yet at the same time I hated her. And I certainly didn't trust her. Then she went away to art school and to her artist's life in Portland. My parents and I went to her wedding to Ken Winterpol. I thought she was part of my past until we ran into each other two weeks before Ken was killed and my relationship to her got complicated again.

Selfishly, I had to make sure Candy wasn't prosecuted because Tod Morgan, doing what he could to defend her, might point to me as the likely killer. I was right there around the time Ken was hit. I was more capable of clobbering him with a poker than Candy was. My motive? To have Candy and her money to myself. I had no such motivation but a jury might believe I did. Even if I escaped a guilty verdict, or even prosecution, just being arrested for a felony would put a big dent in my law career.

I had to make sure that Candy was never arrested, never charged, and certainly never convicted.

The best solution would be to find the person who actually did kill Ken. How could I find that person, or make sure Breuninger found that person, and prove their guilt? After fifteen minutes of drawing nothing but darkly lined boxes on my pad I saw I was hobbled in every direction. I had no access to the physical evidence that Breuninger might have found at the scene of the attack. Neighbors who might have seen something would give Breuninger all kinds of facts they wouldn't give me. Ken's employees in Portland, and friends if he had any, wouldn't have to tell me anything. I couldn't subpoena them or threaten to arrest them for obstruction of justice.

I had no experience in crime investigation. All kinds of people could have killed Ken for all kinds of reasons—a random act of violence, a battle of insults that got out of hand, a business deal gone sour, a jilted lover, or a jealous husband. I didn't know where to start.

23

And yet, I thought. And yet. An idea began to emerge. I had drawn many boxes by now.

It wasn't necessary that I actually find the killer. I wasn't seeking justice. Dead or alive, I really didn't care about Ken. Maybe the world was better off without him. All I cared about was keeping Candy, and me, out of jail. Even better out of court. And it might be within my power to do that. What I could do, even without Breuninger's legal authority, was find other people who might have killed Ken. He was not a likeable man. If he had been as unfair to other people as he had been to my brewpub friends, then Oregon could be littered with people who hated him.

I just needed to find those people. That was legal, wasn't it? Of course. I didn't need to be anyone's defense attorney to do it. I didn't need the power of subpoena or the threat of arrest to get a nice long list. Then if Breuninger and the district attorney started toward trial, I could dog them all the way. "Have you investigated this other person? Have you followed up this lead? How are you going to be able to convince a jury, beyond a reasonable doubt, that Person A committed the crime when there are all these other people, B through Z, who are just as likely to have done it?" And who knew? Maybe I would stumble across the person who actually did kill Ken. Maybe all the facts needed for an arrest would tumble into place.

It was going to take time to assemble my list, with all the information that made each of these people a suspect. But I had time. It wouldn't even affect my training. What would I be giving up? Reading books. Watching videos. Some golf. And some sitting around trying to fill my days. Training more than thirty hours a week was counterproductive. I could use all the recovery time between training sessions, where I had just been passing the time, to search out guilty-looking people.

I grabbed my iPad and started looking at Ken's company on the web. Western Sun Development owned commercial buildings, mostly in Portland but some in Bend. The firm leased them out to businesses, and occasionally bought and sold the buildings. The company claimed to develop high-end properties but the buildings I saw on the website didn't look, to my unpracticed eye, to be first class. None were downtown. None of them looked to be architecturally inspiring. Fair enough, I thought, the world needs second-class buildings as well as first-class buildings. If Ken could serve the market by supplying them, no harm, no foul.

Then I searched eCourt records online for Western Sun and for Ken himself. I couldn't help grinning when I saw how many people had sued Ken's company. He'd sued a lot of them back. Buried in all those dry words and legal mumbo-jumbo I knew there were deep veins of animosity. I identified five promising cases to start with, found phone numbers for the people involved, and made some notes.

CHAPTER 4

Witness

(Leon)

Early in the morning, before Ken Winterpol was attacked, I went for a walk on the cart paths along the golf course. As I always do, I enjoyed looking at all the beautiful houses when the sun was on them and I couldn't see inside. I wouldn't look inside people's houses at night when the lights were on. I wouldn't like people looking into my house, even if all Elizabeth and I were doing was watching television. My attention was caught, however, by the lights on the deck of the Winterpol house that morning. There were two men facing each other and I cast my eyes toward them a few times as I walked along.

What happened next is the reason I came to San Francisco without telling anyone where I was going.

When I got over the shock of what I saw I looked around to see if anyone else had seen it. Nobody. It was a cold morning and even the greenkeepers were not out on the golf course yet. Could I just go home and have a cup of coffee and pretend I never saw anything? I wanted to talk it over with Elizabeth. She was levelheaded in even the most extraordinary situations. But perhaps I would be wrong to burden her with it.

In the wind-whipped fog of my thoughts one conclusion emerged, like a lighthouse growing brighter as I approached it. No one must ever know what I saw. I asked myself what I could do to make sure of that. Short of suicide, I could disappear. Hopefully things would quiet down and I could come back. If they didn't quiet down at least I could take the time away to practice whatever lie I would have to tell when I did come back.

26

I snuck into the bedroom without waking up Elizabeth and took a few things I would need. I raised the garage door, just as though I were going to the store. I took the cloth cover off the Maserati and put it in the trunk. I loved that car and Elizabeth wouldn't drive it. The parents of one of my students gave it to me in thanks for getting their son on the straight and narrow in school. I wasn't insulted that they needed room in their ten-car garage for another vintage car. The Maserati was a 1961 blue-gray Quatroporto with red leather seats and door panels. The dashboard was black and white. It was in perfect condition when I got it and I have taken good care of it ever since. I backed it out of the garage carefully and took off.

At the bank in Bend I stopped to take five thousand dollars out of our joint account, then drove three hours over the mountains to the Portland Airport. I hadn't driven the Maserati that far in years and driving took my mind off the scene I had witnessed that morning. The car hummed along beautifully. It charged up the hills and swung around the curves the way it was built to do. People waved to me. Many would remember seeing this car. But it would be hours before Elizabeth and Dan wondered where I was. It would be hours, maybe days, maybe forever, before the sheriff would want to know where I had gone.

I parked in the long-term lot and covered the car. On my way to the terminal I used my cell phone to book and pay for a ticket to Seattle. Then I turned off my phone and slipped the phone into the side pocket of a young man's carry-on while he was waiting for his baggage at the carousel. If the sheriff got to the point of tracking down my phone he would find it, presumably in Portland, in the possession of a man who did not know how he came to have it.

I didn't take the flight. I got on the airport bus to downtown Portland and walked to the Greyhound station. There I put on a jacket and a Mariners baseball cap that I'd bought in the airport. I didn't think the sheriff would really try to find me so my escape was partly a fantasy, like playing at being James Bond. Near the bus station I bought a prepaid cell phone, what they call a burner phone on the cop shows. Then I got on a bus to San Francisco.

I had the perfect friend to find refuge with. I hadn't seen him for forty years but we always called each other on May 1, International Workers Day. Our families had been close for generations in Valencia. Our fathers had fought for the Republicans in the Spanish Civil War and had escaped together to France when the Republicans lost to Franco and the Fascists. Gabriel and I were born in France and moved together to Los Angeles when we were five. No one in Bend had ever heard of Gabriel Torres, not even Elizabeth as well as I could recall. Gabriel and Maria Isabel had a spare bedroom and were happy to have me.

While I had chosen art, Gabriel had chosen music. He moved to San Francisco so he could listen to Carlos Santana and, occasionally, play alongside him. Now Gabriel favored classic guitar, Spanish melodies, and flamenco. He played every day for himself, for Maria, and for his friends. He played for me during my visit and he swept my heart away. We had known so many people, places, and songs together. The same songs were now tempered by Gabriel's experiences, the world around us, and shades of music we had heard since that time. Maria danced for us a few times, rapping her heels on the floor to a buleria or clicking castanets to a fandango. She said the neighbors objected if she went on too long. I felt sorry for the neighbors not appreciating something we were enjoying so much.

The nightclub owner where Gabriel and Maria used to perform had died years ago and, having had a long dispute with his family, left the nightclub and the building that housed it to Gabriel and Maria. The two of them operated the club for ten years, barely scraping by, in and out of bank loans all the time. Then the dot.com boom came to San Francisco in the late nineties. Everyone wanted real estate. Just when my friends were wishing they could retire someone bought their building for much more than they ever thought it would be worth. So they closed up shop and bought the house I was staying in. With the prosperity of the entire city, the value of the house was still going up.

"I'm richer than an old guitar player has any right to be," said Gabriel.

I too am better off than an immigrant artist has any right to be.

When I married Elizabeth and moved to Bend I started teaching art in the public school system. I earned more money than she did for one year but she has surpassed me every year since. I'm very proud of her. Now that I am a retired teacher on a pension I paint because I enjoy it. I sell a painting now and then. More likely I give one away to a friend. I don't miss teaching though it was fine while I did it and I know I was good at it. The curriculum called for teaching a variety of media—paint, watercolor, collage, clay, ceramics—and mixing in some art history and appreciation. I slanted my time toward teaching my students how to draw from real life. I believed that only one in a hundred of my students would become an artist of any kind, even a commercial artist or, heaven forbid, an art teacher. But all of them would see the world around them every day. I thought the most valuable gift I could give them was to teach them to see what was really there.

Candy was exceptional from the beginning. When she was in my seventh-grade class she continued to work on art projects when the other kids were getting bored and distracted. She once asked if she could take drawing paper and art pencils with her to study hall. I could not do that for everyone so I gave her three sheets and only one big black pencil. She brought back a drawing of another student reading. It showed an innate understanding of proportion and the relations of parts to the whole. I could only give her a little more of my time than I gave the other students but I did what I could. She could concentrate and she came along quickly. I learned from the other teachers that her parents were very poor. Her father was an unreliable worker and an undependable husband. Candy's older sister had run off and gotten arrested in Seattle. Candy wasn't the only student with a bad home. But I could do something for Candy that I could not do for the others. I could teach her to take advantage of her talent. Also, in service to the larger world, I could prevent her talent from going to waste.

Candy has become an exciting artist and I'm proud of her. Critics and the public have recognized her. Our family went to Candy's wedding and we were happy for her on that single day, while we all had reservations about her husband. Ken was going to get what he wanted from that marriage. We hoped that whatever he wanted would not be too hard on Candy.

I took a Bay Area Rapid Transit train across the bay to Oakland with my new cell phone and called Elizabeth from there. Then I left the phone on a train going further down the line. I knew I was a complete amateur at this sort of thing but it seemed to make sense. I was worried that I had overlooked something and the authorities would show up on Gabriel's doorstep. At the same time I thought I was spinning a paranoid fantasy. The Deschutes County Sheriff's deputies might not even bother to look for me and, if they did, they would never get the warrants and the manpower to trace calls to our home phone, find out which cell tower my calls came from in the Bay Area, and then have the resources to find me in a population of six million people. I told Elizabeth I was safe and well and staying with a friend. I'd be home in August. I was sorry not to have told her that I was leaving but something came up suddenly.

"Ken Winterpol's murder," Elizabeth said. It was a statement more than a question.

"That might be it," I said. "Ask me no questions and I'll tell you no lies. I think it would be a lot simpler if I weren't around for anyone to ask me questions. And a lot simpler for you if I don't tell you anything. I can tell you I certainly had no part in Ken's murder. So let's leave it at that."

"I hope you know what you're doing," said Elizabeth. God bless her. She could have told me to come home, tell the sheriff what I knew and be done with it. But she had enough respect for my judgment, or my pride, or some combination, that she didn't say that.

"Ask Dan what he thinks," she said. "You want to stay on the safe side of the law." I said I would.

"But if I don't reach Dan right away," I said, "could you tell him the Maserati is in long-term parking at the Portland airport and see if he can bring it home? It isn't good for the car to sit out there even with the cover on it."

Elizabeth was a little peeved at my request, on top of my skipping town, but she said she would talk to Dan and they would figure something out between the two of them. Then she told me to be careful and to call her again. I said I would on both counts.

CHAPTER 5

The Sins of the Fathers

(Dan)

As I walked back from Candy's house after telling her Ken had died, a man my dad's age stepped out of his house and waved me down. I was sure Bill Stockman wanted to pump me about what was going on.

"Dan," Bill said in a serious tone, "I need to talk with you. I saw the police down at the Winterpol house and I was concerned. I asked resort security and the woman at the gate said someone had died. Then later I saw you and Candy and another man walking to the Winterpols'. What is happening?"

It was none of his business, I thought, but if I brushed him off he would be telling people what a selfish and unfriendly person I was and what a shame that was for my parents. I told him only what I thought he would read in the papers in a day or two. Ken had been found badly injured. Nobody was sure how it happened and the sheriff was investigating.

"Did Candy find him?" asked Bill. Whatever I told him he would repeat at the clubhouse as soon as he could find someone to tell it to.

"I don't know," I said. "I really don't know much about what happened. And I really shouldn't speculate. None of us should, I think."

"Who was the man walking toward the house with you and Candy earlier today?"

"He was an attorney."

"Is Candy a suspect?"

"If the sheriff seriously suspected her she would be in custody," I said. "But it is still a good idea to have an attorney around."

"Aren't you a lawyer?" I was surprised Bill remembered that.

31

"Civil," I said. "I write contracts."

"Well maybe you can advise me anyway, at least for a start," he said. I dreaded this but felt I had to act interested.

"It concerns your father," he said. "I was getting ready to go play golf this morning when I saw your father walking off the golf course. He was hunched over and tense, like he was worried about something. Did he see what happened at the Winterpol house?"

So that, I realized, was why my father wasn't home. He had seen something he didn't want people to know. Or perhaps, God forbid, he was somehow involved in the attack on Ken. He must have been very worried to hunch over as Bill described. My mother said Dad always stood "straight as a matador."

"He didn't see anything as far as I know," I said. "Did you see anyone else around at that time?"

"No. Martha told me there was a frost delay so after I saw your father I sat down to watch CNN. The next thing I knew all the police cars showed up."

"So here's where I need your advice," Bill continued. "Should I tell the sheriff I saw your father at that hour and they might want to talk to him? Am I legally required to? Could I go to jail for saying nothing? I don't want to make any trouble for your father."

No, I thought, you would prefer to threaten to tell the sheriff about Dad, hoping that I will tell you more about what happened. "I can't advise you, Bill," I said. "I'm not your attorney. You should do whatever you think is right. But, if it will help, my understanding of the law is that if the sheriff comes to you and asks you questions, you absolutely need to tell him the truth. But you are not under any legal obligation, as far as I know, to go to the sheriff and volunteer information, particularly if you didn't see any crime committed."

"Okay," said Bill. "I think I should just sit on this and let your father make up his own mind."

"He'd probably appreciate that," I said. "I know I would. But listen, I've got to get home. Thanks for asking about Dad. I'll let you know if I learn anything." I wished I hadn't said that, paying the price of escaping the conversation by virtually inviting Bill Stockman to pester me.

Now, in addition to Candy and me, my father could be suspected of Ken's murder. My father was not a violent man. He had never struck anyone. But injustice made him angry, whether it was a student picked on at school, a teacher wrongly accused of some misdeed, or a whole class of people being unfairly treated. He spoke out against it and, among people he knew, he tried to do something about it. If he thought Ken was hurting or threatening Candy he would not have left it alone. Perhaps he confronted Ken and argued with him. For my father to have hit Ken, the larger and younger man would have had to turn his back. But maybe Ken was on his way to punish Candy for something just to show how little he cared for Dad's admonishments.

My father's mind and my own did not work the same way. I had developed theories, over the years I had known him, about why, in spite of our affection for each other, and my looking like a taller version of him, we were so different.

First of all, Dad was an artist and I was not. When I was a child and he went into his little studio, my mother tried to keep me out of there so he could paint in peace. But if I got in there and was quiet I could see my father concentrating on what he was doing and even see how much he was enjoying it. Much as he loved my mother and me, he also loved his other world. Framed on the wall in his studio I saw the same words every day in beautiful calligraphy. The meaning of the words got richer as I grew up. I thought for years that my father had written them but they came from Pablo Neruda: *"You can cut all the flowers but you cannot stop spring from coming."*

The second thing about my father was that he was Spanish, in spite of spending most of his life in the United States. Dad outgrew his Spanish accent when the family moved to Los Angeles, but he retained the reserve and dignity of a Spaniard. Also like a Spaniard, he could be exceedingly generous. He helped a lot of kids in school, especially Hispanic kids, not so much by teaching them art but by encouraging them to study, to raise their expectations, and to graduate.

Finally, my Dad was a closet Marxist, at least emotionally. His father, my grandfather, fought for the Marxists in the Spanish civil war in the 1930s. He named my father Leon Martinez after Leon Trotsky. Dad rarely talked about Marxism or communism, and never wanted to debate it, but he firmly believed that people with money, the capitalists, had always exploited the working man and that working people had a natural right to own the businesses where they worked. Dad gave me only two real sit-down talks when I was a teenager. One was about respecting women and the other was about communism. I had trouble understanding why my father favored communism while he loathed Russia which, of course, was communist. It wasn't until I took a course in college that I understood. In the Spanish Civil War, my grandfather fought for the POUM, the same Marxist party that George Orwell fought for. The POUM was allied with the anarchists, the Basque separatists, the Catalan Separatists, and the Communist Party. They were all on the "Republican" side, fighting against Franco and the Fascists. But the Communist Party, backed by the Russians, assumed the Republican side was going to win the war and the Communists were just as concerned about stamping out rivals for the ultimate control of Spain as they were about beating Franco. The Communists wound up jailing or shooting many of their POUM allies. Much later, when the Soviet Union broke up, my father put it down to the venality of the Russians rather than any fundamental flaw in communism.

As much as I respected my father, one big inconsistency puzzled me. Why had a man with such intense political inclinations, and such an intense interest in art, married a woman who was as stable and normal as my mother, a woman who had no great feeling for art, had only left small-town Bend to go to college and return, and who was about to become, of all things, a banker—an enabler of capitalism and all the despicable evils that went with it?

When I asked Dad how this happened he said, "I loved her." That seemed to be a more than sufficient answer for him.

"I still do. She, and you, are my life."

CHAPTER 6

The Young Buck

(Dan)

Detective Breuninger had guessed right about one thing. Candy did have a young buck for a lover. I knew who he was and I was worried for him. He would be a logical suspect and Candy's having a tryst with him would make her look guilty too.

The "young buck," and I did like the phrase, was me. I had been with Candy one time, about two weeks before Ken was killed and all our lives changed. I was finishing a run, with nothing on my agenda in life except training for the tri, when Candy stopped her Porsche and rolled down the window. I knew from my mother that Candy and Ken were living at Upriver but I hadn't seen her since her wedding three years earlier. My parents were invited to the wedding and I was included out of politeness. Before the wedding I hadn't seen Candy since she moved to Portland ten years earlier to start art school.

"Can you come by the house this afternoon?" she said, looking up from behind the steering wheel, "I have something I want to show you."

"Sure," I said. "Is two o'clock all right? I'm going for a bike ride later."

"Two o'clock," she said. "See you then."

That was our entire exchange. We were grown up now, I said to myself. She was married. I needed to clamp down my imagination and act like an adult. I rested a bit after my run, then showered and had a good lunch.

I walked over to Candy's house, right down the street, at the appointed hour. I was trying to put our strained past behind me, to act as though I were going into a meeting to review a contract with a client. She kept me waiting at the door until I thought she wasn't home. Then I heard quick hard steps across a wood floor. She fumbled with the lock and opened the door slowly. Her hair was pulled back and she wore a blue painter's smock that didn't quite reach her knees. Her legs below that were bare down to a pair of black suede boots. Was this what she wore to paint? Or was she taunting me? She stood back and regarded me critically from head to toe, as if she were going to paint me, or as if she were rethinking whether to let me in or tell me she had gotten busy with something. She let go of the doorknob and marched back through the hall to the edge of the living room. Then she turned around with a slight look of impatience, as though I should know whether or not I was to follow her. I shut the door and walked her way.

"We decided to build this house so I could get the right light for my painting and Ken could play golf on the weekends. Ken would like to spend more time here but he says he has to go into the office and look people in the eye." Candy was standing in front of the window with the bright afternoon light behind her. I didn't see a bump or a ripple in the smock.

"We can ski in the winter," she said, "and the real reason I'm here is I love the land and I love to paint it. I learned so much about painting looking out the window of your father's studio in Bend. I've painted Mount Bachelor fifty times, like Georgia O'Keefe painted The Perdenal in New Mexico over and over."

"Do you still swim?" I asked, remembering her in a swimsuit.

She gave me a flash of disdain. "No," she said. "I gave up swimming."

The girls I knew in Portland lived in dorm rooms or apartments, usually ones they shared with other girls. Seeing Candy in a house of her own, and a very nice house at that, made me feel she had in some way ascended to my parents' generation. Her voice was deep and resonant for a woman but with a hint of uncertainty, not, it seemed, because she was worried about what I thought, but because there was something she hadn't quite made up her mind about.

"What I have to show you," she said, "is upstairs, where the light is better." She turned and led me up the carpeted staircase that had a finished log for a bannister. The smock hid and revealed, hid and revealed the back of her bare legs as we climbed. We walked down the hall to the room at the end. It was not her studio but the master bedroom. There was an easel by the window and Candy walked to the front of it to regard the painting with a critical eye. I walked around and looked at it too.

I thought I would see some strange abstraction that I would be at a loss to appreciate. I would find something complimentary to say. But I was not prepared for what I saw. It was clearly my father, no mistake, but my father as I had never seen him before. The man I knew was loving but sometimes distracted, optimistic but often burdened by trivialities. The man in the portrait had fire in his eyes.

"I've never seen my father this way," I said. "He looks like Jehovah from the Old Testament."

Candy leaned against me in a way that I thought was almost sisterly. We were both children, in different ways, of the same exceptional man. I thought I would have time to think about what might happen next, to think about what Candy wanted, to think about what I wanted, to think about the implications of what a man and woman, already pressed together, are likely to do by themselves together in a bedroom. But there was no time for thinking. Candy saw to that. Candy wrapped her arms around me in what I sensed might be the start of an embrace. But she clenched the back of my shirt, pulled it off over my head, and tossed it on the floor. She unfastened my belt and bent down to pull my trousers and undershorts down to my ankles. Quick, mechanical, and not the least romantic. One minute I was respectably clothed and the next I was naked as a shorn lamb.

"Take your shoes off," said Candy, sitting on the edge of the bed unzipping her boots and throwing them aside. I sat beside her, shedding my shoes and pants, as though I were in a supervised workout, waiting for my coach's next command. Candy pushed herself back to the middle of the bed and unbuttoned her smock down the front without taking it off. Things were moving awfully fast, even for a guy. I wanted to kiss her, caress her, rub my chest against hers. But Candy was already arching her back. I began to caress and kiss her breasts, breasts I had never seen more than a hint of before. I settled in to give them my full attention.

"That's very nice, counselor," said Candy. "But let's get to the point."

This was obviously not the time for subtlety. Our violent and determined coupling continued until neither of us could summon another thrust. Panting, we lay side-by-side with our heads on a pillow. Only then I saw the room as Candy had seen it. Blocking the light from the window and facing us was the painting of my father. He looked down on us, not necessarily with disapproval, but with the manner of a wizard who sees everything, understands everything, and pities all mere mortals. The painting unnerved me. What had Candy been thinking? Had she dreamed of taking my father as her lover all these years? Was I a proxy for him? Or had she, I shuddered to think, actually been my father's lover? Maybe she wished my father could witness the gift she gave his son. It was some of Candy's artistic weirdness, in a mindset I did not understand.

"The housekeeper is due soon," said Candy. At least it wasn't Ken who was due soon. I hadn't been completely sure Ken wasn't in the house. How crazy could this woman be? Had I been inveigled this far just to provoke her husband? Was I part of some love game the two of them played? Would he suddenly appear with a tire jack in his hand? One of the rules of sex is, I think, the more risk you take, the more you think you really shouldn't be doing this, the more exciting it is. I'd swap a little excitement for a little less terror in the future.

"I'm sorry," I said. "I have nothing left to give the housekeeper."

"Then you better go." She laughed. I rolled myself out of bed to a kneeling position on the carpet. Then I stood up and got my clothes on quickly. Candy got up as well and put on some slacks under her smock. She still had not taken the smock off. It had covered her arms from her shoulders to her wrists through our entire escapade. She was hiding something—bruises, tattoos, needle marks—she did not want me to see. That's why, after Ken was attacked, I had Tod Morgan get photographs of her arms. He never told me what he saw, if anything.

"I'm going to go paint," she said. She headed down the hall and I started down the stairs. "Go out the front door," said Candy. "She comes in through the garage."

I heard a door open as I was rushing down the stairs and I quickened my pace. There was an old red Honda parked in the driveway that hadn't been there before. Old Candy sure didn't mind cutting it close.

I was awestruck and self-satisfied as I walked back to my parents' house. This was still two weeks before Ken was murdered. I suppressed the questions that kept rising the rest of the afternoon. What had just happened with Candy, why had it happened, what did it mean, and what did it mean for the future? Was it a one-time event or did she expect me to show up the next afternoon? Was I unique or was Candy in the habit of inviting young men over? Was this really about my father and not about me at all?

For that matter, what did I want to happen? I knew I would remember this afternoon for a long time. Could I live with myself if, given the opportunity, I didn't go back for more? Or would I be happier recalling this as a once-in-a-lifetime event? Did I want Candy to leave Ken and marry me? Certainly not. As much as Candy attracted me I knew I could never live with her. Could I be her secret lover, repeatedly cuckolding her husband in his own house? That was not the kind of man I thought I was, not to mention that being caught would be embarrassing and, quite possibly, dangerous.

I didn't see Candy after that until the morning Ken died, though I certainly tried to. When I called her house I always got voicemail. I didn't know her cell phone number or email address. I couldn't very well mail her a note. *Thank you for a wonderful time* would sound ridiculous. Several times up until the day Ken died I knocked on her doors, front and back, but she wasn't home or didn't answer. She could have gone to Portland for all I knew. I steered more of my runs past her house and along roads she was likely to drive. At first I was thinking about more sex. Then I was thinking that extramarital sex was a really bad idea for Candy. And, though I had no one I was being disloyal to, and Candy was the original instigator rather than the follower, I was guilty of making her risky behavior possible. The morning I found Ken I was going to give visiting Candy one more try, knock one more time on her door. Now I was embroiled with an unpredictable woman in untangling a felony.

The afternoon of the day Ken died, in spite of everything that had happened, I went to swim laps in Bend as I had planned all along. Keeping to my training schedule and working my body hard helped settle my mind. I even had the energy to give some tips on swimming to a woman in the next lane. She certainly had the muscles and aerobics for swimming but her technique was strictly day camp. She caught on quickly, though, and I guess I really helped her.

Part of my training routine, two or three times a week, was to walk over to the brewpub my two friends owned. I'd have a sandwich and a beer and walk back to the swim center where I left my car. A perfect training diet would not have included beer. The alcohol tended toward toward dehydration, put an extra load on my liver, and was more fattening than pure carbs. But I only had one beer with a glass of water before and another glass of water after. I reasoned that the beer helped my mental health more than it hurt my physical health.

Pete Slesnick and Frank Suyama, my friends from the rugby team at U of O, gave me stock worth one percent of the business when they started out in return for my helping them with legal issues, including helping to negotiate their loan from Ken Winterpol. I wasn't licensed to practice law back then but I thought I knew enough to add some value.

The brewpub was around the corner from Bond Street, one of the two main streets through downtown Bend. The pub had a long sign that said VANDEVERT BREWING in gold letters surrounded by a dark green background. The sign looked English and the green and gold looked like a British variation on U of O's green and yellow. The bar and tables were dark brown wood and the walls were a light honey color. The pub had a rugby theme on the inside, though rugby didn't smack you in the face. The pub needed customers that didn't know or care about rugby. Pete and Frank had a rugby ball high on the wall behind the bar and there were photos of rugby teams, including U of O's, on the hall leading to the bathrooms. One photo showed the New Zealand All Blacks doing the Haka dance.

"When rugby players are in town, they come here," said Pete, "and they drink a lot of beer."

Pete and Frank named the pub after a road called Vandevert that intersected the main highway sixteen miles south of town, near Upriver Ranch. The road got its name from a cattle rancher who had settled there in the nineteenth century because he liked to hunt bear. Pete and Frank called their most popular brew Bear Hunter Beer and it had a bear on the label. After someone came in and made a fuss about the idea of hunting animals Pete added a sign for the beer on the wall that said, NO BEARS WERE HARMED IN MAKING THIS BEER. People liked it and it turned out to be the slogan for the beer.

There were big windows in back of the pub where customers could see the brewery in operation. The tanks and pipes always looked shiny and spotless. Sometimes you could see Frank or one of his helpers turning a valve or opening the hatch on a tank and pouring in a pail of hops. Whenever I saw him back there I wished Frank would act more lively, like Julia Child on TV whipping up an inspired recipe. But Frank was a chemist at heart and I knew, once he and Pete had created a recipe they liked, it was more important to be consistent than to be creative. Pete did convince Frank to make more of a show of holding the samples he drew up to the light to check the color. He was supposed to sip the sample, smack his lips and look deep in thought.

I'd met Ken before he married Candy because he was going to loan money to Pete and Frank to start the brewpub. I was in law school then and my friends asked me to sit with them while they discussed the loan. The first thing that impressed me about Ken was his eyes. When I was a boy, a friend and I discovered a strange trap door in the middle of a field. We lifted it up to find a pool of lumpy brown sewage. That's what Ken's eyes looked like. We dropped the door and ran away, which is what I felt like doing whenever I saw Ken. I wondered whether everyone saw his eyes that way. What kind of a man could have eyes like that, be successful in business, and marry a knockout like Candy? Maybe it was enough that his otherwise good-looking face hid his eyes when he smiled and suddenly made him appealing. It was like a magic trick. Ken was an unsettling person.

We met in the building where the pub was now. Ken owned the building, one of his few investments outside the Portland area, and he said he wanted to help the brewpub thrive. That would attract more business to the building and to the immediate area. We met Ken in the empty first floor and sat on folding chairs around a card table littered with price lists for brewing equipment, beer and ale recipes, contacts information for potential suppliers, projected cash flows, and a cobbled-together marketing plan. Pete and Frank's lease on the building had already been signed and this meeting was just about Ken investing in the brewery. Pete and Frank had twenty-five thousand dollars from friends and needed another fifty to buy the brewing and kitchen equipment and open the pub. Ken said he thought brewpubs had a great future and he thought Pete and Frank were the right guys to make a success of it. He wanted to be part of the company and they wanted his money. Without looking at the reports they brought to show him, Ken offered them a deal that looked very good on the surface—a loan with no payments for four years. My friends and I were too inexperienced to recognize how much leverage the agreement gave Ken. He could demand payment of the entire loan at any time. He said this was standard language. The three of us reasoned that he would never demand immediate repayment. It would ruin the business and he would be cutting off his nose to spite his face. We didn't realize that Ken's right to shut down the entire business by calling the loan gave him immense power to dictate what Pete and Frank could and could not do. If the business did well, he could force them out and take the business over. Further, what seemed a minor detail at the time could turn out to be critical: the agreement said we couldn't get money from anyone else in the future without Ken's approval.

A year later I apologized to Pete and Frank for letting them sign the agreement. They said they weren't worried about it. The brewpub was open and doing well. Ken hadn't made any threats or issued any directives. The only problem: he had a habit of bringing in groups of people whenever he felt like it and insisting on the best table and rapid service. The people who worked there were not fond of him. Pete had to apologize, plead, and give away free beer to get other customers to leave the table Ken wanted.

I settled onto a stool at the bar, said hello to Pete, and told him we needed to talk.

"Not harping on Ginny again, I hope?" he asked with a frown to discourage my mentioning her. Ginny was a waitress and barmaid who worked at the pub and lived with Pete. I'd warned Pete that if Ginny ever fell out with him she could sue the pub five ways from Sunday for sexual harassment, employee intimidation, unfair labor practices, and who knew what else.

"Ginny would never do that," Pete had said when I spoke to him earlier. "She's not that kind of person. She can stand on her own two feet. We live together because we love each other."

"I'm just warning you," I'd said, "if she ever gets mad at you she can ruin the business. You should either marry her or ask her to find work somewhere else." Pete didn't think he needed to worry.

I could see Ginny waiting tables as I sat at the bar. The customers loved her, her long blonde hair with an upturned wave at the bottom, and her enthusiasm. She purposely wore an outfit like the girl on the St. Pauli Girl bottle, a white blouse with puffy sleeves, a low neckline, and big laces that held the blouse together in the middle. The outfit had an apron with big blue shoulder straps that made detours around her chest. The local St. Pauli Girl distributor came in once to complain that Pete's pub was infringing on a trademark. Ginny told him it was a traditional German outfit and she could wear what she damned well pleased. We never heard from the man again. The pub didn't sell St. Pauli Girl but Pete said Ginny probably did more to help St. Pauli sales in Bend than any amount of advertising.

"Tonight it's not about Ginny," I said. "It's about Ken Winterpol."

"Don't tell me," said Pete. "He wants four tables tonight for a gathering of teetotalers."

"No," I said. "He'll never ask you for a table again. He's dead. Died this afternoon. Very likely murdered."

Pete leaned over to me and spoke softly. "Couldn't happen to a more wonderful guy."

"I don't know yet what his will says but his heir, who is probably his wife, may want to collect the loan Ken made to the brewpub. You may have to come up with the cash to pay it off."

"How long have we got?"

"At least a few months, I'd guess."

"You're telling me now might be a good time to find a new investor."

"Time to start thinking about it." I said. I paid for my sandwich. The beer was free—the only benefit so far of being a one-percent owner.

Early the following morning I rode my bike up to the Mount Bachelor ski area. It was a forty-mile round trip and took me about ninety minutes, a real workout going up but fast and easy coming down. It wasn't ideal training for the bike portion of the triathlon, which would be on dirt trails, but it challenged my legs and pushed my aerobics. I ate a second breakfast, took a shower, and read the newspaper. Ken made the front page: UPRIVER MAN DIES IN POSSIBLE MURDER. The article said the sheriff was investigating the death and no one had been arrested. The only thing I didn't know before was that Ken was fifty-one years old. Twenty years older than Candy.

I walked over to Candy's house to see if she and I could locate Ken's will. And to see whether she and Patsy Weil at Oxton, Rath, and Flynn had talked. And, in the reptilian basement of my brain, to see if Candy might welcome some physical comfort. Making a pass at Candy would be incredibly poor taste, perhaps even immoral. But the possibility existed, the old crocodile inside me thought, that she would make a pass at me.

CHAPTER 7

The Undead Rise

(Candy)

I wasn't going to seduce Dan. He was going to have to take some initiative. But if he didn't I was going to be pissed. I'd rape him if I could. There wasn't a single obstacle to our having as much sex as we wanted and take as much time with it as we wanted. Well, he'd want to get back to his training and eventually I'd want to get back to my art. But that would come after we were sated.

I wore slacks and a blouse with buttons. Running shoes with laces. My hair tied back and almost no makeup. I wouldn't look like a woman planning on sex. I'd direct him to Ken's office and tell him to help himself to whatever files he could find. I'd turn my back on him while I searched for something in a file drawer. I would feel his hands on my hips, my shoulders, or my breasts. Which would it be? I'd turn and we would kiss. Would we go fast or slow? Would he carefully unbutton my blouse or rip it off? Or would I? We would sweep all the papers off Ken's desk and do it right there. He could bend me over it if he wanted. I would come to regret the clothes I'd put on. I looked forward to that regret. Then we'd get in the hot tub. He wouldn't drink but maybe he'd smoke a little weed.

Dan arrived with a briefcase. He had on slacks and a golf shirt, still looking very professional. I shook his hand at the front door, smiling as though it were an effort to observe the rules of politeness. My being a widow and all. I came out the front door far enough to let any nosy neighbors see my calculated look—"respectable casual," it might be called. I could have been cleaning house or paying bills or cooking. No new smile for Dan when the door closed. He looked at me intently, as though trying to establish an unspoken sympathy between us and looking for a corresponding look from me. If I'd been a jury I would have decided in his favor no matter what the case was. I didn't want to betray my thoughts to him but I may have. I think all women appreciate a man who can read their mind. I wanted to wrap my arm around his neck and grab his sex but I turned away and I led the way toward Ken's office.

We got as far as the living room when he put his right hand on my shoulder. I stopped walking and hesitated for a second. I so wanted him to worry that I would be offended, or panicked, or tear myself away from his touch, or crushed to discover a friend's bestial intentions toward a grieving widow. All the more rich for both of us when I turned and let his arm curl around me. We stood with our chests barely sensing each other through our shirts.

"Did you want me when you were a boy and I visited your house?"

"I wanted you so badly I hated you. My eyes, my hormones, and my pecker were tortured with wanting you."

"I imagined you jerking off upstairs. Were you thinking of me?"

"You are embarrassing me. That was over ten years ago and I'm embarrassed today."

"No need to be embarrassed. I hope you'll let me to give you everything you imagined back then. I owe you."

"You owe me nothing," said Dan.

"Then consider it a gift," I said. "Christmas in July. Assuming you would still like your present."

"I can't wait to open it," he said.

"Let me help you," I said and pushed my shoes off. I slid my pants and panties off to show I was serious. Dan rubbed his hands over my buttocks. I unfastened his pants and yanked them down far enough they fell to the floor.

"Well," he said, "things are going to be awkward if we don't take the rest of our clothes off." He sat on the couch in the living room to take his shoes and pants off while I unbuttoned my blouse and shed my bra.

"Let's not make a mess," I said, and got a large towel from the powder room. Did he wonder why there was a bath towel in the powder room? It rather shot my pretense of restraint, modesty, and unpreparedness. I pulled his shirt off over his head and made him get up from the couch while I laid the towel on it. Then I pushed him down and straddled him. Then I knelt forward, kissing him and rubbing my breasts against his chest. God, he had muscles. His poor pecker was trying to find the entrance on its own, thrusting wildly between my legs. I sat up and guided it home. The thrusting continued.

"Won't you enjoy this more if I'm on top?" he asked. What a gentleman.

"Eventually," I said. "But right now I like being in control." I leaned forward again for a bit and then raised up again. Each position seemed like the best possible feeling in the world until I began to miss the other one.

"Don't wait too long," said Dan. I climbed off him and let him get up. I lay down on the couch and spread my legs like a two-bit hooker. My legs are slim and pretty. Dan ran his hand along one inner thigh and then the other. And then he licked me. God bless the man. He licked me earnestly in long wet licks. Who was giving who the gift?

"It's time," I said, raising his head. "Climb aboard."

When we were done we lay on our sides on the sofa facing each other. The couch was too narrow to lie on our backs and Dan was so tall his feet lopped over the arm at the far end. Yet our bodies would not part. He had a rich brown tan over his whole body, lighter around his pelvis. His face was handsome but a little gaunt. Not El Greco gaunt, but stretched over muscles with no fat for padding. My skin was pure white, what would have been praised in an earlier age as alabaster. Now the fashion was for more color, the look of having spent time in the sunshine. But my translucent skin looked a little exotic, a little ethereal, and I liked that. The green in Dan's shirt would look better on me than on him. The lavender in my blouse would look better next to his tan. I reached my shirt up from the floor and held it next to his arm. I would paint him with those colors.

"What are you doing?" he asked.

"This color is perfect for you. You should get a shirt like this."

"Why not just take your blouse? I could wear it around my neck like a scarf."

"Racing colors," I said, "like a jockey."

"Every time I ride," he said.

We heard the doorbell ring and both groaned.

"It's FedEx with some paints," I said. "They'll leave it." But whoever rang wasn't going away. The doorbell rang again, longer this time.

"Will you see who it is?" I asked. "Tell them we're in a meeting and I'll call them." Dan climbed over me and stood to put his clothes back on. I lay back on the couch and waited for him to return. I could hear the conversation in the front hall.

"Can I help you?" Dan's voice.

"I'm here to see Candy," said a woman's voice—a voice I recognized. I scrambled up from the couch, turned to snatch up the towel and pad the cushions back into some semblance of order. I grabbed my clothes off the floor and ran to the laundry room in the back of the house. I kept the door open though, so I could hear the conversation in the front hall.

"Candy is right in the middle of something. Can I have her call you?"

"I bet," said the woman. The voice belonged to Ken's first wife. She still called herself Rhonda Winterpol. Ken had a restraining order on her to keep her away from him. We'd talked about revising the order to keep her away from me but we'd never done it. And this was the damned result. I could see months lying ahead of her badgering. Well, I'd put a stop to that. Or what are lawyers for? Or the money to pay for them?

"And who are you?" demanded Rhonda.

"How do you do?" Dan said. "I'm Dan Martinez." This did not sound like what I wanted at all. Ken would have grabbed Rhonda by the arm and flung her on the front walk. Rhonda now thought she had a sucker.

"And what brings you here today, Mr. Martinez?" Rhonda asked as if she were the owner of the house.

"I came to see what papers of Mr. Winterpol's I could find. My law firm is helping Mrs. Winterpol with his estate." Ridiculously polite, I thought.

"Then you are the man I need to see," said Rhonda. She spoke with an aristocratic tone that I had somehow forgotten. She was either from a classier family than I imagined or she watched a lot of *Masterpiece Theatre*. Wherever she had once been in life, she had come a long way down.

I strode to the front door, not as well put together as I would have liked, but I was desperate to head off any presumptions on Rhonda's part or concessions by Dan.

Rhonda was not as I remembered her—now a thin woman wearing big sunglasses and a sun hat. Beneath the hat, sunglasses, and makeup her face was gaunt and pasty with a sore spot, like a red currant, on her right cheek. I hadn't seen a lot of meth addicts but Rhonda looked like the perfect picture of one. Parked on the street behind her was a faded green sedan with gaps in the rocker panels. In the driver's seat a man sat rapping out a rhythm on the steering wheel with two drumsticks. How did these people get in the gate?

"I was sorry to see that Ken died," said the woman. "He had his faults but he was our husband." I recoiled from the idea that Rhonda and I had anything in common, that in some way she, whom Ken had ripped out of his life like termite damage, had equal standing with me. My shock gave Rhonda enough time to push past me and plop herself on the bench in the front hall.

"As you know, I'm sure," said Rhonda, "Ken paid me one thousand every month for alimony. I don't want to miss a payment because he's not around." I'd never heard of Ken paying alimony but with Ken, as Rhonda undoubtedly counted on, you could never be sure what he was doing.

"Get out of my house," I said. I thought of calling resort security or even the sheriff, though I really didn't want the sheriff back again. I thought of reaching in the hall closet for an umbrella to thrash this woman out the door.

Dan interceded and at first I thought things were going the wrong way. "Did Ken usually pay you by check or did he transfer the money into your account?"

"Cash," said Rhonda.

"Do you come here to get it or does he send it to you?" This kind of delaying baloney is, I suppose, what lawyers are good at.

Rhonda thought about this. "He sends it. But he isn't going to be doing that anymore so I need to collect it."

Dan pulled a pen out of his pocket and picked up *The Bulletin* newspaper off the bench Rhonda was sitting on. "Could you write down your address so we know where to send the money in the future?" Now that was fairly clever and I began to appreciate what Dan was doing.

"I want the money today," said Rhonda.

We all heard steps coming up the front walk toward us. The drummer boy from the car stood in the doorway glowering. "What's going on here?" he demanded.

"They won't give us the money, Wade," said Rhonda, now angry at the outrageous miscarriage of justice she had encountered.

"We'll see about that," said the man. He was a thin five-foot-ten but with muscles like ropes. His pocked and battered face bespoke a hard life. "We know Ken kept money here," he said, looking at Dan. "Hundred-dollar bills. Where are they?" Dan didn't seem to know what to do with this angry and crazy man. Dan may have been a little intimidated. He planned on living a long life and Wade had a much shorter horizon.

I thought I saw a solution and offered a plan. "If I tell you where the money is will you go away?"

"That's all we want," said Wade. It didn't seem to bother Rhonda that Wade had just contradicted what she'd said about a regular thousand a month. Cash was king.

"There's five thousand for emergencies in a metal box hidden under the wood pile," I said. "You can have three thousand."

"Let's get it!" said Wade with a leer for all of us, as though Dan and I would be just as delighted as Wade to find the money. We all went out to the porch and Wade began throwing logs into the back yard. Dan joined him, throwing logs at a slower pace to lend credibility to what I had said. Rhonda watched, bent forward with her head cocked like a bird, trying to catch sight of the box. Ken should have divorced her for sheer stupidity.

I slipped back into the house, shut the kitchen door to the porch, and quietly locked it. Rhonda and her friend didn't notice, though Dan did. I called resort security because they could get to the house quickly, and they said they would call the sheriff for backup. I waited in the front hall to watch for the guards. I hoped they would arrive before Wade got down to the bottom of the pile.

I heard a crash of glass from the back of the house and then a loud "What are you doing?" from Rhonda. The back door slammed shut and I heard it lock. I leapt into the powder room off the front-hall bathroom and turned the latch.

"Open this door!" I heard Wade shout from the back of the house. "What the hell are you doing?" I had trouble making sense of this. If he had broken the glass to get in, then why was he yelling at someone else to open the door? There was a yelp of pain and some loud swearing that could have only been Wade. I picked up the lid from the toilet tank and prepared to hit him if he broke down the door to the bathroom. I stood there ten minutes listening to voices I could not understand, the porcelain lid getting so heavy I had to put it down. Finally I heard Dan calling my name.

"Candy? Candy? You can come out now. The sheriff is here. Wade and Rhonda are in custody."

Out the front door we watched the deputies put Wade in one car and Rhonda in another. Wade's hands were cuffed behind him. Rhonda's hands were cuffed in front. Deputy Newton, who seemed more friendly to me this time around, came over to talk with us while a male deputy kept an eye on Wade and Rhonda. We told Deputy Newton what had happened, that Rhonda and Wade had come expecting money and ultimately demanding it. Did they threaten us? Not exactly, but their demeanor was threatening. Dan said we were in fear and that seemed to be enough for the deputies to arrest the meth-heads.

Dan told Deputy Newton how the pane in the back door got broken. Dan broke it, reached in to turn the handle, and then locked it again after he had stepped inside. Rhonda saw him and slapped her friend on the shoulder three times to get his attention. When Wade looked at her she pointed to the door with the broken pane and Dan standing behind it. Wade kicked at the bottom of the door and then thrust his hand through the broken pane and to get the door handle. Dan slammed a pot from the stove onto his hand as hard as he could. Whatever pain it caused Wade, it didn't bother him for long. He tried to grab the door handle again from the inside and seemed mystified that his hand couldn't do what he asked of it. This was when Deputy Newton and another deputy came around the corner of the house, Deputy Newton with a Taser and the other deputy with his gun drawn.

"It sure looks like Wade broke that pane of glass, doesn't it?" Dan asked Deputy Newton. "Even his fingerprints are on the inside door handle. If it served your purposes, you could threaten to charge him with breaking and entering, even though you can't really prosecute him for it. Maybe it will induce him to plead to something else." Deputy Newton did not thank Dan for the idea but I bet she heard it.

"This is perfect," said Dan, beaming at me after the deputies had taken their charges away. "Those are the people who murdered Ken. Who is to say they weren't?" He sat on the couch and let out a long breath. "Where were they the morning Ken was hit? They may not have anyone credible to vouch for them. They may not even remember where they were. I can't wait to tell Tod Morgan."

"Did you have to break the glass in the door?" I asked. "Paloma didn't like cleaning up the blood and now she'll have to clean up the glass." Paloma was our—my—diligent but sometimes excitable housekeeper.

"It will only take a minute," said Dan. "Where's the dustpan?" When I was a child housework was always a punishment for the trash basket of errors I had accumulated. I pointed Dan to the laundry-room closet and sat on a stool in the kitchen while he swept up the glass. When he mentioned papering over the hole in the glass I said I would do it. Certainly I knew how to handle card stock and tape.

"You came to look through Ken's papers," I said. "I brought this box down from the bedroom. You should start here." Dan took it into the dining room and we went through the box. There were no wills. There were car registrations and all the cars were registered to Ken. There were titles to both houses, entirely Ken's. There was a prenuptial agreement in the box that described the property each brought into the marriage—from me nothing but a used car, some clothes, art supplies, a few kitchen appliances, and two sets of skis. All the real assets were Ken's. It went on for pages about how property would be divided if we got a divorce. The provisions for one of us dying were boilerplate. I would have no claim on anything Ken brought into the marriage unless he left it to me in his will.

"The will must be at the Lake Oswego house," I said.

"Is there any cash stashed away somewhere? Don't get the idea you can just take it."

"I never heard of any cash hidden away," I said. "It's not the sort of thing Ken would do." Actually, it was exactly the kind of thing Ken would do. But if he had I didn't know where it was.

"Any accounts in the Cayman Islands that you know about?" Dan asked. "Switzerland? Bermuda?"

"No accounts I ever heard of," I said. That was the truth.

CHAPTER 8

Injured Parties

(Dan)

After my encounter with Rhonda and Wade at Candy's house, I went back to Mom's and called Patsy at Oxton about the documents I had found at Candy's. I told her Candy would be expecting Patsy's call about access to the Lake Oswego house and also asked Patsy to call Western Sun. I said the company might be part of the estate, and would probably need a thorough audit and someone to run it or sell it off. I warned her that Ken had been a shady guy, there were dozens of lawsuits and countersuits, and it was going to take some real time and effort to sort it all out. That, of course, would be music to Patsy's ears. Lots of billable hours for Oxton, Rath, and Flynn.

I changed into workout clothes and went into the garage to lift weights. I'd moved a small TV from my room into the garage and I watched baseball while I lifted and stretched. I concentrated on my upper body because I'd already worked my legs with the bike ride that morning.

My iPhone had an app that allowed me to record outgoing phone calls. In Oregon, it was legal to record calls if one person in the conversation—that was me—knew the call was being recorded. California and Washington were "two-party" states—both people had to know the call was being recorded. I was going to stick to Oregon. I had to stay strictly within the law here so I could present the recordings in court if it ever came to that.

The first person I called was a man named Tom Melillo. He had invested in a strip mall in East Portland with Ken Winterpol and some other people, though Ken was the one who put the deal together. Melillo's lawsuit alleged that Ken borrowed all the money that Ken himself invested from a bank and he invested no real money of his own. Then Ken had other companies, shell companies that he controlled, sign leases for space in the mall for high rental rates. The other investors, including poor Tom Melillo, bought Ken's share of the building from him because it looked like the property was doing great, that it was fully occupied and with good income. For a while they continued to get fat checks. Then Ken's fake companies all defaulted and disappeared. Ken was still managing the property so the other investors didn't know their renters had evaporated. Ken stopped paying to maintain the property, then he stopped paying "income" to the investors, and finally he stopped paying on the original loan. The bank that made the original loan foreclosed on the property and all the investors lost their money. Except Ken, of course, because he sold off his share of the property to the other investors a long time before.

When I called his office, Tom Melillo answered the phone himself.

"Hello," I said, "My name is Dan Martinez and I'm a friend of Candy Winterpol, the wife of Ken Winterpol, whom I understand you know. Mrs. Winterpol asked me to write an obituary for her husband and I'm calling whoever I can find who did business with him."

"Ken Winterpol is dead?" asked Melillo.

"Yes," I said. I didn't say how Ken had died because I didn't want to alert Melillo or anyone else that I was looking for a killer.

"You're sure? He is absolutely dead?"

"I'm afraid so. He's in the morgue and Mrs. Winterpol has his death certificate. She hasn't set a date for a service but I can let you know when I find out."

"I might want to come to that," said Melillo. "The burial too. Open casket, I hope."

"So what kind of businessman would you say Ken Winterpol was?" I asked.

"He was a lying cheating no-good son-of-a-bitch crook. He deserved multiple deaths with all the trimmings," said Melillo. This was just what I wanted to hear.

"Did he cost you anything personally?" I asked.

"He undid all I'd worked on for over twelve years. He almost drove me into bankruptcy. It would serve him right if I spit in his face and threw rocks on his coffin. I had to sell everything I owned when he swindled me. House, car, and all my other investments. My kids had to change schools and my family had to live in an apartment. I may never get back to where I was. The man threw a bomb in the middle of my life. I'm not ashamed to tell you I'm glad the man is dead."

"Do a lot of people feel the way you do? I want the obit to be truthful but I'd like to have a few positive things to say for Mrs. Winterpol's sake."

"That bimbo? She married him for his money and she'll probably be dancing on his grave." I wished he hadn't said that. I wouldn't want to play that in court.

"To all appearances she loved him," I said. "And she's devastated that he's dead." I felt good getting that recorded, even if I knew Candy didn't seem all that devastated and, thanks to an afternoon delight of which I had firsthand knowledge, I could not say under oath that Candy loved the man as well as she might have.

"If anybody loved him he was lucky," said Melillo. "Do you know he borrowed his first-grade teacher's life savings and wouldn't pay it back? He told her that instead of paying the loan he would take care of her the rest of her life. She had the loan agreement in writing and she sued him and won. Can you imagine being so bad your first-grade teacher sues you? The guy's a piece of work."

"Can you think of anything good I can write about Ken? It sure would help," I said.

Melillo grumbled and made me wait. "He wore nice suits and always drove a clean car." Then silence. "But don't say it came from me."

"Thanks very much, Mr. Melillo. I appreciate your help."

"I'm glad you called," he said with sudden gusto. "Spread the word."

We hung up and I sat back for a minute. Melillo could make a wonderful witness.

The next two calls went to voicemail and I didn't leave messages. The fourth person I called was Roger Tucker. The call went to his assistant and I said I was calling Mr. Tucker about Ken Winterpol, who had recently died. The assistant put me on hold for thirty seconds and a new voice came on the line.

"So the old bastard is dead," he said with an amused tone in his voice.

"Are you Mr. Tucker?" I asked in as humble and tentative a voice as I could manage.

"At your service," he said with enthusiasm. I went through my spiel about writing Ken's obituary.

"What can I tell you?" said Tucker. "The man was a goon. He made enemies every time he turned around. He made it harder and harder for anyone to trust him. If he hadn't died he would have sooner or later wound up in the pokey. I guess he found a new way to escape." Tucker laughed out loud. "Tell me, did someone kill him?"

"It looks like they might have," I said, "The Deschutes County Sheriff is investigating."

"And you're calling me to see if I did it?"

"Not at all," I said. "I'm trying to write his obituary. Though I'll tell you I'm having a hard time finding people who have anything good to say about him."

"Well, you can say he made me money. I have no complaints about the man."

"But you sued him."

"Negotiating leverage. He outbid me on a building I wanted. It was next to a building I owned and the property he outbid me on was worth more to me than it was to him. He paid too much for it, of course. He borrowed most of the money and then sold shares in the building to small investors, little people who didn't know beans about real estate. The thing is, he sold one hundred and thirty percent of the building. He always intended the investment to fail, like Max Bialystock in *The Producers*. He paid his investors a nice return for a year without letting them see the books. They were fat, dumb, and happy. Meanwhile he wasn't leasing up the building. I took videotapes of the place, inside and out, for weeks. No cars in the parking lot. There were company names on the directory in the front hall but there was nobody on the floors where the companies were supposed to be. The companies didn't even exist. You couldn't find them in the phone book.

"I showed my videotapes to the bank that gave Ken the loan and they sold me the loan for seventy-five cents on the dollar. Ken had paid some of the interest but his payments were getting later and later. The bank was happy to be rid of him. Then I dug up the individual investors, showed them the videotapes, and bought some of them out for as little as thirty cents. My timing was good. Ken had just stopped paying them their nice little incomes, claiming he needed money to make repairs to the building. Some of the investors went to Ken to ask what was going on and they told him about me. By that time, though, I was one of the owners and had standing to sue him for fraud. At the same time I started foreclosure proceedings on the loan. The jerk sold me his equity in the building for a dollar."

"So you leased up the building and made money?"

"It was a piece of crap. I tore it down and built a twin to the building I already had. Matched the landscaping and built a shared parking lot. Made a pile and I still own the buildings. I raised the image of the whole neighborhood."

"Have you still got a list of those other investors?"

"So you are looking for a murderer!"

"Along with writing an obituary."

"Sure. Give me your fax number."

"I don't have a fax machine. Can you email it to me?"

"I don't like email. Give me a postal address and I'll send it to you." I gave him my name and my parents' address.

"Thanks for your help, Mr. Tucker," I said. "When we know when and where the service is would you like me to let you know?"

"Hell no," he said. "I'll just be glad to know he's in the ground. You could send me a copy of the obituary, though. That should make good reading."

"It's a deal," I said. "Thanks again."

Before I could make another call the doorbell rang. I could hear my mother going to answer it and I listened to see who it was.

It was Breuninger. He introduced himself to Mom and said, "I am looking for Leon Martinez. Is he here?" I leapt from my chair to join my mother at the door.

"No, he's not," said my mother.

"Good morning, Detective," I said. "Neither my mother nor I know where he is. He called yesterday afternoon to say his car was at the Portland Airport and asked me to pick it up. But he wouldn't say where he was. He says he's on a sabbatical."

"You realize," said Breuninger, "that if you are not telling me the truth you can be charged with lying to a police officer and obstruction of justice?"

"We've already told you more than we're required to," I said. "We could just decline to answer. But it doesn't matter. We're telling you the truth."

"Now I am going to ask your mother some questions and I don't want you to interrupt. Can we agree on that?"

"I won't answer for her but I may tell her not to answer."

"Are you her lawyer too?"

"For the time being," I said. "I know it is our duty to help you find my dad if we can. But my mother is not required to say anything that might lead to his prosecution. Spousal privilege."

"Doesn't apply here, Mr. Attorney," said Breuninger. "She's not under oath. She's not testifying."

"Communications between spouses are privileged in or out of court," I said. Breuninger scowled at this and turned to my mother.

"Do you know where your husband is, Mrs. Martinez?"

"No," said my mother. "I told you I don't."

"Do you know who he is likely to be with?"

"No."

"Do you know where he is likely to be in the future?"

"Right back here," said my mother. "And when he comes back he will tell the truth." I wasn't so sure of that myself but I glared at Breuninger as though I agreed with my mother completely.

"Has Mr. Martinez told you anything about what happened the morning he left?"

I leapt in before my mother could answer. "We're not going to get into that," I said. Breuninger was clearly annoyed.

"What number did your father call you from?"

"He called me on our house line," my mother said. "The phone doesn't display the calling number."

"We are going to want to search his car."

"If you'll show me a search warrant," I said, "I'll give you the key and you can find it at the Portland airport. Or you can wait for me to drive it back here and then search it, if you have a warrant." Then something occurred to me. "Mrs. Winterpol has retained my old law firm, Oxton, Rath, and Flynn, to handle her estate. They need to look through the Winterpol's house in Lake Oswego to see what documents they can find. Do you want to search that house before they go in?"

Breuninger frowned. Of course he'd like to search the house in Lake Oswego but he couldn't get a warrant to sweep the premises. The warrant had to specify what thing or things he was looking for. And whoever ran Breuninger's budget was not going to authorize a trip to Lake Oswego, near Portland, without a good reason. "We don't need to do that," said Breuninger. "But your firm needs to tell us if they find anything that might shed light on this case." I looked up Patsy Weil's number on my phone and recited it to Breuninger. "Please call Ms. Weil and tell her what she should keep an eye out for. I am not part of the firm anymore and need to step out of the loop."

"Fine," said Breuninger. "And we may be back with a search warrant for this house."

"And what will you be looking for?" I asked. He couldn't be looking for the murder weapon. They'd already found the poker Ken had been hit with.

"That's for us to decide," he answered.

"The trash goes out tonight for pickup early tomorrow," I said, trying to seem cooperative and professional and to avoid any hint of sarcasm. Breuninger would not need a warrant to search the trash once we put it out on the street, but the image of his coming back at night to paw through the garbage was unavoidably laughable. "I'll tell you what," I added, "we'll dump all the wastebaskets in the cart for Frontier Garbage and wheel it out to the street right now. That will save you coming back." If he were diligent, he would go through the trash. If he didn't stoop to dirty work, then we could later say he had not been thorough in his investigation.

My mother stepped forward. "We want you to find the killer," she said. "Everybody in Upriver wants that. We want to help you do that. But the killer is not my husband. You need to look elsewhere."

"We're just following the evidence," said Breuninger.

"Well, I have a lead you might want to keep in mind," I said. "When I was out running the morning Ken Winterpol was attacked there was a gray pickup truck parked by the bridge over by the Deschutes. At the time I thought it belonged to a kayaker. Whoever owned the truck could have hopped the fence and gotten to the Winterpol house and back with a good chance of nobody seeing him. It's just an idea." As with my phone calls to people who hated Ken, I was trying to increase the pool of Ken's possible killers. Breuninger, I'm sure, recognized what I was doing and resented it. I told him I thought the truck was a two-door. Nothing in the truck bed. I didn't know the make, model or year but it hadn't looked new.

I gathered up the trash, put it in the green cart that Frontier Garbage picked up, and wheeled it out to the street. Standing in a shadowed part of the kitchen, I watched Breuninger dump all the trash out and put it back in again. I didn't want to embarrass him any further by letting him see me. But I wanted to know if he took anything as evidence. As far as I could see he took nothing.

I was deciding what to get done before lunch when my cell phone rang. It was my former boss from Oxton, Greg Lyman.

"Thanks for the business!" he said. "Sorting out Western Sun is going to take us man-years. This will definitely move you up in the queue of who the firm hires back when it is able to."

"That's good," I said. "In the meantime, how about a referral fee?"

"Instead, how about we hire you on contract to help us settle

Winterpol's estate? You know the client and you're living near her, which none of the rest of us are. Maintain the relationship. Let us know if she isn't happy. That's pretty much it. We'll call it something else on the invoices." I wondered whether having sex with Candy would count toward "maintaining the relationship" and whether I could bill Oxton for the time. I decided to pose a different question.

"How about a referral fee and I contract for five hours a week?" I was tempted to offer Greg ten hours a week. But I couldn't bill Oxton for the time I spent digging up more suspects in Ken's murder. I could only bill for helping with the estate. Or, to tell the truth, doing whatever it took to keep Candy's account at Oxton.

"We can probably do that," said Greg. "Let me talk with the partners."

"More immediately," I asked, "how about flying me to Portland to help search the Winterpols' house for his will and his financial records?"

"If that is what you want, then sure," said Greg. "You're not going to get carried away with expenses, are you?"

"No," I said. "But I think Mrs. Winterpol would prefer to give the key and alarm code to me rather than to a person she's never met."

"Set it up with Patsy and come ahead," said Greg. A good deal all around.

I looked at the local newspaper from Bend, *The Bulletin*, while I drank a thick smoothie for lunch. There was a follow-up story on Ken's murder. It quoted the Deschutes County Sheriff: "*The department is vigorously pursuing this investigation. We are collecting and analyzing the facts surrounding the crime. No arrest warrant has been issued and no suspects are in custody at this time.*" Then the article gave some background on Ken. He'd grown up in Burns, Oregon and gone to Portland State on a football scholarship.

When I called Candy about picking up the key to the Lake Oswego house she said she was just about to start painting and would leave it on the back porch early the next morning. I seemed to be just another contractor she had to deal with. Then she asked me, in an oh-by-the-way manner, if I would pick up Ken's sister in Portland and bring her back to Bend for Ken's memorial service. I said I would and Candy gave me the address. I couldn't very well say no and I thought a side benefit might be the sister, Linda Winterpol, could give me more ideas about who might want to kill Ken.

The following day, when I went to pick up the key, the firewood Wade and I had thrown on the lawn while looking for the mythical cash-filled metal box, was still there. Out beyond it were brown spots on the lawn that looked like roughly shaped footprints, as though a family of Bigfoots had stepped off the porch and walked over to the fountain. The footprints hadn't been there when I was there before. And, I realized, with a flash of pride in my own cleverness, that the footprints had been made the morning of Ken's murder—probably by Ken, his killer, or both.

All the footprints, rough as they were, seemed too big to be those of a woman. I tried to remember Candy's feet and I could not. She would be annoyed if I knocked on her door and asked her what her shoe size was. Did these footsteps tend to incriminate Candy or my father? Or tend to exonerate them? I couldn't see it one way or the other. I took three photos of the footprints with my phone and messaged them to Breuninger. The footprints were evidence and I thought informing him would indicate my sincere intention to find the killer. And the footprints would give him that much more to think about. One more thing to investigate and to account for in any prosecution.

Then I called Breuninger and left him a voicemail about the photos. How did I know the footsteps had been made the morning of the murder? Frost delay. On very cold mornings the pro shop at Upriver would not let golfers on the course until the sun had melted the frost on the grass. If people walked on a frosty golf course they fractured the frozen blades of grass, the blades died standing up and two or three days later the grass turned brown. The footprints I saw could have been made in the middle of the night but it was very likely they were made in the early morning by Ken's killer or killers. By the time the sheriff's people arrived, and wandered all over the lawn, the frost had melted and they didn't break any grass.

I had walked on the stone walkway that came around the corner of the house and hadn't touched the grass.

I sent the same photos to Tod Morgan and followed up with a similar voicemail. This is what detectives do, I thought with satisfaction. I almost forgot to pick up the key to the Lake Oswego house that Candy had left. The next time I saw her I would take a good look at the size of her feet.

The other thing I resolved to do, as I drove to get gas in the Upriver Business Park, was to take pictures of the license plates on every gray pickup truck I saw. I could imagine Breuninger testifying at trial and Tod Morgan asking whether, after Breuninger learned from me that I saw a gray pickup parked near Ken's house early the day he died, did Breuninger ever pursue this lead? Had he found all the gray pickups in the area and had he identified their owners? I found two gray pickups at the hardware store and one more, covered with soap, in the self-service carwash.

That evening I wrote up Ken's obituary. I'd talked to ten people he'd done business with but the only thing I quoted was Melillo's comment about Ken wearing nice suits. The stories I'd collected about Ken's unscrupulousness I saved for Breuninger and Tod Morgan. I emailed the obituary to Candy and she answered immediately that it was fine. I wasn't sure she'd taken the time to read it. Then I sent it off to the *The Bulletin* with a scanned image of a photo that Candy had left out for me with the key.

CHAPTER 9

Lake Oswego

(Dan)

Next morning Mom drove me to Redmond Airport, north of Bend, to catch an early flight to Portland.

"Don't tell me where Dad is, if you know," I said. "But do you know where he is?"

"No," said Mom. "He's called me a few times. He says he's fine and he'll be home in August. But he doesn't tell me where he is."

"Are you worried about him?" I asked.

"Worried and annoyed," said Mom. "But not too much. He's always gone off in the summer to visit some friend or other. You remember that. They're all artists or musicians I don't have much in common with. I can take only so much talk about art. And they struggle, some harder than others, to be polite to me. So this is normal, except that he hasn't told me where he is."

"You are not as worried as I am," I said.

"Your father and I have known each other a long time."

My mother's remark reminded me of a question I'd been thinking about for years. There was still enough time for her to answer it before we got into the traffic in Bend. "How did you and Dad know you would have a good marriage? You are from such different backgrounds."

"You may not appreciate how dashing and romantic your father was when we were young. He was creative, always thinking of things that nobody else thought of. And he had a certain dignity. Though he could be funny he took himself seriously. It mattered to him how he behaved. He was pretty exciting for a small-town girl like me. We fell in love. I'm not as sure why your father chose me. I was rather attractive back then."

"You still are," I said.

"Not like I was," she said. "I think your father wanted stability—someone he could pledge his loyalty to for the rest of his life and who would do the same for him. His family had changed countries twice and his parents always remembered Franco chasing them out of their home and persecuting their relatives. People his parents knew had been tortured and killed."

"So you promised not to torture him?"

"I never promised that. He was playing the odds."

"And he took you to Paris?"

"After we married and had a little money. He'd been there as a boy. I ate snails for the first time. We went to museum after museum while I listened and remembered what I could. I wasn't a dummy. But seeing your father so excited about it, that was the best part. And having him try to share it all with me. At night we would just walk the streets. It was so romantic. You were conceived in Paris."

"So you've told me. And to think I owe it all to snails."

"Don't be flip about it," said Mom. "Your life has turned out pretty well."

"Yes it has," I said. "Thank you very much."

"Speaking of your life," my mother said, "are you planning on running triathlons for a living?"

"I just have to pick up some sponsors and I'll be set. I think Nike and a sports drink company."

"Don't you have to win a few races before that happens?"

"Details," I said. "At the moment I am not thinking beyond the Upriver Off-Road. I only want to focus on that. Then we'll see."

I'd always found the road between Bend and Redmond, where the airport was, kind of discouraging. Twenty miles of straight road with nothing much to look at. Most of the landscape was a juniper forest, though "forest" was, in this case, a misleading term. The junipers, scraggly evergreens no more than twenty feet high, were spread out over dry land that grew mostly sagebrush, thin dry grass, and rocks. The land was a desert, interrupted by a few green irrigated fields and, incongruously here and there, a willow tree. An irrigation canal, totally artificial, ran alongside the road for a few miles. I preferred the long-needled ponderosas of Upriver or the broadleaf trees of the Willamette Valley. Yet this morning, with the sun coming up and long shadows stretched across the landscape, everything looked fresher than I remembered it. I could imagine a cattleman looking out over this dry land and being supremely content with it.

I jammed my six-foot-four body into a window seat on the flight to Portland and watched the Cascades go by below me. The view compensated me well enough, I thought, for not being able to stretch for an hour. We flew close to Mount Hood. Mount Adams and Mount St. Helens shone brightly in the distance.

As long as I was going to spend a day in Portland, I arranged to meet my triathlon coach, Mitch Avery, after I'd gone to Candy's house in Lake Oswego. I'd found Mitch when I first started training, while I was still working for Oxton. Mitch told me I had to make my goals crystal clear. He said they had to be focused on the race, they had to be measurable, and they had to be under my control, or mostly under my control. He agreed that was a tall order.

Saying I would finish in two hours and forty-five minutes wouldn't work. On the day of the race my time and every racer's time would be affected by the course conditions: How hot would it be that day? Would the trails be dusty or damp? Would there be waves on the lake? Would I get bunched up in a clutch of competitors?

Saying I would win the race would be ridiculous. The top racers would have trained for years and I would have trained for less than twelve months.

I suggested to Mitch that my goal be to train and run as well as I possibly could.

"No," he said. "There will always be something you could have done better. And once you fall away from perfect you've already failed to meet your goal."

We decided on only two goals. First, that when I got to the start of the race I could tell myself I had done virtually everything within my power to prepare for a great race, that I deserved to do well and could expect to do well. To make this goal as measurable as possible, I would assess my diligence before every training session, set intermediate performance goals, estimate how well I would do against them, and then measure the results. I would get to know my capabilities, both physical and mental. I would know myself like a car I had taken apart and put back together. Gaining that knowledge of myself was, in fact, one of the key reasons for the entire triathlon experiment.

My second goal was to finish within twenty-five minutes of the winner in my age group. Mitch said neither one of us knew whether twenty-five minutes was the right number but it was something to shoot for. It was something to compare myself against. As imperfect as the goal might be, it would keep me motivated both in training and in the race itself.

Setting goals had led me to think about why I was focusing so much of my life on a triathlon. I decided it was because I had an opportunity, before my life got complicated with a wife, a house, a family, and a job I couldn't do without, to pick a single clear mission to accomplish, where other duties and objectives wouldn't compromise my efforts, where life would be clearer than ever before or later, and where accomplishing my goals would depend almost entirely on myself, not on the economy, or the fortunes of my employer, or the judgment of my boss or of anyone else. This would be my one opportunity to live a single-minded life. Now, of course, keeping Candy, myself, and my father out of jail was distracting me. But I could handle it. I hadn't missed a training session yet.

Mitch told me my mindset for sports would have to make some serious changes. "In rugby, you exert maximum efforts for short periods of time," he said. "Then you drift with the play looking for what to do next. In tri the key is to make steady efforts at the fastest pace you can sustain. It's totally different.

"And you can't think like a lawyer either. Triathlon training is not like racking up billable hours. More is not better. You don't get stronger while you're working out. You get stronger while you're recovering. You need to have the discipline to stop." I had come a long way, I thought as I gazed down on the suburbs of Portland, and I was looking forward to seeing Mitch again.

The Maserati started on the third try. I drove it through a

carwash on the way to Ken and Candy's house so I could feel more professional, representing Oxton with my best foot forward. I also knew my father would want me to keep his car clean.

The nicest houses in Lake Oswego were on the lake itself and were surrounded by big trees. Lake Oswego was where Portland's rich had lived for generations, though some of the wealthy had decamped across the Columbia River to Washington state, where there was no income tax. I thought Ken must have picked Lake Oswego to give himself the aura of old money. I bet his neighbors described him to each other as nouveau riche, an arriviste, and whatever other snobby words they could come up with. Candy was not old-money either but her art, and its presence in some of the galleries these people visited, gave her cachet. And Candy, I thought, probably knew how to act snobby herself, if not about money then about taste, particularly in art or design.

The house was stone with sharply pitched slate roofs. It was medium-sized for the neighborhood and it sat squarely in the middle of the lot, surrounded by lawn, rhododendrons, and a few large pine trees. It had a 1920s look to it.

Candy and Patsy at Oxton had given me letters authorizing me to access and search the house. Patsy had lined up a locksmith to open any locked drawers or closets I couldn't find a key for. The locksmith had not arrived and I entered the front door with the key that Candy had given me. I found the alarm panel in the front hall closet and turned the alarm off. The house was more contemporary on the inside. It looked to me like an art gallery with furniture. Most of the color was on the walls in the form of paintings, some of them Candy's work. I couldn't say whether Ken loved his wife. But he was certainly proud of her.

In the left hand file drawer in Ken's desk I found folders related to his personal finances and maintaining his houses. The labels included INSURANCE, MEDICAL, PROPERTY TAXES, CARS, LAKE OSWEGO MAINT., UPRIVER MAINT., and WILLS. I pulled out the WILLS folder and opened it on the desk. The top sheet was handwritten and it shook me to the core. It was the original, not a copy, and it was dated only a week ago here in Lake Oswego and signed by Ken. It said very simply that he left his entire estate to his sister, Linda. There was no mention of Candy at all. Had Ken found out about Candy's tryst with me? Had I been the instrument that had cost her the inheritance? I had opened the folder but had not touched the will itself. I folded a large yellow Post-it over a corner of the document so my fingerprints would not be on the will and slid it into a manila envelope. I didn't know what I was going to do about the will but I wanted to be able to say I didn't know it existed. One thing about a handwritten, so-called holographic will, was that only the original had legal standing. A copy of it counted for nothing. Another thing: it didn't require witnesses the way a normal will did. It just had to be in the deceased's handwriting.

The other documents in the WILLS folder were typewritten, witnessed, and notarized wills for both Ken and Candy, dated two years earlier and with no additions or codicils in the folder. I flipped quickly through Ken's will. He left fifty thousand to his sister Linda and the rest 50-50 to Candy and to his children. To the best of my knowledge Ken didn't have any children but Oxton was going to have to make an effort to find out if any existed. Children or no children, this will was going to make Candy a rich woman, unless Ken's company had more debt than its investments were worth. The typewritten will was the one I wanted to see the light of day.

I paged quickly through Candy's will. If she died first her entire estate went to Ken. If Ken predeceased her it left her estate to her children if she had any, then to Linda. I would give both typewritten wills to Patsy and make copies for Candy, Tod Morgan, and myself.

But I would not give Patsy or anyone else Ken's holographic will—the recent, handwritten will that left the entire estate to Linda. Hiding or destroying it would be illegal, immoral, and unethical. I would be disbarred or even go to jail if anyone could prove I had done it. But who was to say I had ever seen it? If someone claimed Ken had told them about the will it would be hearsay, irrelevant without the will itself. However, if Ken gave someone a copy of the holographic will there could be a problem. The copy would not be valid. But a copy would prove that the holographic will existed, and Linda's attorneys would ask me hard questions about whether I had found the will and what I had done with it. I decided I would take the will with me and keep its existence to myself for now. I would leave my options open.

The most recent mortgage statements, less than a month old, showed that Ken was up to date on both houses. The mortgages each had about twenty more years to run. I'd bought some cardboard filing boxes on my way from the airport and I put all the files from the drawer, except the holographic will, into the box for Patsy.

In the right-hand drawer were files related to Candy's art. Most were labeled with the names of specific galleries and contained contracts, lists of pieces shipped and returned, and paperwork that recorded sales. One folder contained newspaper and magazine articles about Candy and her paintings. In the back of the drawer there were files labeled HUNTING and FISHING. Those were for Ken, I thought, since I had never heard of Candy pursuing either sport.

I looked through the other smaller drawers in Ken's desk, finding stamps, paper clips, a stapler, a ruler, blank sticky notes and other detritus common to desks in the world. I kept my eye out for a key that might open the heavy wood cabinet behind Ken's desk. There was no key but lying in the right bottom drawer I found a revolver. The handle was black and the rest of the gun was a dull silvery gray color. Was Ken worried about someone trying to kill him or was he just one of those people who thought he should have a gun around? I didn't want to touch the gun but I did want to see the sheaf of papers beneath it. I could see it was a typewritten letter, dated almost a year earlier, that started *Dear Children*. I pulled a sheet of paper out of my briefcase and, cupping it in my hand, I eased out the stack of papers and let the gun slide off them into the bottom of the drawer. With the unstapled and unclipped papers lying on the desk, I used another Post-it note to turn over some of the pages. I was relieved to see the children Ken was writing to were children he expected to have with Candy, not children he already had somewhere. There didn't appear to be another will or any other document mixed in. I didn't need to be so careful about fingerprints on this document but I still picked it up with a blank sheet of paper and put it in the box for Patsy without touching it directly. I would make copies and give Candy the original. It might give me more ideas about people who wanted to kill Ken.

The locksmith still hadn't come and I spent the time until he did searching the house for more documents and for a safe. Candy said she'd never seen a safe but Ken had owned the house long before he'd married her. If he had hidden it well, there might be a safe she didn't know about. I looked behind all the art and in the back of all cabinets. I found a flashlight in the kitchen and looked into all the vents. No safe. I found the attic was full of old furniture and cardboard boxes. There could be a safe hidden in a dark corner or under something. It would take hours, maybe days, to look through all the dusty accumulation. I doubted that much of that stuff was Candy's or that she would want to bother sorting it all out. I decided Patsy could have an auction house or an appraiser go through it. I wasn't even going to start.

When the locksmith arrived the only thing I had for him to do was open the tall cabinet in Ken's study that I hadn't found a key for.

"Do you care if I damage the lock?" he asked.

"Better not, if you can avoid it," I said. "We may need to lock it up again."

"So you want me to make new keys for it."

"I think so," I said. "It depends on what's in it when we open it up."

"It'll probably take me an hour, maybe more."

"And if you damage the lock?"

"It will probably take five minutes to drill it. If I use an electric lock pick it will take even less time and it may or may not damage the lock. And, the electric lock pick may or may not work."

"Let's spend the time and money to keep the lock and get new keys," I said. The man rolled out a cloth with what looked like dental instruments in it, picked one up, and inserted it into the lock. I wished I could leave and go for a run while he worked. But I was responsible for the house and I wanted to be there when he opened up the cabinet.

I'd brought nothing to read so I retrieved Ken's thick file on hunting from his desk and sat down in a stuffed chair to leaf through it. There were photos of an elk-hunting trip with some other men. The hillsides were rocky and dry with yellow grass, faded sagebrush, and scattered juniper trees. It looked like Eastern Oregon or Northern Nevada. There were articles about hunting elk, deer, bear and all kinds of birds—ducks, geese, chukar, pheasant, quail. There were flyers for outfitters and for hunting lodges.

I came across a much-handled sheet of lined paper with handwritten notes on it, one entry per line, spread over five columns. I imagined the notes were records of animals Ken had shot or hunts he had been on. Each entry had a date, some initials, a number, a second set of initials, and then, in the fifth column, an entry that could be either a number, a word, initials, or some combination of them. There were no headings on the columns. The dates went back twenty years, and the entries, all in the same handwriting, were made with different pens in various shades of blue and black ink.

Rather than get up and retrieve Ken's fishing folder to scan through it, I tried to see if I could break the code on this record that Ken had kept so carefully. I thought that some of the initials could be those of guides or hunting companions. A few initials in the second column appeared more than once but most of the initials in the fourth column repeated several times—BP, CD, FJ.... I couldn't see how they might correspond to the game that was hunted. Maybe they referred to hunting locations or names of lodges.

The numbers in the third column were much too big to be anything like the number of birds or animals shot. They ranged from 500 to 45,000. Maybe they were the price of the hunt without the dollar sign, though $45,000 seemed too high for any hunt I could imagine in Oregon.

Some of the words in the last column happened to be the names of Portland suburbs. One was the name of a street I knew in Portland and some of the others could easily have been street names—Ponderosa, Fremont, Vancouver, Beech, and Emerson. I picked one of these entries that was both a number and a word and looked it up on my iPhone as though it were an address in Portland. To my surprise and great satisfaction, 4028 Crondall Avenue was a legitimate address. It was a small office building and, with a little more searching, I learned that the landlord was none other than Western Sun Development, Ken's own company.

"I've got it," said the locksmith. When he swung the cabinet doors open we were looking at six rifles and shotguns set vertically in a rack. "I hope these aren't loaded," he said.

"It doesn't matter," I said. "We're going to lock them up again and leave them right where they are." There were two shotguns, one of them break-action and one with a magazine. The four rifles ran from a .22 for small game to a .30-.30 for elk or deer. All designed for hunting, not military or home defense. No antiques. Ken was a hunter, not a survivalist. Growing up in Burns, surrounded by good hunting country, it made sense. He probably hunted from an early age. I took a picture of the guns with my cell phone.

There was a large envelope in the bottom of the cabinet and I picked it up. It was from a lab of some kind with a report inside that had something to do with DNA. It took me a minute to figure it out. The report compared the DNA of two people. Aside from saying Person A was male and Person B was female it did not identify who the people were. The people had 25 percent of their DNA in common. The report stated that 25 percent was consistent with all kinds of relationships—grandparent/grandchild, aunt or uncle/niece or nephew, or half-brother/half-sister. So who was Ken testing? The report was dated less than a month ago. Had it led Ken to change his will? Had it led somehow to his death? If he'd learned that Linda and he were half-siblings instead of full brother and sister, why had he changed his will in her favor? Or had some woman contacted him from Burns claiming to be the illegitimate daughter of Ken's father? Or were the people not related to Ken at all but there were inheritance implications in some real-estate deal Ken was working on? The possibilities were endless. I would pass the report on to Patsy Weil at Oxton in case somehow it turned out to be relevant to Ken's estate.

I had to wait while the locksmith made a new set of keys and I went through the fishing folder to see if there was another lined sheet with strange notations on it. There wasn't and I went back to the paper I'd been working on. I looked up four more of the entries that appeared to be street addresses. Only one belonged to Western Sun. Maybe the others had belonged to Western Sun in the past but it would take an offline title search to find out. The other entries in that same column were the names of smaller cities around Portland or what looked like street names without specific addresses. Clearly the record I was looking at was related to some of Ken's properties. But why was it so cryptic? Why was it handwritten? And why was it hidden away in a folder labeled HUNTING? Ken certainly didn't want anyone to find it, or understand it, or even think it was important if they did find it. He hadn't allowed that someone like me would be sitting in his home office with time on his hands.

The locksmith came back in and I tried the keys. They all worked and I signed the work order acknowledging what he'd done. I hadn't wanted to turn on the computer on Ken's desk while the locksmith was there but I turned it on now. The screen asked me for a password and I thought that would be the end of my time at Ken's house. I called Candy to see if she knew the password.

"I don't have any idea," she said, sounding a little bored and annoyed.

"Do you know what Ken's thinking was behind keeping a revolver in his desk?"

"I pretty much stayed out of his office and his business. I'm not surprised he had a handgun but he never discussed it with me."

"He also had a cabinet of hunting rifles and shotguns behind his desk."

"Well, I know he went hunting. I saw him put guns in his car but they were always in bags with handles. When he shot something he had the meat stored somewhere and then had someone in to cook for dinner parties. Over the table he'd talk about the trip where he shot whatever it was. I think the women found it boring. But the moose was good. Everybody liked that."

"I found Ken's will from two years ago," I said. "Do you know if he made a new one after that?"

"He didn't say anything about it. We made our wills together and I never changed mine."

"Well, unless some children pop up from somewhere, you inherit everything except fifty thousand to his sister. To determine how much you'll get, or whether there is anything at all, Patsy will have to sort out Western Sun. You may not know for months. If I were you I wouldn't go on a spending spree."

"I wasn't planning on it."

"I'm done," I said. "By the way, I really like all the paintings I see here."

"Good," she said. She really wanted to get off the phone and we said goodbye.

What a strange kind of marriage she and Ken must have had, I thought. Whoever I married I would both love and trust. I was not going into a devil's bargain like the Winterpols.

All the time I'd been talking with Candy I'd been staring at Ken's computer screen as it waited patiently for me to enter a password. On a whim I entered *Candy*. A cheery *Welcome* replaced the password prompt. Ken might have been a crook but he wasn't very good at defending himself against other crooks, at least not computer crooks. The folders and files on his computer had to do mostly with maintaining his two houses, hunting and fishing, or personal investments outside of his business. I selected all the document folders and copied them onto a twelve-gig thumb drive I had in my pocket. Patsy could find a nerd to sort through it all. I carried the box of paper files out to the car and checked the house to make sure everything was in order before I retrieved the thumb drive, shut down the computer, and locked up.

On my way to Oxton I stopped by the track at Lewis & Clark College for a training session with Mitch. I'd sent him weekly reports and we talked every two weeks by phone or Skype. I hoped that by watching me run, Mitch could suggest a way to make me faster or more efficient.

After I warmed up he said, "Why don't you do a lap at the pace you want to race at and then pick it up twenty percent when you get back here?" I took off, concentrating on maintaining my best running form. I accelerated past Mitch, stopped, and jogged back to him.

"Okay," said Mitch, "your right foot is landing over ninety

times a minute and that's good. You're landing midfoot, which is okay and I don't want you working on forefoot landings. It'll take you years to get that right and you're too close to race time to monkey with it. I think you could work on reducing the vertical oscillation. You're wasting energy just moving up and down. Try leaning forward from the ankle a little bit more." I ran around the track another time attempting to do that. It felt awkward and slow.

"That's better," said Mitch. "Work that into your runs over time. And keep your pace above ninety."

Mitch had brought two bikes and we went to the parking lot behind the stadium so I could ride one. I rode a big loop around him at speed on the asphalt and then slowed to ride back and forth across a rough unpaved triangle of ground in the center of the parking lot.

"It doesn't look like any bad habits have crept in," he said. "Let's try the trails." There was a forest just north of the stadium that belonged to a cemetery on the other side of the woods. The trails were not designed or maintained as bike trails and sometimes you had to navigate through a homeless encampment. But the trails were single-track with not many people on them. I led so Mitch could watch me ride.

"You're not getting everything you could out of the bumps," he said. "You're pulling up on your bike as you start up the front of the bump. And that's good. But before you get there you need to push down. Then your body and the bike both act as springs and you can rise up the bump quicker and easier." I started to get the hang of it on the way back to the parking lot. But I overdid it one time and landed in the trough on the far side of the bump, rattling my bones and losing all kinds of energy. I would need to practice this on my own bike back home. I had built a practice area for myself in the woods at Upriver and I would be spending more time there.

I needed to take a shower before I went into Oxton to deliver what I had found in Lake Oswego. I went to the apartment I'd shared with two friends from law school while I was working in Portland. I had asked them if I could use it and they said sure, they'd hide a key outside for me. They hadn't replaced me with a new roommate and the friend I'd shared a bedroom with now had it to himself. They had new drapes, a new rug, and a new sofa. They had a real bookcase instead of boards and cinderblocks. We had all said that gentrification cost money and we would put it off as long as we could. Apparently I had been holding them back.

With a clean shirt and pressed pants, I tried to sneak in and out of Oxton's offices as quietly as possible. I knew everyone would make a point of saying hello and asking how I was. I didn't want to take the time. And I didn't like being in the office again. I had made a big decision to leave and here I was back, doing low-level stuff by attorney standards, something any associate would resent doing.

I copied everything I'd taken from Ken's house except the holographic will and gave Patsy the originals. She copied the electronic files I'd lifted from Ken's PC and I told her the password in case she needed to explore the computer further. After Oxton I drove to Forest Park, changed in a park restroom, and ran for ninety minutes. The day was clear, the trails were dry, and the woods were beautiful. I had run these trails many times before, first while I was at Lewis and Clark and then while I was at Oxton. It felt good to be running them faster, stronger, and more easily than I had ever before. To cool down I walked the last half mile to the parking lot and stopped to look out over the city. Portland was not my home but it was hard not to love it.

I spent the night at the Heathman, one of the best hotels in the city. I did get the cheapest room because I knew that Oxton would bill Ken's estate for my stay and that would be a little less money going to Candy. I did some weights with the machines and medicine balls in the hotel gym, then took a shower and ordered room service, chicken salad with a beer and berries for desert. Over dinner I started reading Ken's letter to his anticipated progeny.

CHAPTER 10

To My Children

(Ken)

Dear Children,

I am writing this now, before you are born, because I want this letter to remind us all how much I looked forward to knowing you. I want you to have happy lives and I want to enjoy that hope in advance of our being together as a family.

The most important lesson I can pass on is that life can be good or bad and it can change quickly from one to the other. You need to be prepared for both and you need to be ready to fight for yourself if you have to. Bill Gates, a very successful man, said, "Life is not fair. Get used to it." Life was not fair to me but I prevailed.

I want life to be unfair to you too, but outrageously unfair in your favor. Let's let other people get the short end of the stick. I hope you get your mother's good looks, her gracefulness, and maybe her artistic talent. I hope you get my killer instincts and my determination. Even if you have none of those advantages, you will grow up in a loving household and never have to worry for money. I will teach you the importance of hard work and make sure you get the best possible education.

Another lesson I want to pass along comes from a movie made by a man I respect. The key line is "Protect yourself at all times." The hero teaches a young woman how to be a champion boxer. But she forgets the simple rule he gives her and is badly injured. I don't want that to ever happen to you. You can always trust your mother and me but beyond that remember, "Protect yourself at all times."

Your mother and I have a very special bond. We both grew up in poor homes with bad parents. My mother may have been good but she was weak and she died young. Your mother's parents were both horrible *to her and told her she was no good. Your mother and I are resolved to do much better. We may not be perfect but we love you and we will do right by you. Even before you are here we are making ourselves people you can be proud of.*

I hope to tell you about my life when you are old enough to understand. But there are people who will lie about me. So I want to tell you the truth. Where I have done things that I am not proud of, or which you may not be proud of, in those cases I want to explain the situations that led me to do what I did.

As for me, my mother died when I was twelve. My father lost his job and became a drunk. My older brother, who had graduated high school and could have helped us, left my sister and me to take care of our father and fend for ourselves. My sister Linda, who was a good girl and should have had a decent life, found the only way she could support us was to go with truck drivers. I knew what she was doing but didn't understand at first the risks she was taking. She would come home tired and sit in my mother's old chair staring off into space. Between working and taking care of my father and me she had to quit school. Sometimes she would come home with cuts and bruises. I said I would come with her to protect her but she wouldn't let me.

"You shouldn't see what I do," she said, "and the way I act when I'm doing it. And if you tried to argue with anyone you could get hurt." I promised myself I would make money so she would not have to work. I looked around and saw guys, not much older than me and a lot dumber, driving around town with money to spend. This was in Burns. It didn't take me long to find out what they were doing. They were selling marijuana. They were sloppy and stupid about it and they used pot themselves. I found a guy who could get some, persuaded some of my classmates to sell it for me, and we all took a pledge never to use the product ourselves. It was a kind of game and we were so young that the older guys ignored us for a long time. They were too disorganized to bother.

I bought Linda some nice clothes and she went back to school. She only had to stay back one grade. If anybody insulted her I sent some guys to beat them up. We hired a neighbor to cook and clean house for us. My father liked that but resented all the money I was bringing in, more money than he had ever made in his life. Pretty soon I had to stop giving him money because he would go buy drinks for his friends, stay out to all hours, and drive home drunk. I gave him enough liquor to stay home and watch television. He was hit by a car when he was drunk and trying to cross Highway 20. I swore I would never end up dependent on booze or drugs or anything else.

Some people looked down on my family. It made me resolve to beat them at their own game—to be wealthy and successful. I looked at the established fat cats in town, way more secure than the drug dealers, and found that what made these people rich was owning land and buildings. Rent money came in every month and they didn't have to hustle for it. So I decided I would get into the real estate business. I took the money I had accumulated from the marijuana and buried it in three places out in the desert. I got a scholarship to Portland State, majored in business, and finished in three years.

The woman I married before your mother was a mistake. Rhonda was ambitious, like I was, but what I took for refinement was only a collection of appetites. She was greedy for clothes, classy cars, and jewelry. The flashier and more expensive the better. One of the things she wanted was a horse so we joined a horse club near Portland. I'd worked on a horse farm near Burns when I was a boy and I'd had my fill of horses. They smelled bad and produced mountains of manure. They kicked you if you gave them the chance.

The place Rhonda and I joined was called a horse club but that was a fancy name for a big stable with corrals and trails where you could board your horse. Rhonda wanted a horse, I realized later, so she could wear a snappy riding outfit. Her horse was a chestnut that threw her twice. We went to social functions with other horse owners and I saw Rhonda in a new light. She couldn't talk about horses or anything else the other people wanted to talk about. All she could do was wave her jewelry in front of them. She drank too much and complained at length about the salespeople at Nordstrom, as though that made entertaining and instructive stories. Her point was she was too rich to be treated the way they had treated her. After a while the other members avoided her. There were people there I could have done business with but Rhonda held us back.

Rhonda's drinking was always a problem. But her starting on serious drugs broke it for both of us. I had seen what drugs could do to *people who had some backbone, unlike Rhonda who had none. I knew where this would end up. So I protected my money as well as I could and filed for divorce. I got a good settlement by offering her five hundred dollars in cash right there on the table in the lawyer's office if she would sign the papers. I'd starved her for cash the last few months we were married and she jumped at the hundred-dollar bills. She held out for a thousand dollars for eighty-one seconds. I timed it. Then she signed the papers and left in a hurry to go get a fix. After that I was much more careful in sizing people up. You need to learn to do the same, especially with people of the opposite sex. You need to know what they really want and which way they'll jump if they're cornered.*

Your mother and I are ideally suited for each other. You are lucky. We are not similar by any means. Your mother is an artist and she has a dancer's grace about her that comes from I don't know where, certainly not her parents. She says her savior was an art teacher she had in high school named Leon Martinez. It wasn't just art, she says. He had a noble air about him without being stuffy. And he concentrated on whatever he was doing, including teaching her. She said he could see right through her and know what she was thinking. But he never lorded it over her or embarrassed her. I think she would have married Martinez if she could have.

I am not an artist. I am just a street fighter who keeps getting smarter. I complement your mother by being tougher and more persistent. Sometimes the world gets to be too much for her and she's inclined to drop everything—all plans, commitments, opportunities, and people—until she gets her bearings again. That's when she needs me.

We both want to be better people. That's what we have in common. We want to be gracious and generous and associate with the best sorts of people. We want you to be part of that. We want your lives to be much better than ours.

We are learning from the people we meet. We plan strategies for conversing with them and later discuss what worked and what didn't. Some rich people really are as good as they seem. But some of them hide how selfish or deceptive they really are. Or they are in such a favored position they can be vicious and get away with it. Upriver Ranch is easier than Portland. There is no old guard. Nobody's job requires them to live there. Everybody wants to be neighborly and welcoming to newcomers.

You children will live lives where you don't have to look over your shoulder. I hope you are so far removed from such concerns that you don't even appreciate what you are free of. I did some things back in Burns that people hate me for. I don't regret what I did. People deserved what they got. People got too greedy and too careless. When they got into trouble I could see they would start ensnarling me in their own stupidities. So I went to the district attorney for Harney County and made a deal with him. He wouldn't charge me with anything, trivial as it might be, and I wouldn't have to testify if I told him the names of a dozen criminals, where and when to find them with evidence of their crimes, and how to find more evidence against them. I even told him which of those people he could get to turn state's evidence on the others. He was never going to get those guys without my information. It was the biggest bust in Harney County history. They brought in State Police from all over to help out. The DA was a hero and got re-elected two more times. People went to prison, got out, committed more crimes, went back. People died of drug overdoses. The two who turned state's evidence disappeared. But some who went to prison are still around. To threaten me they would have to risk my destroying them.

If I am not around, some people may tell you I cut corners in business, that I broke the law or cheated people. None of that is true. I've just been a good businessman and they are jealous. They wish they had the smarts and the courage to do what I did. There is only one thing I did that was wrong and I'll tell you about so you'll know that was all there ever was. And I more than made up for it. My first real investment in Portland was a parking lot. I collected rent every day, not just once a month. On the stalls I did rent by the month, if they were late in paying, I didn't have to go through eviction procedures, I just had them towed away. What I did wrong was I hid revenue and avoided paying some taxes when the lot got busy, especially around Christmas. I sat in the attendant's shack myself and collected cash from people driving in. The customers got what they paid for. What was illegal and what I regret was about half the revenue never got recorded and I didn't have to pay taxes on it. I've paid so much in taxes since then I've more than made up for it. That's it. That's all there ever was. Not that big a deal.

In any case, that's all in the past. You'll never have to worry about it. Your mother and I look forward to having you in our lives. We look forward to knowing you and we look forward to doing everything we can to make your lives happy and successful.

With much love,
Your Father

History Lessons

(Dan)

Well, that was enlightening. Ken was a liar, even to his unborn children. His letter hadn't mentioned the frauds he had perpetrated on Tom Melillo and other people I had talked to. The good news was Ken's letter brought in a whole new group of suspects for his murder. I was excited about that. I would have to give Breuninger a copy of the letter and see if I could find the people Ken sent to prison thirty years earlier. Or let Breuninger find them. He would have to pursue this lead.

The biggest surprise, though, was how much Ken was counting on having children with Candy. He imagined Candy was signed up for this but I had my doubts. Candy didn't seem the mother type. But then, who knew what was going on in her head? Maybe she wanted children.

I was intrigued with the parking-lot story. If Ken were still dealing drugs, a parking lot would be excellent for laundering money. Ken could just print parking passes for nonexistent customers and move his ill-gotten cash from drugs into the parking lot as cash receipts.

Back in my hotel room I pulled out my copy of the handwritten ledger I'd found in Ken's hunting folder. On the entry I'd lined up earlier with Ken's building at 4028 Crondall, the first set of initials was JC, the number was 13,000 and the second set of initials was DC. What did JC stand for? Jesus Christ came immediately to mind but I didn't think that was it. If it were a person, there would be thousands with the initials JC. It didn't seem to be much of a clue. DC brought Washington DC to mind. Then I made an association that I thought was too unique to me to be relevant. At Oxton I was once asked to draw up a chart showing all the cases we had worked on for one of our clients and note what the final disposition of each case was. One of the abbreviations I used was DC. It meant "dismissed case." It meant a judge had dismissed a case.

I humored myself. If DC meant "dismissed case" on Ken's little ledger, then JC might be the initials of a judge. In fact, I knew, there was a judge in Portland with the initials JC. His name was James Curtin. He had been on the bench a long time and wasn't thought to be a very good judge. "Past his prime" was apparently being kind. An Oxton partner opined to me that Curtin had always been marginally competent.

I looked for initials in the same column as JC that were more unique and I found one, XT. The only first name I could think of that began with X was Xavier. The number next to the initials was 5,000, the next initials were BP, and in the last column was the name of a suburb of Portland named Windsor. Thinking all the entries had to do with real estate, I guessed that BP stood for "building permit." I did a search for the name of the head of the building department in Windsor. Lo and behold, his name was Xavier Tapia. Unless I was mistaken, it looked like my buddy Ken paid Mr. Tapia $5,000 six years ago to issue a building permit. Maybe Mr. Tapia merely expedited a building permit. In any case, if the entry said what I thought it did, Xavier Tapia accepted a bribe.

This whole sheet of paper—perhaps Ken's only copy—hidden away innocuously in a folder on hunting, appeared to be a record of bribes he had paid to obtain favorable judgments in court, have cases dismissed, get building permits and occupancy permits, and who knew what else. Did Candy know about these bribes? Probably not, I decided. Ken had no reason to tell her and the fewer people who knew about them the safer Ken was. Also, the pace of his payments had tailed off in the last four years. He was really trying to become a respectable member of society.

I took out a fresh sheet of paper and started a new list of my own, trying to match up some of the data. But among the advantages and disadvantages of serious triathlon training, I learned, was that when it is time to sleep, you are out like a light. As beguiled as I was by Ken's cryptic ledger, I fell asleep in ten minutes.

The next morning I crossed over the Willamette to the address where Candy said Linda lived. Ken's letter had made me wonder about the woman who would be my passenger on the ride back to Bend. Would she be a nice middle-class housewife with a long-forgotten shameful past? A successful businesswoman in her own right? Or an overweight hard-bitten woman who spent her time in bars and smoked? If she smoked we would have to stop the car and get out for every cigarette. It could be a long trip.

When I got to the address I shook my head at Candy's carelessness. It wasn't a house or an apartment building. It was a school. I called Candy in hopes she could find the right address but she didn't answer. I didn't have a phone number for Linda and my cell-phone provider could find no listing for a Linda Winterpol, if that were still her name. I stewed in the car for a few minutes while I tried to figure out what to do. My only hope was the address was close to being right and, if I knocked on enough doors in the neighborhood, someone would know where she lived.

I started with the school, the Saint Cecelia School for Girls, announced in gold letters on a brown wooden sign in the lawn. The tan stucco walls, rusty red tile roof, and heavy dark wood door and window trim made it look like it belonged in California. The double door opened onto a spare hallway to the back of the building. On the right was a narrow door with a small wooden sign hanging out into the hall that said OFFICE. The office had a counter wide enough for two people at most to stand in front of it. Behind the counter was a desk where a bright-eyed middle-aged woman in a functional dress looked up from her computer.

"Can I help you?" she said in a businesslike but not unfriendly tone. I told her I thought I had the wrong address but perhaps the woman I was looking for lived in the neighborhood and could she help me find Linda Winterpol.

"Just a minute," said the woman, "she's expecting you." She picked up her phone, punched in two digits and after a short pause announced, "Please tell Sister Catherine her ride is here." She hung up the phone, gave me a smile, and said, "She'll meet you here right away."

Linda, or Sister Catherine, appeared at the other end of the hallway and walked toward me. She was husky, like Ken, but not fat. She had long brown hair barely beginning to go gray and she wore a plain patterned dress, not the habit I might have expected on someone called Sister Catherine. I gave her a big smile, extended my hand, and introduced myself. I thought the name "Martinez" might receive a slightly warmer reception than "Smith" or "Parker" in a Catholic institution, though I had hardly ever set foot in a church in my life.

"Should I call you Ms. Winterpol, Linda, or Sister Catherine?" I asked. This seemed a polite question when I thought to ask but it sounded a little mocking when I said it.

"Sister Catherine will do just fine," she said, with a steeliness that seemed like Ken. But she shook my hand and looked me in the eye. She had a small light blue suitcase that I put in the back of the Maserati. When we got underway I told her how sorry I was that she had lost her brother. She said she had prayed for him every day when he was alive and she would pray for his soul every day now that he was dead. "He was a good man," she said, and I chose not to argue the point. There were a number of things I chose not to say— that I knew that Sister Catherine herself had once been a prostitute and that I had in my suitcase a holographic will that could make Sister Catherine a very wealthy woman. I wondered whether she had taken a vow of poverty.

"What do you do at the school?" I asked.

"I teach biology and physiology to eleventh- and twelfth-graders," she said.

While I said nothing more, I began to wonder why Sister Catherine said nothing. We had driven out of Portland and all the way to Gresham before it occurred to me that she might be grieving for her brother. I still couldn't believe that anyone had really liked Ken. His death was a shock to Candy, no doubt, and his death did not auger well for Western Sun employees, but I had been assuming, without being aware of my own assumption, that everyone else was secretly pleased he was gone. Even I, who hardly knew him and was spending more time on him than I had ever planned to spend, thought the earth was a slightly better place, that the ship of human progress had made a subtle but positive course correction. From his shit-colored eyes to his predatory business practices, to his apparent corruption of government officials, he had been a liability to the world at large. Yet here was a woman who didn't seem to think so.

"Were you and Ken close?" I asked.

"We were loyal to each other," she said. That wasn't the same thing as close, I thought. But loyalty was not to be sneered at and at least Ken was loyal to somebody. I wondered about the character of Ken's loyalty to Candy, a loyalty that encompassed leaving her all his money while at the same time apparently beating her arms so badly she wouldn't take off her smock when she invited me to her bed.

When we escaped the traffic lights in Sandy and started over the pass by Mount Hood, I raised an issue I thought Linda would have some insight into. "Was there anyone from Ken's past in Burns that might be angry enough to kill him?"

"A few," she said, and paused to think about it. "There were some rotten people in Ken's past, in both our pasts. Some dead. Some in prison. Some too confused to find Ken or do anything to him."

"Gosh," I said, "what did Ken do to make these people so angry with him?"

"We were broke. I mean my family was broke. My father was laid off from the mill and he got injured cutting trees for firewood. No medical insurance and his unemployment ran out. My mother had no skills and couldn't find a job. She killed herself when I was fourteen and Ken was two years younger. We had an older brother who didn't help us at all. He just left. Ken went out and put food on the table by hunting. In season, out of season. Public land, private land, Indian land. It didn't matter. We had to eat.

"Then Ken started bringing home cash instead of meat. Serious money. He wouldn't tell me where it came from. But we could eat decent food and I could go back to school.

"I learned what Ken was doing, when he wasn't hunting. He

89

was going out into the desert and making meth. He sold it to biker gangs. That drug has ruined lives and I'm sorry Ken was ever involved in it, even if his intentions for me and our father were good. Ken hid the equipment in abandoned mines and he'd watch the mines for a whole day before he went back in them. It was small-time but for us it was a lot of money. He was still going to high school, doing well in his studies, and playing football. When he left for Portland State he quit the drug business, thank goodness. The Mexican cartels got into the meth business right after Ken quit. They killed some of his friends.

"While Ken was in college he managed apartment buildings for landlords. He got free rent. When he graduated he became a landlord himself. He owned a parking lot for a while and then bought an apartment building the landlord hadn't taken care of. Ken fixed the place up and raised the rents. Meantime he kept sending money back to my father and me. When Dad died and I decided to take holy orders, Ken started giving money to the Dominicans instead of to me. He still does. Or did." Sister Catherine gazed out the window at the deep pine forest going by.

"Ken's love allowed me to save my soul. If I knew who killed him I would tell the police in an instant."

I waited half a mile before taking Linda up on this. I wanted to seem thoughtful, and concerned rather than reveal what I was, eager and impatient. "So," I said, "do you know the specific people he angered so much in Burns?"

"I never wanted to know anything about his business and he kept me out of it. But you could start with every drug dealer convicted in Eastern Oregon about twenty-five years ago."

We had just passed the turnoff to Timberline Lodge and things were looking up. I would have much to tell Breuninger.

"Did you know Ken's first wife?" I asked. I didn't say I'd already had a run-in with Rhonda.

"Oh, I knew Rhonda. I knew she was a mistake for Ken the moment I met her. Pride led him astray. He thought Rhonda was his ticket to polite society. She knew how to make herself pretty and she could be arrogant enough to make Ken think she was smart and sophisticated. Ken wouldn't listen to me. After I took my vows Ken said I had lost touch with the real world. But I had learned to be humble and to depend on God in a way that Ken had not. Ken's weaknesses were pride and vanity."

"Avarice, I should think," I said, "thinking of how hard he worked to make money."

"Avarice too," said Linda, "but it was secondary to pride."

"So why did he and Rhonda break up?"

"Ken learned she couldn't get him into polite society. And then, of course, she started using drugs. Ken abandoned a sinking ship."

"Do you think he learned his lesson or was he after the same things with Candy?"

"Still pride and vanity but he got smarter. At least Candy didn't pretend to be something she was not."

"And her talent as an artist seems to be the real deal," I added.

"It helps to be beautiful," said Linda, which seemed a bit snippy for a Dominican Sister.

We were driving through the Indian reservation now and I idly wondered what the laws on wills and inheritance were here. Unlike the rest of Oregon, the laws that applied on the reservation could be tribal, federal, state, or some combination of them. I vaguely knew that land owned by a single Indian might revert to tribal ownership no matter what somebody said in their will or who their relatives were. At least we were going to escape that complication unless Ken had bought land from an Indian. I wouldn't be surprised if he had.

I drove Linda to Candy's house and carried her small suitcase to the front door, along with an envelope for Candy that held the original of Ken's letter to his hoped-for children and copies of the wills and bank statements from Lake Oswego. Candy gave Linda what appeared to be a sincerely happy smile. Linda seemed to be pleased to see Candy as well, though they were both a bit subdued. I put the suitcase down on its wheels just inside the door, leaned the envelope against it, and stepped aside.

"Thank you, Dan," said Candy, over Linda's shoulder, and then turned into the house, shutting the door behind her. Linda didn't say goodbye at all. I was a little miffed at both of them. But then, it was their brother and husband who had died, not a member of my family. I put the Maserati back in my parents' garage where I was used to seeing it. It would probably not be driven as far as Portland again in its life.

That afternoon I emailed my discoveries about Ken's mysterious ledger to Patsy and told her where to find the original in the files I had left her. Half an hour later I called her.

"We should send the evidence of bribery to the Multnomah County District Attorney," said Patsy. "Could you draft a letter I can send him describing where and when and how you found the record?"

"What's the penalty for bribes?" I asked. "Could they wipe out the estate?"

"Bribing a public official is a Class B felony in Oregon, maximum of ten years and a two-hundred-and fifty-thousand-dollar fine per count. How much of a fine the court actually assesses usually depends on how big the bribe was and how big a benefit the briber derived from it. But if the dates you are telling me are right, the statute of limitations has run out. No threat to Ken or his heirs. Some of the decisions Ken got as a result of the bribes could get reopened. But the courts and the cities are likely to decide what's done is done. There's no way to predict the results."

"And the officials who were bribed?" I asked.

"Statute of limitations again," said Patsy. "But the ones who are still working may not be working for long."

CHAPTER 12

Coming into the Country

(Amy)

I'd found two other girls online who wanted to share an apartment and we were just moving in. It was near the Juniper Swim and Fitness Center in Bend, which was where the yoga instructor and I wanted to live. The third girl, who had a job raising goats in Tumalo, didn't care where we lived. I was coming down the stairs to get another load from the car when an older man at the bottom of the stairs caught sight of me and froze in place. He kept staring at me with his mouth open as I slowed my pace coming down the stairs. I kept my eye on him, more out of curiosity than alarm. It was broad daylight and my new roommates would be coming back and forth on these stairs very soon.

"Can I help you with something?" I said. His mouth snapped shut and he shook his head as if trying to wake up. Then he spoke in a surprisingly authoritative tone of voice.

"Are you a tenant here?" he asked.

"New tenant," I said. "Just moved to Bend." That was perhaps more information than I wanted to give but, if we were going to be neighbors, I couldn't seem too unfriendly.

"How do you do?" he asked, now smiling. "I'm Ken Winterpol." He seemed to be watching me closely for a response. The name meant nothing to me.

"Do you live here as well?" I asked.

"No," he said, "Not at all. I just bought the building."

"I thought some company owned it."

"Western Sun," he said. "That's my company."

"Are you the manager?" I asked.

"No," he said. "My office is in Portland. But if there is anything wrong with your apartment I'd like to know about it. I'll see that it gets fixed."

"It seems perfect," I said. We were still standing on the stairs. I walked down a few steps and stuck out my hand.

"My name is Amy De Santis. How do you do?" His hand was fleshy but strong. He had a nice smile but not an attractive face. If eyes are the windows of the soul Ken Winterpol was deeply in need of salvation. But I hope for the best in everyone.

"Amy De Santis," he repeated, as though demonstrating his friendliness by taking care in remembering it. He glanced at my left hand. There was no ring on. "Are you from around here?"

"No, I'm new to Bend."

"Where were you born?" he asked. Not "Where did you move here from?" or even "Where are you from originally?" But "Where were you born?"

"Denver," I said. Then the yoga instructor, asked me to help her carry her mattress upstairs and that was the end of my conversation with Ken Winterpol. He creeped me out a little but I try to look for the best in everyone. I remembered Western Sun and Portland. If we ever had a serious problem with the apartment or the manager I'd call Mr. Winterpol.

I realized later I might call him for another reason. I kept wondering why he looked so stunned when he first saw me. I'm pretty but not that pretty. And I certainly didn't look my best in the old clothes I had on for moving. Maybe, I thought, I looked like someone he knew. I would have liked to know who that was.

Western Sun, Ken Winterpol's company, sent an invitation to all the residents of the building to come to a barbecue on a Saturday two weeks away. Ken's secretary called my roommates and me individually to make sure we were coming. She had our cell-phone numbers, I guess, because we'd given them to the manager of the apartment.

The people in my building said they'd never had a landlord throw a party for them before but there would be real barbecue, beer and wine, and live music. The music turned out to be a guitar and a banjo played by two older men. They played Hank Williams and other old country-and-Western songs, including some funny ones. I'd heard plenty of C&W growing up in Colorado and these guys were pretty good. There were rented tables and chairs for us to sit at. If the party was supposed to make us feel a little lucky to be living in Ken Winterpol's building, it accomplished its goal. My goat-farmer roommate said there must be a rent increase coming but we'd signed a year's lease and figured we could move out when it was up if we didn't like the new rates.

Ken Winterpol came and introduced himself to many of the residents. It seemed awfully neighborly—very much the picture of Bend I liked to imagine. Ken asked me to sit down with him for a minute and he poured me a fresh glass of lemonade after I said I'd pass on a beer. He said he wanted to learn more about why I came to Bend and how I chose this apartment building.

I told him I came to Bend for a good job and the outdoor sports. Two of us wanted to live close to Juniper. And we liked the apartment. It was a little old and tired but it was sunny.

Then he asked me whether De Santis was the name I was born with. It was an odd question but our conversation was on a roll and I'd told my story many times before. I was adopted. My mother died giving birth to me and she left no record of who the father was. She hadn't even given me a name before she died. I got my name, first and last, from the couple who adopted me. They couldn't have the children they wanted and I was the answer. They were wonderful parents to me and I had a great childhood in Boulder.

I felt sorry for my birth mother, I told him. When I turned eighteen I started trying to find out who she was, where she was from, and where the rest of her family was.

"What was her name?" asked Ken.

"Vickie Coate. It said that on my birth certificate. I was able to get that much. But there was no father listed, and not even an address for her. Vickie Coate may not even have been her real name. I called every family named Coate in Colorado but none of them had a relative named Vickie they couldn't account for."

"How do you spell Coate?" asked Ken and I told him: C-O-A-T-E.

"Thanks," he said. He looked around the lawn at the other tables where some people had finished their food and were standing up thinking about leaving. The music had ended to enthusiastic applause. "And now," said Ken, "I thought we'd take a group photo." Then, when he got up, he did a sort of odd thing. He took our empty paper cups and walked toward a barrel set out for trash. He threw one cup in the trash, pulled a big plastic Ziploc out of his pants pocket, put the second cup in the bag and sealed the bag. He carried the bag around with him while he asked everyone, in a loud and enthusiastic voice, to gather in front of the building for a photo.

About thirty of us stood facing the sun while Ken took our photo, camera in one hand, plastic bag in the other. Then he asked us to look toward a tree in the lawn over to our left. We obliged. The goat farmer said it was a little like getting a group mug shot. Anyhow, Ken thanked everyone for coming, he was happy to have us in his building, and to be sure and call the manager if there were any problems. Then he was gone.

My new roommates and I agreed the party had been a little odd, but certainly nice enough.

I worked for a small company called Greenwood Biomedical. The job didn't pay all that well but they promised to involve me in everything the company did. It would be a good start on a biotech career. I liked the people I met, especially Grace Wray who was in charge of testing. My essential responsibility was to find people willing to test our product. The company made a tiny chip to go inside pills. When the pill hit a patient's stomach, the chip sent a signal to a patch the person was wearing. The patch updated a cell phone and the cell phone sent a message to the patient's doctor so they would know the patient had taken the pill. People often didn't take their medications and wound up in emergency rooms because of it. This chip would help solve that problem. The pills we gave our test subjects were placebos and the chips, before they dissolved completely, were smaller than a grain of sand.

Bend appealed to me especially because when winter came I could ski Bachelor. I grew up in Boulder, Colorado and skied all my life. When I went to college at UC-Santa Barbara I went home to ski three times every winter. Like Boulder, Bend was a good place for outdoor sports. And better than Boulder, it was much smaller. People said Bend was the way Boulder used to be.

My goat-farmer roommate had a degree in agriculture from Wyoming. She took me and the yoga instructor out to see the farm. All the goats on a big bare hill were female and they came down the hill when they saw us. They thought we were going to fill their trough. They were kind of sweet and didn't mind being petted through the fence though what they really wanted was food. The five rams that serviced all the nanny goats were kept in a separate pen. They were bigger than the nannies, they smelled awful, and they looked anything but sweet. Male horses can look noble. Bulls can look strong. Billy goats have none of that. They just look ugly and mean.

I worked afternoons and evenings, when I could better reach possible test subjects on the phone. In the daylight hours I wasn't working I decided to train for the Upriver Off-Road Triathlon coming in September. Off-road meant the biking and running would be mostly on dirt trails, not on paved roads. On the bikes we would be climbing hills, steering through tight turns, jumping over rocks and logs, and trying to get the most out of the bumps and dips in the trail. I knew how to swim, run, and ride a bike though I had never trained in any of these sports. At Santa Barbara I was on the rowing team. My legs and back were very strong, my shoulders almost misshapen. I had only one nice dress that fit me. My aerobics were excellent but I would have to work on my endurance. I was great for a six- or seven-minute row. The off-road tri would last over two hours.

I did my running on the quieter streets in Bend, including up and down Pilot Butte. Because the Upriver Triathlon would be off-road, I ran on the dirt and grass in Pilot Butte Cemetery. It was a little sad to run there but it did make me appreciate being alive and burning along in the sunlight. To get on real dirt trails in the forest, where I needed to do more of my running and most of my biking, I needed to find people to go with me so it would be safe.

It would have to be in the mornings because my job at Greenwood Biomedical had afternoon hours.

Juniper was certainly a friendly place, as was Bend as a whole. One of the first times I swam there a guy in the faster lane next to me asked me if he could give me a few tips. I said I could use them. I was just starting to take swimming seriously.

"You're a strong swimmer," he said, "but you are wasting a lot of energy. You can go faster with much less work. Don't kick so much. Just kick enough to keep your feet level with the surface so they don't drag. Keep your head down in the water. That will help keep your feet up. And let your breath out slowly until you are just about to breathe in. That'll keep more air in your lungs and make you more buoyant."

"Okay thanks," I said. He said good luck and pushed off the wall for more laps. This was certainly an encouraging place to swim. And what a nice guy. He wasn't trying to pick me up or act superior. He just saw an opportunity to help. I hoped there were more guys in Bend like that.

I tried to do everything he said on my next few laps. It took some concentration but I got the kicking and the head-down part. Getting the breathing right consistently was going to take a few more sessions.

When we stopped again he said I was doing much better. "Try keeping your body straight as an arrow but without tensing up." I tried that too and it seemed to help. I practiced what he told me every time I swam. My times got better and I wasn't as worn out at the end of my workouts.

I tried to read *The Bulletin* every day. Bend was my new home and I wanted to get to know it. I didn't read the obituaries but I turned the pages. I sucked my breath in sharply when I saw Ken Winterpol's picture. He was not only dead, he had been murdered. This strange man I'd just met the month before. There was nothing in the article that hinted at why anyone might kill him. He was a successful businessman whose other interests, at least the ones stated in the article, were horses and hunting. The article didn't say "killed in a robbery attempt" or anything like that. It just said murdered by an unknown assailant. It said Ken was survived by a wife named Candace, a brother in Prineville named Richard, and a sister in Portland named Linda.

So I went to Mr. Winterpol's funeral. Curiosity got to me. There was a reason Ken Winterpol was interested in me and I wanted to know what it was. It was at a Catholic church near downtown Bend. I wore the same shapeless black suit and white blouse I had worn for my job interview. I hung back from signing the register in the front hall but when no one was coming up the steps to enter the church I looked through the names. The only name I recognized belonged to the manager of our apartments. None of the other tenants came. If anyone asked me how I knew Ken—in other words, what was I doing there—I would just say I was grateful for the party he threw for the tenants in my building. People might think I was daft but at least it would be plausible. And true.

At first I sat in one of the back pews but I moved up when I saw there were only twenty people in a church that could sit hundreds. Most of the people were older but there was one tall younger woman in the first row in an expensive-looking dark red dress. The service was a real Mass, with readings done by a woman who was a volunteer from the church, not a friend or relative of Mr. Winterpol. The priest gave a brief homily, trying to make the most of the same information I read in the obituary. Before Communion the priest made a point of asking those who were not Catholic to not take part in that sacrament. I would not have gone up to the rail in any case.

Near the end of the service a nun who was sitting in the first row went to the pulpit. I thought she was associated with the local church but she said she was Ken Winterpol's sister. She looked out over the congregation and when she saw me her head snapped back and her eyes widened. So Ken wasn't the only person my face brought up short. Undaunted by the surprise, she talked about the wisdom and fortitude Ken showed as a boy, in spite of difficult circumstances she didn't go into. When their mother died and Ken's father was too ill to hold a job, Ken worked hard to support the family. He was the first one in their family to go to college and his generosity had allowed Linda to follow her heart into holy orders and teaching. His charity to the Dominicans and the Saint Cecilia School continued through good times and bad. The sister rejoiced that Ken found success and love in his life, in his business and finally, in his marriage.

When the service was over the congregation walked out in order—first the coffin wheeled away by two funeral home attendants, then the first row and then the other rows front to back. When I got to the back of the church the nun was waiting for me.

"How do you do?" she said. "I am Sister Catherine. Ken Winterpol was my brother."

"I'm Amy De Santis. I live in an apartment building Mr. Winterpol owned. I talked with him twice, that's all. But he was very surprised when he saw me, like I think you were. Do you know why that was? Do I look like someone you know?"

"Yes, you do," said Sister Catherine. "You look like me."

The way I examined her face would have normally been rude. But she bore my inspection patiently, even eagerly. When I ignored her headpiece and allowed for age, I was looking in a mirror. It was a shock to see the person I was going to become, though I certainly wasn't going to become a nun. Excitement welled up in me cautiously. It seemed I might finally find my birth mother's family and know where I came from.

"Yes," I said, "I do look very much like you and you look very much like me. I was adopted and don't know my birth parents. We could be related."

"We must find out," said Sister Catherine with determination. "If Ken had a child I want to know that child. And you want to know your family. It's only right that you should. And there may be legal implications as well. Ken's will leaves money to his children. None of us thought he had any. We should have DNA tests and have the lawyer who is settling Ken's estate arrange them so the results are binding. I don't know how that works. I will call him. His name is Dan Martinez. You better write down your phone number so I can give it to him."

I wrote my name, number, and email address on a scrap from the back of the funeral program. It was the only paper we could find. Sister Catherine wrote down hers at the Saint Cecilia School in Portland. I left the funeral elated, not the way you're supposed to feel. I had to keep myself from skipping down the steps of the church. I was sorry Ken was dead but only for selfish reasons. If he was my birth father I would never get to know him. I'd always resented that obscure figure because he had clearly abandoned my birth mother and me. I never wanted him to have the satisfaction of knowing he had a daughter who had turned out well. But I couldn't help wanting to know what he was like, and what happened between him and my mother.

CHAPTER 13

Threats and Celebrations

(Dan)

Back copies of *Burns Times-Herald* were online and I got the names of ten people who had gone to jail for meth in the early eighties. It took longer to find obituaries or court records that put some of them in prison or in the ground when Ken was killed but I still had three who, for all I could discover, were out and about and capable of mischief. And that was as far as I was going to go down that road for now. I would give the names and the best information I could find on these people to Breuninger and leave it at that. My decision not to get any closer to these people was influenced by a voicemail I'd gotten while Linda and I were out of cellular range on the ride over from Portland.

"A word to the wise," the man's voice said. I might have heard the voice before but I couldn't place it. The man might have been drunk. "I'm coming for you. You're going to get it sure as shootin'. Only you won't know where or when, will you? I'd sleep light if I were you." My cell phone reported the number that had called me so I called it back. It rang and rang and rang. On my third try someone answered. It was a pay phone at Shari's Restaurant in Bend. The man clearly wanted to scare me. But would he actually harm me? I decided, and there was some rationalization in this, that I should assume he would not. He didn't ask me to do anything or stop doing anything. Scaring me seemed more important to him than actually hurting me. I could leave town and live like a coward or I could go on with my life and assume nothing would happen. It was the brave response, in a way, but it was also the lazy response.

The trip to Portland had thrown off my training schedule so I skipped Ken's memorial service and went swimming at Juniper. I locked my cell phone, watch, and wallet in the car and took my combination lock for the locker. The coach asked us all who was planning to swim at Elk Lake and about a third of the hands went up. So we worked on keeping a steady pace for the entire workout. In a long race like Elk Lake the swimmers would need to gauge how fast they were going when there was no clock to check. It would be easy to swim too fast at the beginning and get tired. We swam a routine of 50, 100, 150, and 200 meters with fifteen seconds rest between each distance, trying to keep the same pace as we went from shorter to longer lengths. We had to start at a pace much slower than we would normally swim for fifty meters so we could still be swimming at the same pace when we got to the 200.

Mom went to Ken's service. When I saw her at lunchtime she said it was bare-bones Catholic with a minimum of prayers. Linda/Sister Catherine spoke briefly about how kind Ken was to the people he loved. I wondered how many people that amounted to and how long he loved them. Mom said Candy looked beautiful. There weren't many flowers but the ones on the altar were pretty. I suspected Candy had ordered them. Mom said Breuninger was there and I wondered whether he was trying to show the family that the sheriff's department cared or he was hoping someone suspicious showed up. He was probably disappointed on both counts. Mom said nobody there looked like they could hurt a fly.

The priest invited everyone to a little reception with white wine in a side room but Candy left with Ken's sister shortly after it began. Mom said it was pathetic, even for a man with hardly any friends. She said it would have been better to have no reception at all.

Someone at the service pointed out Rhonda and Mom was horrified, or at least as horrified as my mother could get. Mom didn't like to say anything negative about anyone. She said Rhonda looked like she'd had a tough life and, at the reception, Rhonda put away glass after glass of white wine. She accosted Mom, not knowing who she was, and cross-examined her about property values at Upriver, whether they were going up or down and whether my mother thought they were a good value. Rhonda said she was evaluating houses at Upriver for investment. As if, I thought.

That afternoon I researched holographic wills online. I was hoping there was a way I could come clean about the will and still make sure Candy got the inheritance. The answer was much better than I hoped. I had assumed handwritten wills were legitimate everywhere. They are valid in California and Idaho and a lot of other states. But in Oregon a will had to have the signatures of two witnesses. Ken's handwritten will didn't have any witnesses. It was completely invalid, irrelevant—what we had learned in law school to call "nugatory." What a relief. And great news for Candy. But that still left me in an awkward position. If Ken told anyone he had written that will and where it was—especially if he gave them a copy of it—then a court, or even Patsy, would ask me very pointedly what I did with it, invalid or not. I didn't dare destroy the document, much as I wanted to.

Importantly, the holographic will, invalid as it was, showed clearly that Ken had a radical change of heart about Candy a week before he was murdered. It might lead Breuninger to find out about Candy's little tryst with me, or an escapade with some other man, or some other bad faith on Candy's part. If the holographic will came to light it would shift more suspicion onto Candy for the murder. And if the district attorney worked hard on uncovering the reason for Ken's sudden change in attitude, he might find I was a likely culprit.

My training schedule was jammed for two days because I had an event coming up I had to work around. My high school basketball team was having a mini-reunion on July Fourth at Sean Wray's house. Sean was the team's student manager all four years I was on the team. He was a funny guy, very good in math, and to everyone's surprise, including his own, he was now a multi-millionaire. He had gone to Oregon State and graduated with a BA in software engineering. By luck, as he himself would admit, he was hired very early by Facebook and snagged stock options that wound up being worth a fortune. He still worked for Facebook because, as he said, "I'm an engineer. I like being an engineer. What else am I going to do?"

When Facebook opened a data center in Prineville, thirty-five miles from Bend, Sean got himself assigned to it. He bought a house in Bend on Awbrey Butte, where the Bend upper crust lived. The house looked out over all of downtown Bend and, beyond it, south to Newberry Crater and Lava Butte.

Almost in the center of Sean's view was an extinct volcano, small as volcanos go, named Pilot Butte. Only four cities in the country had volcanoes inside the city limits and Bend was one of them. Every July Fourth the city shot fireworks off the butte. The cap of the evening at Sean's would be watching the fireworks from his deck. Sean and his wife, Grace, had been in the house for less than a year and Sean was more excited about the fireworks than anyone else. It almost seemed that the fireworks were the reason he had bought the house. His children, a girl of five and a boy of four, were getting special permission to stay up late and watch the show.

"How did Facebook decide to build a data center in Prineville?" I asked Sean. "It's a long way from Silicon Valley."

"Cheap land, cheap electricity, and cool air temperature," said Sean, "and Prineville was happy to have us."

"And cheaper labor than Silicon Valley," I said.

"Labor wasn't a factor," said Sean. "It only takes a few dozen of us to run the place. The building is all computers and disk drives. Just whirring away, keeping track of who your friends are, when their birthdays will be, and what funny thing your cat did yesterday."

"What difference does the air temperature make?"

"All those electronics give off a lot of heat. If we used regular air conditioning it would take too much electricity. So we start with air that is cool, especially at night or in the winter. If we need to cool the air further we run it through a big spray of water. Then the cool air drops straight down onto the electronics. We don't have to run air conditioners and we don't have to pump the air through ducts." Facebook sounded like Prineville's good luck.

We started shooting hoops in the driveway. Grace asked Sean and two more of us to move the table with the drinks and potato salad farther away from the basket. We went back to shooting hoops at leisurely pace, barely a warm-up. Then some guys suggested a game, three on three. I said I'd bow out. Even a slight injury could set my training back for weeks.

I stood by the food table next to Robbie Thoreson, a guy who had been a few years ahead of me, in Candy's class. He was another Norwegian whose family had moved to Bend for the lumber business and never left. We had been exactly the same height in high school and were matched up in one-on-one drills all the time, though he was a more experienced player than I was. Outside of basketball season Robbie ran cross country in the fall and track in the spring. I played football in the fall and threw discus and shot put in the spring. Back then I was the bulky one and Robbie was thin as a sapling. Now I'd gotten slimmer, especially training for the tri, and Robbie had added some muscle. He hadn't gone to college and had started work as a mason's apprentice. Now he had his own one-man masonry company, and hired part-time workers when he needed them.

"How's business?" I asked him.

"Not as good as before 2008," he said, "but it's coming back. I'm getting by."

"You doing any running?"

"On weekends," he said. "It helps me stay limber."

"But no basketball?"

"It was never really my sport," said Robbie. I was a little sorry to hear Robbie say that because he had been a better player than I was. It only dawned on me halfway through my freshman season that, though he was beating me in the drills, I was learning more from him than he was from me. I was getting better at a faster rate.

"Mine either," I said. We were grand old men now, and could admit these shortcomings without regrets. I think we took some satisfaction in our shared maturity.

Robbie used to walk around the halls of Bend High School holding hands with Candy when they were both seniors. He was a handsome guy and they made a head-turning couple. I think, for Candy, that was the point, though I didn't figure it out until much later. Robbie was the perfect accessory. They didn't talk much. As far as anyone could see they never kissed or embraced. No one ever saw them out on dates. Candy didn't even come to the basketball games. But still, my friends were fascinated by the question of whether Robbie was getting any. As time went on it seemed less and less likely. But if he wasn't, we wondered, what was in it for him?

"Did you know that Candy Bailey's husband was murdered?" I asked.

"I saw it in the paper," said Robbie. "It's too bad." He turned back to the game. He probably wished everyone would forget he was ever connected with Candy. He was Candy's dupe and he eventually realized it. He had even moved to Portland and worked construction when she went to art school. That lasted less than a year. Apparently she had met more interesting people. I'm sure he knew absolutely nothing about art.

A guy I didn't recognize was talking to Sean with great intensity and lots of smiles. "I wish I could find a way to get you more pumped up about this opportunity. The possibilities are infinite. Everybody is sitting around trying to figure out how to get into this space and we're already there. We're there."

"Give me an update next week," said Sean.

"Just remember," said the man. "the window is closing. I'm just trying to get everybody flying in the same direction." He gave Sean a deeply serious look and left the party without thanking his host.

"What was that all about?" I asked.

"Everybody thinks I want to invest in their startup. They want me to be their angel. But I am not a business genius. I am an engineer who got lucky and has enough brains to hang onto his money."

"What does the guy's company do?"

Sean laughed. "I don't even remember."

Sean had two beers on tap, Black Butte Porter from Deschutes Brewing and Apocalypse IPA from 10 Barrel. Then he had three more beers from local brewing companies in bottles. Nothing from Vandevert. I nursed one bottle of Diablo Rojo all evening, only 5.5 percent alcohol. I asked Sean what beer he liked himself.

"I like 'em all," he said. "Who would have thought Bend would be famous for beer? Yet here we are. I can find a good local beer for every day of the month. If I weren't in high tech I'd want to be brewing beer. I mean Facebook is a huge success and all but I don't get to see people enjoying it. Look at this party. Lots of people drinking beer and having a good time."

Grace came up to us with a nice-looking girl I didn't recognize.

"Dan," she said, "this is Amy and she is new to Bend. Amy, this is Dan Martinez."

CHAPTER 14

Biology and Fireworks

(Amy)

Grace, the testing supervisor at Greenwood that I liked so much, invited me to a July Fourth party. She and her husband had a house up on a hill overlooking Bend and Pilot Butte where the city was going to shoot off the fireworks. It was a pretty nice house for people who weren't that much older than I was. Grace's husband, Sean, worked for Facebook.

Most of the people at the party were about five or six years older than me and a lot of them were tall. I'm five-nine and wasn't used to having to look up so much when I met people. Many of them were from Sean's high-school basketball team and they all seemed to know each other. But Grace, being a good hostess, greeted me as soon as I came in the door, got me a lemonade, and spent a good twenty minutes introducing me to people, mostly her girlfriends. Some of the other women had brought food and I hadn't. I whispered to Grace how sorry I was. She said she hadn't asked me to bring anything on purpose.

"You've got enough to do," she said. "The people who brought food volunteered to do it. They wouldn't like it if I told them not to. And, as you can see, we are going to have more than enough." That made me feel better.

"Now," she said, "I'll introduce you to all the single guys."

"Oh, Grace, don't do that," I said, embarrassed at her agenda and her assumption about my own. "I'm just happy to be here."

"I'll be doing all of them a favor," said Grace. "But first I want you to meet Sean. He's not single."

"Grace really likes you," Sean told me. "You could do anything at Greenwood and she would want you to stay." He seemed like the nicest, happiest guy.

"Do you want to recruit my guests to swallow your magic pills?" he asked.

"I don't want to interrupt what looks like a great party," I said. "Besides, young people don't make very good subjects. They're not used to taking pills and they hate wearing the patch."

"I wouldn't think older people would like those things either," he said.

"But they see the benefit. Some of them have to take other pills and they're happy to include the placebo with the chip just to have a record. Or they have a relative struggling with medications and they want to help advance the technology."

"Where do you find your subjects?"

"I try to find them in Bend. I'm meeting a lot of people."

"Well, here's a candidate. Hey, Robbie, do you want to take a pill?" Sean called out to a tall man taking a swallow from a beer glass. The man looked wide-eyed at Sean. "It's the perfect pill," said Sean, "it has no effect whatsoever." Now the man looked a little annoyed, as though he thought Sean was making fun of him but wasn't sure exactly how.

"Help this lady out," said Sean. "She works for Grace's company and she needs people to experiment on."

"Beer is really the only medicine I need," said Robbie. "Thanks anyway."

"Well," said Sean, "there's plenty of that. So drink it up." Then Sean turned back to me. "Guy's passing up his chance to make history. What a shame."

"Thanks for trying anyway," I said, though I knew Sean had only tried to enlist Robbie for fun.

Grace seized the moment to walk me over to another tall man. "Amy, this is Dan Martinez. Dan, this is Amy De Santis. She is new to Bend and she works with me at Greenwood."

"Pleased to meet you," he said. He had such intelligent eyes. I liked him immediately.

"You're exactly the man I'm supposed to talk with!" I said. "Do you work for a law firm called Oxton?"

"I did," he said.

"But aren't you working on Ken Winterpol's will right now?"

"Sort of," he said. "How do you know that?"

"Well," I said. "I met his sister, and we think we look enough alike to be related." Dan drew his head back and examined my face.

"I can see some resemblance," he said in a politely agreeable way. He wasn't convinced but it didn't really matter.

"I was adopted," I said, "and I don't know who my father was. The sister is willing to do a DNA test with me to find out if I am related. But she wants you or your law firm to arrange it." Dan studied my face a little longer and thought before he spoke.

"Ken wanted to have children in the future," he said, "but nobody thought he had any so far. I'll have to check the will to see exactly what it says. There may be no inheritance for you even if you are his daughter."

"I don't care about any inheritance. All I really want is to find my mother's family."

"The law firm is supposed to find anyone who might have a claim on the estate. Even if the will says you don't inherit I'll make the arrangements for the DNA tests. Tell me where to reach you." We held up our cell phones and swapped information.

"There's something else," I said. "Didn't I meet you swimming at Juniper? You gave me a quick swim lesson?" Dan looked at me again. I think I was overloading his circuits.

"I guess that's right," he said. "You just started swimming, or training for swimming?"

"Yes," I said. "I'm training for the Upriver Off-Road."

"Well, so am I," he said with a smile. We'd finally made a connection that didn't involve a dead man and inheritances.

"Where do you ride?" I asked.

"Up to Bachelor and back on the road and then some short trails around Upriver. But the best trails are just west of Bend and I don't get there that often. It's hard to get other people to ride there on the same schedule."

"And you don't want to ride there by yourself?" I asked.

"Not a good idea. If you have a bad fall you need somebody to go for help."

"I'd like to ride those trails too," I said, "and I have the same problem. How are mornings for you?" I was being presumptuous. But we were both into training. I didn't think I was out of line.

"I can do mornings," he said, now faking more enthusiasm than I think he really felt. I was asking a lot of him on very short notice, getting him to spend hours helping me in one capacity or another. Also, I'm sure, he was thinking I would slow him down on the trail. But he agreed to meet me at Phil's trailhead at eight thirty two days later. I think we were both taken aback by how quickly we committed to spend a couple of hours together. We took a second to size each other up. He was a pretty good-looking guy. Probably married, I thought. Well, it didn't matter. We were only training together. I had enough brains not to look for a ring. He might have wondered if I wanted to date him. We turned away from our discussion as though, once we had concluded our very practical agreements, we had nothing more to say to each other.

At five minutes to ten everybody went out on the deck to watch the start of the fireworks. The sky was finally fading and the lights of Bend had gotten brighter below us. Amateurs were shooting off small rockets all over the city. The trajectories looked feeble from up on the ridge where we were. At ten o'clock exactly the first city-sponsored rocket took off from Pilot Butte. It exploded into a glittering white shower. It was followed by a green rocket and then a red one bigger than the others.

"That's the best one," said Sean. Two more followed until, after the next one, Sean said again, "Oh, that's the best."

"You mean the best so far," I heard Dan say. I looked at his hand. No ring.

"It's the best," said Sean. The next one was shaped like a flower with white petals and a purple center. "Best one," said Sean with conviction and a note of finality.

"Sean," said Dan with a laugh, "they can't all be the best one. I mean, they're all beautiful but they can't all be the best." Sean was putting us on and Dan was enjoying it. It was fun to watch. Sean rocked back and forth and grumbled like an unjustly reprimanded child. He let the next two rockets pass unremarked. Then they fired off two at once, one red and one gold.

"That's my favorite," said Sean.

"It's a pretty one," said Dan. The next one, a white center surrounded by circles of red and blue, was the biggest yet.

"Favorite," said Sean.

"They can't all be your favorite," Dan said in mock protest. They fired off three rockets in quick succession, white followed by gold, followed by red.

"Favorite," said Sean defiantly. He was very much enjoying himself. Dan was enjoying himself too and I was laughing just listening to them.

"Pick a favorite," Dan said, "and stick with it." Another rocket went up.

"Oh, that's the best one. That's the one I love," said Sean.

"Forsaking all others?" Dan asked. Sean didn't answer until the next rocket went up.

"Favorite!"

Two days later I got to Phil's trailhead, west of Bend, a little ahead of eight thirty. I had my bike off the car rack and was ready to go when Dan drove up. We both started with sweatshirts on. Dan's was green with OREGON RUGBY lettered on it in yellow. Mine was gray with a blue silhouette of a girl with a ponytail doing a jump on a mountain bike. We both had all-mountain bikes with twenty-six-inch wheels and six inches of travel in the suspension.

"I need to tell you," Dan said before we mounted our bikes, "I checked on Ken Winterpol's will. It says that after fifty thousand goes to his sister, the rest of his estate goes fifty percent to his wife and fifty percent to his children, held in trust until they turn thirty. We don't know yet what his estate will be worth but it is likely to be in the millions. You're the only possibility on the horizon. I thought you'd like to know."

"I told you I don't care about that," I said. "Did you order the DNA kits?"

"Yes," he said. "Expedited. And I confirmed that Linda agrees to the testing. I think she'd like to have a niece. I'm also going to collect some of Ken's things, like his razor and his toothbrush, to get further confirmation."

"Good," I said. "Let's ride."

Dan volunteered to lead and started at a medium speed so we could warm up. Then he gradually stepped up the pace, checking, I'm sure, how well I could keep up with him. The leg muscles I had developed rowing served me well and I think I surprised him. He only stopped once to wait for me and he was still breathing hard when I caught up. And I wasn't getting slower. The pace I set was the pace I kept.

When we got to the highest point and turned to go down I told him I would lead and I took off down the one-way singletrack. I'm sure he was annoyed at the prospect of reining back his speed to stay behind me but I knew what I was doing. I'd grown up mountain biking for fun in Boulder. He told me later that he rationalized that going second allowed him to make sure I was safe. After all, we were not riding together to keep each other company, but to have help available if one of us fell and got injured, or even had bike trouble. It was mutual. We were theoretically equals. But he still felt a protective male responsibility for me, including running off any creep who might think a woman riding by herself was a tempting target. Neither of us acknowledged the difference in our roles at the time. It smacked of chauvinism.

I raced down the trail, watching like a hawk for roots, rocks, and turns. When I got a chance to look back, Dan was nowhere in sight. I was afraid he had fallen and I waited until I saw him come down the trail a minute behind me.

"You're fast," he said.

"Yeah," I said, "I'm pretty good at this part." I took off again and didn't wait for Dan to follow. He couldn't keep up. I waited for him several times. He was more likely to fall and break something than I was.

"You need to get into the rhythm of the trail more," I said. "Use your eyes. You need to look three or four moves ahead and plan what you're going to do. It's not just one move at a time." I could tell he was annoyed, not at me, or only incidentally and temporarily at me. He was frustrated at not being as good at downhill as he thought he was.

"If I try to do that can you watch me?" he asked.

"Sure," I said, and hitched my bike out of the way so he could go ahead. He went slower than before and I could tell he was concentrating on seeing further down the trail. I'm sure he felt uneasy not focusing on what was right in front of him. He rode for five minutes and stopped.

"That's better," I said. "You just need to concentrate on it." Here I was, younger than Dan, telling him what to do. Well, I was right and he was gracious about it.

"Thanks," he said when we got back to the cars. We got our phones out and set three more times to go riding together. It felt like we should go get a cup of coffee but I wasn't going to suggest it and I wasn't going to pause one second waiting for him to suggest it.

Dan apparently made a greater impression on me than I realized. Walking into work the next day, I thought I saw him. I drew in my breath, my heart sped up, and my eyes widened. I very much wanted to say hello. But it wasn't Dan. It was the man Sean Wray had jokingly tried to recruit to be a test subject for the Greenwood chip, the one at Sean's party who said beer was the only medicine he needed. The man was laying cement to repair the walkway into Greenwood. I said hello and re-introduced myself. He said it was nice to see me again and gave me a nice smile. He waved his big hand, coated with gray cement dust, as a substitute for shaking hands. He didn't tell me his name again but Dan would be able to tell me who he was. Seeing someone I actually had met before was a sign I was getting to know people in Bend.

CHAPTER 15

Heritage

(Dan)

My father called me on my way back from my ride with Amy. I was crossing the Deschutes on the Reed Market Bridge. There were kayaks and rafts on the river below and I was remembering all the times my friends and I had paddled upriver from here and come down again through the rapids. No helmets, no life vests, no brains. Yet we all survived. Logically we should be reckless when we're old and don't have that many years to live. But we are reckless when we're young and cautious when we're old.

My father was in good spirits but he missed Mom and me. I missed him too but not as much as I was worried about him. He told me he was safe and happy.

"There are things I like that your mother doesn't. So I'm taking this opportunity to enjoy them without dragging her along." I knew what those things were likely to be—art museums and galleries, flamenco music and dancing, and speaking Spanish. My mother didn't speak Spanish, had only a passing interest in art, and could barely tolerate flamenco unless there was singing, in which case she couldn't stand it at all. She said it sounded like screaming. Dad would play Diego El Cigalo, El Cameron de la Isla, and Paco de Lucia when Mom was out of the house. When I was a boy I used to play at flamenco dancing, looking very severe and rapping my heels on the floor while turning in slow circles like a matador holding a cape in front of a bull. "More fire in the eye," my father would say. "You have powerful emotions inside that threaten to explode. Yet you are holding them in to maintain your dignity, your pride. The conflict is consuming you." I never did learn to sing, play the guitar, or dance in any proper way. But I learned enough to like flamenco. My father said I had a touch of Gypsy blood in me.

Before my father said anything more on the phone I told him, "Don't say anything about what you are doing, Dad," I said, "or I will figure out where you are. And don't tell Mom what you are doing or she will figure it out."

"It's a big world," he said.

"Dad, you're either going to come back here and cooperate with the sheriff or you're going to stay unreachable. If you stay away but hint about where you are then you put Mom and me in a dangerous position. We're only safe if we can honestly tell the sheriff we have absolutely no information about where you are. Flat zero, zilch."

"They haven't issued a warrant for my arrest, have they?"

"No. But they want to talk to you. The sheriff even could try to arrest you as a material witness."

"Material witness means they think I know something important, right?"

"Right, Dad."

"Well, let's just assume that I don't."

"Dad," I said, "you're walking on a narrow ledge here. If the D.A. gets frustrated enough he could try to arrest you for the murder itself."

"It will never come to that," my father said. "My son is an excellent attorney."

"An attorney with no experience in criminal law," I said.

"You should have more confidence in yourself."

"Dad, this is not a high-school debate. This could mess up the rest of your life. And Mom's for that matter."

"Not to worry. But listen, the other thing I called to tell you," said Dad, "is that I'm going to be incommunicado for a few weeks. I told your mother I won't be doing anything the least bit dangerous. Very relaxed, reading, listening to music, surrounded by good company, no women around. As safe as I could possibly be. So if there is anything you want to ask me, aside from where I am, you better ask it now."

"No questions, Dad, just a request. Don't discuss any of this with the good company you're going to be hanging out with. Agreed?"

"Agreed." he said. "I'm going to do what my lawyer has told me to do. Hasta la vista, son."

"Vaya con dios," I said. He hung up. The thought that I wouldn't speak with him for a while evoked a sadness that surprised me. I had gone for a month or more without speaking with my father when I was in college. Now knowing that I couldn't speak with him if I wanted to got to me. There would be a time, hopefully far in the future, when all possibility of speaking with him would be gone.

As the road home climbed toward Lava Butte I remembered the trip Dad and I took to Spain, just the two of us, when I was sixteen. He had only visited Spain a few times over the years and, except for speaking the language fluently, he was almost as much a tourist as I was. He had memories of previous trips to Madrid and Valencia but Seville, Granada, and Barcelona were as new to him as they were to me. We visited the town near Valencia where his family had lived and we met people who knew my grandparents. According to family legend, my grandfather met Ernest Hemingway during the Spanish Civil War, but my father said that might not be true. My grandfather, who never went back to Spain, would only say that it was in another country and a long time ago. I remember that my grandfather limped from a wound he received at the Battle of the Ebro.

There wasn't much to look at in the little town and I was a bit impatient at first with all the sitting around and talking we did, even though I could follow the conversation and occasionally make a remark. But I was a good son and sat it out. My father spent a long time talking with a woman his age that he had known in France when they were small. "I've never forgotten her and she has never forgotten me," he said. My father looked younger than she did. I'd always thought my father looked very Spanish. But there in Spain, in the little town, he suddenly looked very American. He was relaxed and confident, polite and considerate in spite of not knowing the people as well as they knew each other. I was proud of him. I think our hosts were thrilled to see him but they weren't entirely sure what to make of him.

A brief but violent cyclone caught me up during our visit, a romantic cyclone. There was a beautiful young woman at one family's house who gave me a friendly smile when I first saw her across the room. Then she completely ignored me for five or ten minutes, though my eyes kept coming back to her. When I finally focused on a conversation I was having with an older woman about her visit to New York years ago, the younger woman caught my eye. She was looking right at me. Our eyes met for a few seconds as though we understood, at a profound level, that we had waited all our lives to meet each other. The bond between us, ordained by fate, was on a level of importance and power elevated far above anything else that had ever happened to us. She was waiting, with growing frustration, for me to approach her. Then she lowered her eyes slightly in disappointment at my cowardice, and looked away. I was crushed and at the same time, in a panic. The woman was married. I had met her husband earlier in the day. If that woman's look meant what I imagined it meant, then I was interfering between a man and his wife. Was I willing to do that? If she led me by the hand, I guess I was. I dismissed the niggling little thought that her being recklessly drawn to a sixteen-year-old virgin, no matter how deep his soul might be, was extremely unlikely.

I tried to catch her eye again as I fumbled through the conversation about New York. But the beauty would not look my way. She had given up on me, sadly for both of us. Twenty minutes later an old man was telling me about a horse that brought him home in a rain storm. Suddenly the woman was looking at me again, this time with a "this is your last chance" expression on her face. I tried to excuse myself from the horse conversation but the man grabbed my arm and added more urgency to his story. "And Buttelo never stumbled," he said. "Never stumbled." When I looked back at my soul mate she was in conversation with a man in a suit and tie who was twice my age. I decided, with sorrow, that I had to give up. I was unequal to the challenge and, sadder still, might never be equal to it.

I went back to the story of Buttelo and the stormy night. I tried to tell a story about a high-school friend whose family kept horses in Tumalo and who rode horses in the rodeo. Explaining calf roping put my Spanish to the test and the man I was talking to was struggling to show interest. I fared no better describing my friend's skill in cutting, how well he and his horse separated one cow from a herd and kept it from getting back with the rest of the cattle. I just couldn't make it sound very interesting. The man I was talking to suddenly looked past my shoulder to greet someone who had walked up behind me.

"Hello, Marta," he said. "I'd like you to meet Daniel Martinez. He is telling me about rodeos in the United States."

"Con mucho gusto," she said to me and I was struck dumb. Here was the beauty I had been staring at from across the room. My jaw dropped and I stood there unable to move. The smile on her face was friendly now, with no hint of the signals that had passed between us. Or which I thought had passed between us.

"Do you ride?" she asked.

"A little," I said. "I have friends who compete in riding events. They ride every day."

"Bronco busting?" she asked in English. She had a slight accent but she wasn't the least bit embarrassed about it.

"Yes," I said, "and bull riding."

"But not for you?" she asked.

"No."

"What sports do you do?" she asked. My brain was underwater and I was grateful for the easy questions.

"Football, American football." I was still in high school then and hadn't discovered rugby.

"Are you a quarterback?" she asked. She meant me to be impressed, pleased, and put somewhat at ease with her interest in the game.

"No. I am a tight end." She clearly didn't know what a tight end was. "Sometimes we catch the ball and run with it."

"Touchdown," she said.

"I have two to my credit," I said. I didn't tell her it was junior varsity.

"And how are your children, Marta?" asked the man I'd been talking with.

"Both well," she answered. "Sebastian is in second grade and Mateo will start school next year." She was talking to both of us. "I hope they will play sports. But not American football. It is too dangerous."

"Rock climbing?" I said. She shook her head. Then someone else came up. Those were the last words I exchanged with her. How could the same woman be outrageously exotic one moment and so friendly and nonchalant the next?

My father seemed very happy when we left the gathering. "Marta Velasquez took you on a merry ride, didn't she?" he said.

"She certainly did" was all I could say. "Was she trying to make me feel like an idiot?"

"Not really. She likes you or she wouldn't have bothered. But she likes you as a sixteen-year-old boy. She gave you a gift and she knows it. You will remember her for a very long time." He pulled the tiny rental Fiat away from the curb where he had parked it.

"Just for her amusement?" I asked. "She made a fool out of me."

"She was teasing you but not maliciously. You will be swept away again someday when you're older."

"And what did she get out of it?"

"Well, for one thing," said Dad, "in your memory she will always be young."

"Yes, I don't suppose I'm going to see her again," I said.

"You might. She is your cousin three times removed. Her father's name was Leon, as mine is, after Leon Trotsky. In your generation, of course, nobody knows or cares who Leon Trotsky was."

I wondered what memories of women my father carried around with him, women he met or maybe even saw across a room before he met my mother. His memories of what they looked like would be rich. Was he disloyal to my mother when he thought of them?

When I went riding with Amy again we had lunch at a brewpub on the way back into town. We were dirty from the workout and our riding shirts were sweaty. So we sat outside as far as we could get from other tables. I had a burger and a beer. Amy had a salad with chicken, water to drink, and a bite of my burger. I offered her some of my fries but she declined.

The sun beat down on us and caught Amy's sandy blonde curls. It was the first time I'd seen her in full daylight when her head wasn't in a swimming cap or a bicycle helmet. She was very pretty, and I wondered if I was biased because I was enjoying my time with her so much. And, thank goodness, she didn't have Ken's shit-colored eyes. Her eyes were blue tending to gray.

"Where did you grow up?" I asked.

"Boulder, Colorado," she said, "Then I went to UC Santa Barbara for college, then I got a job here with Greenwood Biomedical."

"Did your family get to Colorado by covered wagon or airplane?"

"VW bus. They were hippies when they arrived and got more and more normal over time. They only got married so they could adopt me. The only parents I've ever known are the ones who brought me up. I was very lucky. They were excellent parents."

This seemed to me a sign of maturity. Not all people fresh out of college are ready to admit what good parents they had. "How much have you done to find your father or your mother's family?"

"I had my birth certificate with mother's name on it, Vickie Coate. She died giving birth to me. I couldn't find any more information about who she was or where she came from. She didn't go to school in Boulder and she was never arrested in Colorado. For all I know she had just landed in town when the time came to have a baby. I feel bad for her but I probably have a better life than if she had lived. I love my parents."

"Your biological parents must have had some athletic ability," I said. "And some smarts."

"Nature versus nurture," said Amy.

"Have you tried 23andme to see if they can find any cousins online?" I asked. "Or tell you what your ancestry is?"

"I tried it," she said. "But it only came up with fourth or fifth cousins, many of them in Australia. I didn't like the idea of letting all these unknown people into my life. I couldn't tell if we were related on my mother's side or my father's side. I didn't care about my father and I didn't want him to even know I existed. What I really wanted was to find people who knew my mother, who knew what she was like, what kind of life she had, and how she came to have me. All those distant relatives were irrelevant. They might even be creeps."

"Ax murderers," I offered. "Or Republicans." I did get a laugh out of her with that one. "Or perhaps they are wonderful people. You never know."

"I think I got some good genes for rowing," said Amy. "That was my sport in college. I learned some good lessons from it. Excellence comes from focusing. To succeed you need other people. Your brain will give up long before your body does."

If Amy was Ken's daughter it looked like she got his drive to succeed without his compulsion to cheat. She would have been born about the time Ken switched from being a drug dealer to a real-estate developer, presumably trying to put his past behind him and at least appear respectable. In some ways Amy was what Ken had wished to be.

CHAPTER 16

Right and Wrong

(Leon)

Ken was not the kind of man Candy should have married. I saw it when I first met him on their wedding day. But what could I do? Elizabeth said she agreed with me but was still hopeful for them. She said that sometimes things had a way of working out in a marriage.

Candy needed love more than she needed money but she didn't know it. If I had told her in time I might have made a difference. Now her mistake, and my failure to counsel her, had laid waste to the landscape. Her husband was dead and Candy was a widow. And the devastation from that death extended to my son, my wife, and myself.

If an artist could ever wish to be blind, my moment was watching the attack on Ken Winterpol. I was standing on the golf cart path a hundred yards away from Ken's house looking over a marshy meadow and the Winterpol's back lawn. I saw two powerful-looking men arguing on the deck. The shorter, heavier man looked like Ken Winterpol. The younger, taller man with dark hair looked like my son. Ken stood with his arms crossed, holding something against his chest and under the opposite arm. I thought it might have been a gun and I feared for Dan. I thought of shouting at them to break up their dispute. But Ken turned back toward the house and I thought the discussion was over. Then the young man took one stride toward the fireplace, snatched a black iron fire tool off the stone chimney, and, in one long sweep of his arm, cracked Ken on the side of the head. Ken crumpled onto the deck. The other man stood over him a moment, the weapon still raised, then strode off toward the fountain across the lawn. He flung the instrument into the water with a splash. He didn't look up and didn't see me standing on the golf course, frozen in place by what I had witnessed. Then he ran off.

If I could have forgotten what I had seen I would have. At least I wasn't going to tell anyone about it. So I hustled away and escaped to San Francisco.

Had that tall young man really been Dan? It certainly looked like him. But how could he have gotten himself in a situation where he would strike another human being that hard? I accepted that I didn't know Dan as well as I had in the past. He was a man now, not the teenager we had sent off to college.

I could only think Candy was at the heart of the problem. For months Dan had been coming and going from our house at unpredictable hours, sometimes dressed for running, sometimes for biking, sometimes golf, and sometimes in street clothes to go into Bend and swim. But in the last two weeks he'd gone out in street clothes for a short while and come back. Who bothers to go for a walk when they run for miles five days a week? I thought he might be going to see some girl who was visiting her parents nearby. When it occurred to me that it might be somebody's wife I put the thought out of my mind.

But Candy. Candy was a young woman with a husband who was away for days at a time. She had seen enough immorality in her parents, and perhaps in her husband, to be vague on the lines between right and wrong. Dan should have had more sense than to share a bed with her. Ken was not the kind of man you cuckolded. And now look what happened. My son killed a man, putting himself in danger and cracking open a divide between himself, his parents, and the rest of society that could never be healed. Painful as it was to me, at least I could spare Elizabeth this knowledge for a few more weeks.

Maybe Dan didn't have an affair with Candy. Maybe it was something else. It's a mystery to me that he killed Ken at all so why shouldn't it be a mystery why he did it? I kept asking myself where I had gone wrong as a father. If not me, then where had his teachers let him down? I found myself considering the anguished American

Muslim parents, raising a child to lead a happy life, only to discover their son or daughter has gone to join nutcase terrorists in the desert. But Dan had not been seduced by some medieval ideology; he had let his emotions overcome his morals and his common sense. The flaw was not in his thinking; it was in his character.

When I found I wasn't sorry that Ken was dead I had to question my own standards. I had never liked or trusted him. Perhaps the world, and Candy in the long run, were better off without him. But any violent and unjust death is a crime against society. It upsets our faith that our nation and our neighborhood, particularly a gated community like Upriver Ranch, are peaceful, safe, and fair.

I had mulled over these ideas ever since I walked off the golf course that morning. But then, in my last few days at Gabriel and Maria's house, I thought more slowly and carefully about where my duty lay. I sat in the bay window overlooking San Francisco. It was a sunny day. And I asked myself the critical question. Knowing what I knew and what I didn't know, what should I do? Should I tell the sheriff what I saw, as I would if the killer had been anyone else? Should I protect Dan by saying nothing? Should I insist to Dan and Elizabeth and all the world that I had never seen anything at all?

All my life I thought I was a truthful man. Truth was the basis of my art. Truth was inherent in the rights and duties I had as a citizen. My father had risked his life in Spain for what he saw as the truth. Should I trample the truth to protect a family member, like some illiterate tribesman in a backward country?

Yet Dan was the peak achievement of my life, the product of the love between Elizabeth and me. A Neruda poem called "The Son" had always warmed my heart. But sitting in San Francisco on a bright summer day its lines haunted me. "We shook the tree of life... and you appear now singing in the foliage...." To hurt Dan, to see him go to jail or even be executed because of what I said, would rip my heart out. It would bring my life to nothing. It would be better to die myself.

Son or not, Dan had brought this on himself. Some men's sons die young, in war, in accidents, or in some other way. Dan's mother and I had twenty-eight good years with him and then he changed.

We should count our blessings for what we had. Then, perhaps, we must give it up. I still did not know what to do. For the time being, though, I would protect Dan. Once I told someone what I saw there would be no going back.

I sat unmoving in Gabriel and Maria's chair for a long time. The house was quiet until I heard the rustle of Maria's skirt behind me.

"Leon," she asked in a tender but penetrating voice, "what happened in Oregon that led you to visit us?" I concocted a story so quickly I surprised myself. I'm sure Maria believed me.

"I witnessed a murder. I don't know if the murderer saw me but if he did I am afraid he will kill me too."

"Do you know the man?"

"No," I lied again, "but I could recognize him and, if he saw me at the time, he could recognize me now."

"I'm so sorry," said Maria. "Are you afraid to go home?"

"Yes, I am," I said, "but I will go home soon enough. They will have caught the man or they will have given up looking. If they haven't caught him I will have to bet that he thinks he will be safer lying low than killing yet another person. It's a position I didn't expect to be in at my age."

"Can we help?" she asked.

"Your company and hospitality have helped me immensely already. I wish I'd come to visit you long before this and I hope you will come visit us in Oregon."

I asked Maria not to tell Gabriel what I had told her and I didn't think she would. But she didn't like to see me deep in thought, I could tell, and she proposed that we all go to Berkeley that evening to hear a flamenco guitarist they were both fond of, an American with a fiery Gypsy spirit. We set off at eight and arrived at the tapas bar where El Keni would play. We ate fried calamari with sweet aioli and a salad with ham, pistachios and dried cranberries. El Keni played powerful flamenco while a slight Japanese-American woman danced ferociously. That was America for you, a kid from Massachusetts and a woman whose ancestors played the shamisen, both loving and mastering music from Spain. Choices for them, choices for me, and choices for all those Mexican-American kids I taught in high school.

CHAPTER 17

Debt Collection

(Dan)

On a morning's drive to go swim at Juniper, I called Patsy to see what she had learned about the health of Western Sun and the prospects for Ken's estate. I was hoping the business was rich and the inheritance would be substantial. I was also hoping there were people that Western Sun owed money to who might be angry enough to murder the owner.

"He's short on cash," Patsy said. "He's paying contractors and service people late. He's way behind on his property taxes. But he's current on his bank loans and it looks like the properties are worth much more than what he put into them. So it should be a sizable estate when it all gets settled."

"That's good news," I said. "Do you have a list of the creditors, contractors and whatnot he's late in paying, how late he is and how much he owes them? Can you email it to me?"

"Sure," she said. "But listen, the most immediate problem is there is no one running Western Sun. The company needs to choose a way to raise cash. The employees are directionless and some of them will leave if we don't get a manager in there. How would you like to take this on? It would pay well. It would help a lot that Mrs. Winterpol knows you and trusts you."

"Aside from not being qualified," I said, "it would throw all my own plans into a tailspin."

"Do you know of anyone else we can get to do this?" asked Patsy. "Ideally we'd get someone who knows commercial real estate but who isn't a competitor or a potential buyer of the business." It was a longshot on Patsy's part to ask me. She, or other people at Oxton, must have known far more developers than I. But, as a matter of fact, I did know of someone who was at least a possibility.

"You might talk to Tom Melillo," I said. "He's a developer who is not very busy these days. He says Winterpol ripped him off and he's got no money to invest. He'd be happy for the chance to get back into development. He was successful, apparently, before he got mixed up with Ken. I'll send you his contact information."

"I'll check up on him," said Patsy. "If he's qualified he might be our man."

At home that evening I opened an email from Patsy that listed all the people Ken was late in paying. Some debts were six months overdue and a few creditors had threatened to take Ken to court. There were thirty-seven names overall. They appeared to be mostly small companies that maintained different aspects of Ken's buildings. Ken could easily replace any of them if they stopped providing service.

I wondered how I could identify contractors who would seem dangerous enough to become plausible suspects. I decided I would call the contractors to tell them Ken was dead, that I was working with the law firm settling his estate, and that I was checking on claims against him or his company. All true and reasonable. Then I would ask them how urgently they needed to get paid, as if their answer might have an effect on the speed of payment. That question should bring out some desperation or anger if I hadn't evoked a strong reaction by then. Finally I might ask them if they would be willing to forget what Ken owed them for the sake of his widow. I would record the conversations to present in court if necessary. I wouldn't need to reach all thirty-seven people I had listed. I only needed a few to sound like potential killers. But I was beginning to think I might happen across the person who actually did kill Ken. Whoever had called and threatened me clearly didn't like the course of my endeavors whether or not he was the killer. If I thought I had stumbled on the real killer I would tell Breuninger right away. I didn't want any murderer turning his sights on me.

When I next met Amy for a bike ride I was so happy to see her I wanted to kiss her. I guess I hadn't realized how much I liked her.

We were friendly, even enthusiastic, but we focused on our bikes and the task we had set ourselves for the day. We left from the same trailhead but rode further and over a different set of trails. We worked hard going uphill but paced ourselves as though we were in a triathlon and were going to have to run afterwards. Then we flowed downhill again, with me trying to focus on the trail as far ahead of me as possible. I was getting better at it but Amy was waiting, not even breathing hard, when I got to the bottom.

"I have an idea you might be interested in," I said. "There is a swim at Elk Lake in August. It is for swimmers, not part of a triathlon, and I would expect both of us to finish back in the pack somewhere. But it would be a good experience—cold open water, a timed race, and competing with a mass of other people."

"Most of whom will be trying to drown us."

"Exactly," I said.

"Sounds like we could use that. I haven't swum in open water with so many people before."

"Fear of death can play with your mind," I said.

"I've been practicing lifting my head every twelfth stroke to look where I am going. In a pool I don't need to. It would be good to practice in a big lake where we have to do it."

"Okay," I said, "we're in."

In between my running, biking, swimming, and strength training I started calling the people Ken owed money to and I'd found two, an electrician and a plumber, who had done work on a strip mall for Ken and whom he hadn't paid for six months. In the meantime Ken had sold the property. The new owner had no obligation to pay them for their past work and Ken had no reason to keep their goodwill. The electrician in particular was out a lot of money for lighting fixtures and was very upset about it. He said, and I had his whole speech recorded on my cell phone, "Serves that bastard right if he's dead. What was he thinking? That other people were just going to stand by and let him rip them off? I hope whoever killed him put a stake through his heart." Wonderful.

When I had to leave voicemail the vendors were pretty good about calling me back. They wanted to get paid. One that didn't call me back, and I had to call again, was Little River Masonry, the only vendor with an address in Central Oregon. It turned out the company belonged to Robbie Thoreson, my old basketball teammate whom I'd just seen at Sean's party.

"I did the rock work for the new fountain in the back yard," Robbie said when I reached him. "Winterpol said it wasn't built right and he wasn't going to pay me. I told him I'd fix it but I needed the money now. I had bills to pay. He said he'd pay me when I made it right—wouldn't even give me partial payment. I figured I'd go back to it when I had a slow spell. Now Winterpol's dead I don't know if I'll ever get paid." I told him I'd see what I could do.

I called Candy about the fountain and she said she didn't know what Ken had told Robbie. So I told her Robbie promised to fix the fountain but he really needed to get paid. I said the estate could legally wait until Robbie corrected the work but, since Candy knew him, and we all had friends in common, it would be a nice gesture to release the money now.

"Do whatever you want, Dan," she said. "I don't want to get involved with Ken's business." This debt was personal, not business, but Candy didn't have time for fine points like that. She'd given me the okay to pay Robbie so I called Patsy at Oxton and asked her to send him a check. She said no problem.

I organized all the material I'd gathered on possible killers and put it on a CD to give to Breuninger and the DA. First I thought I should check in with Candy's attorney, Tod Morgan, to tell him what I was doing and see if there was any way I should slant my report for a better result. I made an appointment to see him on a morning that Amy and I weren't riding. I filled him in first on the progress of Ken's estate. He was gratified to hear it looked like Candy would have plenty of money to pay him.

"There may not be much of a fee to collect," said Tod. "I met with Breuninger and Mrs. Winterpol once. I can't tell you what she said but you'll be relieved to know Breuninger gave her an opportunity to throw suspicion on you and she didn't take it. Breuninger didn't have many questions and she had fewer answers. She's a good client that way. The downside is she won't tell me much either. Nothing about the relationship she had with her husband. That's all right for now but if we go to trial she'll have to tell me everything. I'd like to go through the evidence Breuninger has collected but, of course, he has no obligation to show it to me until my client is charged. My guess, frankly, is that she will never be charged and I'll return most of the five-thousand-dollar retainer."

"I hope you're right," I said. "Especially when Breuninger sees my long list of other people who had good reasons to kill Ken. We could theorize all day. Winterpol got his startup capital by dealing meth, even producing it. He turned on his buddies, helped put them in jail instead of him. There are dozens of people he cheated in business. And there's a string of people he owes money to he hasn't paid. I have their names and statements from some of them about the harm Winterpol did. I have voice recordings of some of them telling me how much they hated Ken. I also have a record of what looks like bribes Ken gave to government officials. Oxton and the Multnomah District attorney are still sorting that out but all the people he bribed had an incentive to keep Ken quiet on a permanent basis. I brought you a full report on a CD along with the recordings and pictures of all the gray pickup trucks I've seen in the Upriver area."

"You want me to look at it?"

"Just hang onto it. There is no need to dive in it if Candy isn't charged."

"And you're going to give this to Breuninger?"

"Absolutely. I'm sure any case against Candy will be circumstantial, not conclusive. Then you can ask Breuninger about all these people, all the other avenues of investigation, and whether he pursued them. He can't have investigated all these possibilities thoroughly enough to say he's sure Candy did it and none of these other people did."

"Who's paying you to dig all this up?" he asked.

"Nobody," I said. "Candy's a friend of my family and I have the time to do it."

Tod was no fool. He knew perfectly well that I was protecting myself as well as Candy. He might or might not know I was protecting my father too. I hadn't told him Dad had left town the day of the murder and Candy might not have told him that either.

"There's one odd thing about this case," said Tod, "and maybe you can make some sense of it along the way. Why would law enforcement come to the scene of what appeared to be, from what you've told me about your 911 call, a stroke, a heart attack, or a straightforward household slip-and-fall?"

"I don't know," I said, "and Breuninger got there quickly, right after the EMTs."

"And that's another thing," said Tod, "on TV shows the detectives come to the crime scene right away. In real life that almost never happens. Regular police officers or sheriff department deputies gather evidence and interview witnesses at the scene. The detective doesn't get involved until later. So why was Breuninger there at all?"

"Beats me," I said.

"I asked him why he came to the house after your call," said Tod. "He avoided giving me an answer and, of course, he doesn't have to tell me unless I get him on the witness stand."

"Ken skirted the law in his business dealings," I said. "Maybe Breuninger was onto him for something and finally had an excuse to look at Ken's home life."

"Well," said Tod, "there's something going on here that we don't understand. Keep your eyes open."

"I will," I said.

My next stop was the county sheriff's office to drop off Breuninger's copy of the CD. The detective was out so I left it for him but I got him live and in person on his cell phone as I was driving away. I told him about the CD and all the people I'd found with a motive to kill Ken.

"So now the amateur defense attorney is playing amateur detective?" he asked.

"Yes," I said, "and doing a bang-up job of it too."

"We'll see about that. Sounds to me like you're trying to waste my time. Sounds to me like you might know something you want to steer me away from."

"Facts are facts," I said in as calm, confident, and friendly manner as I could muster.

"Thanks a lot," he said. "Is there anything else about this case that you think I might like to know?" This sounded more like a complaint than a question but Breuninger was clever. If he could catch me telling him a lie I would be open to prosecution.

"Everything I have to report is on the CD," I said. I could have said, "Everything I choose to report." I certainly wasn't going to mention Ken's holographic will.

"Are there any suspects you left out?" asked Breuninger. "Anybody else who stood to gain from this man's death?"

"Winterpol hurt a lot of people," I said. "I'm sure there are dozens of possibilities I've left out."

"Lawyers," he said in a disgusted tone and hung up. But the question Breuninger had asked me, about who else stood to gain from Ken's death, gave me a thought I didn't like. The person who actually stood to gain the most from Ken's death, if she were his daughter, was Amy. The friendship we had would shatter immediately if I got her dragged into Breuninger's murder investigation. I also thought of Linda's gain if the handwritten will had been valid. If Linda knew about it and believed it was good, she picked the right time to kill her brother. But Sister Catherine did not look likely. I laughed at the idea of presenting her to a jury as a possible killer.

I'd gotten a call from Patsy while I was on the phone with Breuninger and I listened to her voicemail before I went in to swim. Candy had agreed to let us retrieve what we could of Ken's DNA from his medicine cabinet in Upriver. She was in Portland but her housekeeper would be at the Upriver house the next day and Candy had told her to let me in.

That afternoon I lifted weights and took it easy because I was going to do a "brick" the next morning. In the triathlon world a brick meant training in two events back to back. After a long night's sleep I rode my bike from home to the start of the trails above Upriver, leading up to the Cascades, and rode about twenty miles uphill and down. Then I quickly locked my bike to a tree, changed

134

my shoes, and ran eight miles over some of the same trails I'd just biked. I concentrated on my form rather than power and speed. Still I kept up a pretty good clip.

After the run I rode my bike back towards Upriver at a cool-down pace. On the paved road cars came down the hill behind me every minute or so. When I am in a car I think bicyclists are reckless to be riding so close to thousands of pounds of steel going by at fifty miles an hour. When I am on a bike I think I am safe as long as I stay in the bike lane. In any case, I couldn't see the cars coming from behind and I could only trust that each driver was paying attention and wasn't angry with the world.

I heard one car slow down behind me, in spite of there being no car coming the other way. I glanced behind me and realized, just in time, that the driver wasn't slowing down for my safety. He was taking aim. I yanked my bike handles hard right down the embankment, using all my mountain-bike skills to avoid rocks and to stop at the bottom without splitting my torso in two on the bike.

The driver of the car was not so lucky. He had fully committed to hitting me and he ran his Chevy off the side of the embankment. The Chevy flipped and slid to a rocking and banging halt on its roof in the dirt. Dust rose up all around it. I spun my waist pack around and pulled out my cell phone to call 911. I told them who I was, where I was, that a car had tried to run me off the road on my bike, and that the driver was in his upside-down car and likely injured. The operator, a very calm woman who sounded as though she had been doing this job for a while, put me on hold to dispatch help.

"Are you injured?" she asked when she came back.

"No, I'm fine."

"Can you see the extent of the man's injuries?"

"No," I said. "I can't see from here. But he's not getting out of his car."

"Can you go to the car and see?"

"This man just tried to run me over on purpose. I don't know why. But he might be armed and I'd rather keep my distance. As a matter of fact, if you don't mind, I'm going to move back up the road about a hundred yards and wait for the sheriff."

The operator put me on hold again and then came back. "You need to remain at the scene of the accident," she said.

"I am not leaving," I said. "I'm just moving a little further away."

"You need to remain at the scene of the accident."

"I understand," I said.

"So you will not leave the scene of the accident?"

"I'm not leaving," I said, already walking my bike back up the embankment.

"Don't make or receive any other calls," she said, and we hung up. I turned and looked back at the car. Still no sign of the driver or any passengers. I thought whoever was in the car must be badly injured or caught in some crushed part of the car. Maybe I could help them or even save a life. Evil as the driver might be, and possibly going to prison for attempting to murder me, I believed I had a duty to pull him out, if I could, before the car caught fire. I coasted down the road again, parked my bike on the edge of the bike lane and cautiously approached the car. Through the back window I could see the outline of a man upside down, hanging from his seat belt with his shoulders resting on the ceiling. I crept up slowly to the driver's door, watching for movement all the time. When I looked in the window I could see it was Wade, Rhonda's boyfriend, who had somehow been released from jail. I was sure he resented me for duping him about the supposed money under the woodpile at Candy's house, and for getting him into the jail from which he had somehow been released. Running over me and killing me must have appealed mightily to his emotions. But it was a really dumb idea. He wasn't likely to have gotten away with killing me if he had succeeded. Prison for the rest of his life. And if he was willing to kill me that was one more indication he would have been willing to kill Ken.

With that happy thought I rested my eyes on Wade a little longer. He was breathing hard in quick short breaths. I noticed, much to my relief, that both his hands were empty. He wasn't moving his limbs at all. Blood was trickling out of his mouth and running over his upside-down face.

"Wade," I said, "there's an ambulance on the way. Hang in there."

"Son of a bitch," he said, in a voice just above a whisper.

"Wade," I said, "Did you kill Ken?" If Wade was in enough pain, and upset enough, he just might tell me the truth. It was a little like using torture to extract a confession except, of course, that I was not administering the torture. And if Wade died, anything he told me on the way out would be a "dying declaration", admissible in court. If he lived, however, I would not be able to testify to what he said. Even if I couldn't testify to it, though, a confession from Wade would encourage me, and Breuninger if I could persuade the detective, to investigate Wade very thoroughly.

"Wade," I asked again, "did you kill Ken Winterpol?"

"Hell, no," he said with an anger I hadn't imagined he could muster. "He was going to pay me money."

"Why was he going to pay you?" I asked.

"Fifteen thousand dollars," he said. "That would have really set me up. Then he goes and gets killed and next thing I know you've gotten me arrested. Why does nothing ever, ever work? It was going to be so simple." The voice that had threatened me on the phone was now coming at me from Wade's mouth. Had he been serious when he threatened me in the voicemail or had sudden inspiration hit him when he saw me on the bike?

"What was going to be so simple?" I asked.

"I just had to get those people out of that house," said Wade.

"What house?"

"It was next to property Ken had in Bend. It was right on the corner. But the people wouldn't sell it to him and he couldn't develop the rest of the property without removing the house."

That was too much for me to process all at once and I returned to the most immediate concern. "Do you have a gun in the car?" I asked.

"Fuck, no," said Wade. "Come on and get me out of here. Unfasten the goddamn seat belt." I wondered why he didn't unfasten it himself. When I looked more closely one arm was behind his head, wedged between his head and the car ceiling. The other arm was lying free but at a funny angle. I thought it might be broken.

"I don't think I can reach it, Wade." Actually I thought I could if I tried. But I didn't trust Wade not to have a gun. I was content to let him hang.

"Damn," he said.

"How were you going to get the people out of the house?"

"I dumped garbage next to the house. Really smelly stuff. I fired off shots in the middle of the night. I left them a note that Rhonda wrote. It said we knew there were witches in the house and we were going to burn the house down to exorcise them. Real crazy. And Ken had this idea I should tell all the lowlifes in town they could buy drugs there. The people in the house were just about ready to move and I was going to get paid. It was going to be a big score. Then Ken goes and gets himself killed." Wade wriggled around under the seatbelt but couldn't get free. "Then Rhonda has one shot at getting some money from Candy and you come along and mess up the plan. You should be here busted up instead of me," he said.

"You said you were coming to get me," I repeated from Wade's voicemail.

"Damn straight," he said.

I could hear a siren so I got up, stepped away from the car, and walked up the embankment to my bike. Two sheriff's cars arrived together and the deputies, both men and neither of whom I'd seen before, got out.

"Are you the one who called 911?"

"Yes. The man in the car is Wade something-or-other. He was recently released from jail, probably on bail, and he just tried to run me over. He's in the car and injured. I didn't see a gun and he says he doesn't have one."

"Okay," said the shorter deputy with the moustache, "you stay right here. Don't move." He looked back at me twice as the two deputies approached the car on both sides, guns out. I heard them speaking to Wade but I didn't hear him speaking back. Finally Moustache put a latex glove on one hand and reached into the car for half a minute. "Dead," he said.

"Should we pull him out of the car in case he isn't dead?" asked the other deputy.

"The EMTs will be here in a minute," said Moustache. "Let them decide whether he's dead or not."

138

By now there were cars backing up in both directions and the deputies were shouting at people to get back in their cars. Moustache told the group coming from Upriver to move ahead. He didn't want them to block the ambulance whose siren was coming closer. The people coming down the other way were just going to have to wait where they were.

I thought about what Wade told me. Ken was intimidating people so he could buy their house. It was extortion. That could explain, perhaps, why Breuninger, a detective, showed up at the Winterpol house in response to my call to 911. There was no suggestion of violence or any crime in my call. Somehow Breuninger knew about the extortion and here was a chance to explore Ken Winterpol's house from top to bottom. Once the attack on Ken turned into murder the detective got more than he had bargained for.

Now there were more deputies on the scene, including Deputy Newton, the woman who had given Candy and me a ride to my parents' house. I waved to her but she said something to the deputy with the moustache, whose name turned out to be Scofield, and did not come over to talk with me herself. I gave Scofield my identification and my parents' address. He confirmed that Wade was dead, apparently from internal bleeding.

"There will probably be an inquest and you'll be required to testify," he said.

"I'm not going anywhere," I said. "Just tell them to call me."

CHAPTER 18

Identity

(Dan)

I rode my bike home, took a shower, had a shake, and went over to Candy's house to catch the housekeeper while she was still there. Candy had said the housekeeper's name was Paloma Rodriguez and that her English wasn't very good. The woman who answered the door was a Latina of about forty with a concerned look on her face. I introduced myself in Spanish. She didn't let her guard down right away but as we continued to speak Spanish she started to relax. I asked if I could sit down on the steps leading up to the second floor. Not only did that put me more at her eye level but I thought it engendered some sympathy for whatever pain or fatigue might make me want to sit down. Also it put Paloma in charge of the house as if she owned it. I told Paloma that my father was a teacher and he had tutored Señora Winterpol when she was a girl. I told her I had known the Señora for a very long time. I also told her I had earned a doctor of law degree. I was sure the word "doctor" would impress her. I didn't think I could ask her direct questions but I might draw her into a conversation to find out what Breuninger had asked her about the murder and what she had told him.

"I'm so sorry about the death of Señor Winterpol," I told her, still in Spanish. "I think he was a real gentleman." Paloma agreed he was a caballero and a man of authority. "Señora Winterpol was lucky to have such a man," I said.

"Yes she was!" agreed Paloma, so emphatically it took me back.

To get more on Paloma's good side I said, "Maybe Mrs. Winterpol should paint nothing but portraits of her husband for a year to show her respect."

Paloma looked down for a moment and said, "Maybe." I gathered Paloma did not care much for Candy's painting.

Our discussion was worth pursuing but the DNA samples I had come for were the first priority. I explained I had come to collect some things Ken had used and asked whether Paloma had washed or thrown out his razor or his toothbrush. She said she had left everything in the bathroom where it was. I asked if there was anything else that might have his spit or his blood or his skin on it. She said there was a brush in the shower that he used on his back. Mrs. Winterpol only took baths. I asked Paloma if she had some baggies and trash bags I could put things in and she went to the kitchen to get them while I waited on the stair steps.

"I still don't like going into the kitchen," she said, coming back. "The poor man died there." He'd died at the hospital but I didn't correct her. I asked her if she had been the one who cleaned up the blood and whether she had any sponges or rags that might still have his blood on them. She had used a mop, a sponge, and some rags. She had thrown them all out. She had cleaned very thoroughly so no one would ever see a trace of blood.

"Can you come show me where Mr. Winterpol's things are?"

"Yes," she said. I stood up and turned to go up the stairs when I heard a gasp from Paloma. When I looked around she was standing at the foot of the stairs, looking up at me with her hand over her mouth.

"It was you!" she said. "It was you!" I sat down on the steps again. The trust I had earned with her was obviously shot. I tried to look as surprised and non-threatening as I could.

"Paloma," I said gently, "there is no need to get upset. What are you thinking?"

The woman crossed herself and backed away with a look of horror in her eyes. She turned and hustled frantically out the back door. I heard a whoop from outside. Then a car started and drove away.

Dumbfounded, I sat on the stairs, wondering what had just happened. What did Paloma mean by "It was you"? She couldn't possibly mean that it was I who I killed Ken. She wasn't here when he was attacked. She could only mean, I thought, that she had

141

glimpsed me leaving the house after my intimate rendezvous with Candy. If she told Breuninger it would increase his suspicion of me. But her supposedly recognizing me from the back would never hold up in court, probably would not even be admitted into evidence.

Who knew what the woman was thinking anyhow? She was skittish and, I thought, not very bright. In any case I should not let her distract me from my mission. I picked up the plastic bags she had dropped and climbed the stairs to the master bedroom. The bed was made and the bathroom was sparkling clean. There were two sinks and two medicine cabinets. I set my cell phone down on top of a towel in a towel rack and leaned it back against the wall so the camera in the phone was facing the two medicine cabinets above the sinks.

I started the video camera and stepped back. I gave my name, the date, the time, the location, and stated why I was there. With latex gloves on my hands I opened a medicine cabinet that turned out to have cosmetics in it. Then I opened the other cabinet and put the toothbrush and safety razor I found in there in separate bags. I also took a stick deodorant though I didn't know whether it could be used for DNA. All the time I was doing this I was describing what I was doing for the recording. I wanted this evidence to be as solid as possible.

I carried the cell phone over to the shower and picked up the back brush off the showerhead. Then I put the phone back on the towels while I put the brush in a trash bag and tied it shut, still describing what I was doing as I went along. I announced the time out loud for the recording and walked downstairs with the camera pointed in front of me. I checked that all the doors were locked and then locked the front door behind me on the way out. I kept the recording going so I could establish it was continuous. I wanted to make it clear that the items I sent to the lab were the exact same ones I had taken from Ken's bathroom.

My mother came into our garage with me to hold the camera while I put the bags down next to a tool box my father had on a workbench. There was a lock on the toolbox and the key was in it. I took some tools out of the box and put the bagged items into it.

I locked the box, took the key, and added it to my keychain. Then I announced the time again and shut off the camera.

My mother, naturally, wanted to know what was going on. I explained that I had met a woman who might be Ken's daughter and I was collecting DNA to find out. I said she might inherit half of his estate.

"How did you find this woman?"

I told Mom how Amy had gotten my name and then run into me at Sean's party. I told her how we were now training partners and I'd seen her a number of times.

"And you like her?" my mother asked. How did my mother know that? What had I said that gave me away? I said yes I liked Amy but I didn't know her very well yet. And whether I liked her or not, I was trying to fulfill the directive in Ken's will.

"Am I going to meet Amy?"

"You might, Mom, but we're not to that point."

I offloaded the video to my PC and then backed it up online. Until the DNA test kit arrived from the lab I could stop thinking about Amy's possible parentage and go back to training. I lifted weights until it was time for supper. Mom had rented a movie that we watched together. Its title was the name of a Japanese actor but the movie was in Danish. My mother said she couldn't speak Danish, but she had grown up hearing Norwegian at home and it was similar. She said the subtitles made it easier for her to understand the spoken words. And she enjoyed hearing the sound of it in any case. There was a crazy brother in the movie. It was funny in places and touching in others.

Life got back to normal for a few days while I waited for the DNA test results to arrive. I stayed on my training schedule, riding with Amy when possible, and sometimes seeing her at the pool. We were friendly but we had things to work on. By silent agreement, it seemed, we weren't going to complicate our lives by building a relationship.

I was getting ready to drive into Bend to meet Amy for a bike ride when I saw a sheriff's car out in front of the house. I opened the front door to find Breuninger standing there beside a uniformed deputy. The deputy was resting one hand casually on his gun.

CHAPTER 19

The Law Descends

(Detective Carl Breuninger)

Dan Martinez was a thorn in my side from the very beginning of this case. When Winterpol wasn't even dead yet Martinez kept me from getting facts from Mrs. Winterpol. When I wanted to talk with his father, Leon, Dan had spirited the man out of town. Then Martinez came up with more and more people who might have killed Winterpol but very probably didn't. I would eventually have to track many of them down before we could prosecute. Alerting me to the footprints in the grass was, I suppose, relevant to the investigation. They might or might not be. But the gray pickup that Martinez supposedly saw a quarter mile or more from the Winterpol house was a complete red herring. He didn't have the license plate, the make or model, and wasn't even sure whether it was a two-door or a crew cab. He was slowing down my investigation. There were things he didn't want me to find out, and I felt that knowing what they were would go a long way toward solving the case.

If Candy Winterpol killed her husband by herself and nobody saw her do it, we were never going to convict her. The crime scene didn't offer enough evidence. A jury would doubt, with good reason, whether she could swing the poker hard enough to kill Ken. And if she wanted to kill him, why just hit him once and leave his death to chance? Finally, even if someone saw her hit Ken, she could claim self-defense.

We had a better chance at conviction if Mrs. Winterpol conspired with someone else. We could play the other person off against her. Dan Martinez seemed the most likely, followed by his father or by both of them together. After that, Ken's first wife,

Rhonda, and her drug-addled boyfriend were good candidates. Their motive wasn't clear to me but it may not have been clear to them either. Just crazy people.

Or, quite possibly, and as Mrs. Winterpol and young Mr. Martinez would prefer I believe, someone else entirely killed Ken Winterpol and neither of them had any idea who the murderer was. I started with this third-party theory when I interviewed Mrs. Winterpol the day after the murder. Right or wrong, it was the theory most likely to elicit information from our conversation.

We met in Morgan's office. I knew him from previous cases. Morgan would protect his client well but he was experienced. He wouldn't spew all the legal objections he could recall from *Law & Order*, valid and invalid, the way Dan Martinez tried to.

I established that Mrs. Winterpol played golf and had played tennis in the past. So perhaps she could swing a poker hard enough to kill her husband. I slipped that question past Morgan. It sounded like the usual rapport-building at the start of an interview. Mrs. Winterpol answered all my trust-building questions—where and when she was born, where she went to school, when she and Ken were married—but she did not warm to me the way I wanted.

She said she thought Ken had business disputes but she didn't know who the people were or what the disputes were about. That was no help.

"Are you concerned that whoever attacked your husband may want to attack you too?"

"Not very," she said.

"Help me understand," I said. "None of us knows right now who killed your husband or why they did it. Yet you seem to think that no matter what was going on they won't assault you as well?"

"I'm only an artist. Who would have any reason to kill me? Besides, they may get away with killing Ken. Why push their luck?" She was right, I thought, but imagining what the killer was thinking seemed a stretch for a grieving widow.

"Who is the beneficiary of your will?" I asked.

"My children. If I don't have children, then the arts program at Oregon State in Bend. They don't even know I put them in the will."

I tried another line of questioning.

"How well do you know Dan Martinez?" I asked.

"I've known him since high school in Bend but I haven't seen him for years until recently."

"And why did he come to your house so early that morning?"

There may have been a flicker of alarm in her eyes but she answered the question smoothly. "I don't know," she said. If she and Martinez had conspired to kill Ken they might well have agreed on an explanation. Now would be the time to trot it out. But the "I don't know" gave no hint of a conspiracy.

"When I was at your house that morning, Mr. Martinez told me he had come to talk with your husband about a brewpub they had both invested in. Do you remember that?"

"I don't remember that," said Mrs. Winterpol. She gave Morgan a look but he didn't say anything.

"Is it possible they argued and the argument turned violent?"

"You are asking Mrs. Winterpol to speculate," said Morgan. "I'm going to advise Mrs. Winterpol not to answer that question."

I tried a different tack. "And how were things in your marriage to Mr. Winterpol?" I asked. Her eyebrows came down and her mouth tightened. She seemed more angry than alarmed, or at least she pretended to be angry. It was Tod Morgan who was alarmed.

"If Mrs. Winterpol is a suspect," he said firmly, "then this is an interrogation, not an interview. You need to read Mrs. Winterpol her rights and I will advise her not to answer any questions at all."

"Mrs. Winterpol is not a suspect," I said. "Forget the question." That was the end of the interview. I never asked how Mrs. Winterpol got the bruises on her arms that Deputy Newton had seen. I might ask Mrs. Winterpol later or I might leave the question for the district attorney.

Candy Winterpol, I thought, could claim to be out of touch with the world, to choose what she couldn't remember and get away with it. The pose went with being an artist. But inside, I thought, she was hard as a diamond and smart as a fox.

My next interview was with Paloma Rodriguez, who cleaned house for the Winterpols. The house was big but easy to clean. The

Winterpols had no pets. Hardly ever any guests. Mr. Winterpol was often away in Portland and Mrs. Winterpol shut herself in her studio while Paloma cleaned the downstairs. When Paloma made the beds and vacuumed upstairs Mrs. Winterpol generally left to do errands. Paloma didn't see the two Winterpols together very often because Mr. Winterpol was mostly there on the weekends. She never saw them fight. Mrs. Winterpol left cash for Mrs. Rodriguez in the laundry room every time she cleaned. Hardly anyone came to the house while Paloma was there except workmen, UPS, and FedEx.

Mrs. Rodriguez spoke enough English for me to interview her but I brought in a Spanish-speaking sergeant near the end to see if she might tell us more. Mrs. Rodriguez said Mr. Winterpol was a good, strong, and generous man, and that Mrs. Winterpol was lucky to have such a man for a husband. I picked out the words "rico y masculino" and the sergeant relayed the rest to me after Mrs. Rodriguez left. Mrs. Rodriguez felt that having to clean the blood off the kitchen floor was not right. She thought the sheriff's department should have done that. Lastly, she asked the deputy whether she would still have her job at the Winterpol house. The sergeant relayed this question to me and I said I had no way of knowing. But, I told her, I thought Mrs. Winterpol planned to keep the house. I knew of no reason she would not continue to employ Mrs. Rodriguez. Mrs. Rodriguez was guarded throughout the interview. We all breathed easier when it was over.

I was getting pressure to make more progress on this murder. Upriver Ranch was an upscale place that created hundreds of jobs in the area. Residents had paid a lot for their nice big houses. Tourists paid two hundred dollars for a round of golf and forty dollars or more for dinner afterward. People needed to feel safe there. But I was nowhere near making an arrest. The footprints on the back porch were faint and there were so many of them on top of each other we would not be able to prove a match even if we found the shoes the killer wore. Dan Martinez kept enlarging the field of people with a motive to kill Winterpol. It would take hundreds of man-hours to ask all these people where they were when the murder took place and hundreds more to check whether they were telling the truth. My best hope for progress was to arrest Dan Martinez and watch him try to squirm out of telling me what he was trying to hide.

I finally caught a break when Mrs. Rodriguez showed up at the front desk several weeks after her interview asking for me. No one around spoke Spanish so she and I sat on a bench in the front lobby and I asked her in English what she had come to see me about.

"I know who killed Mr. Winterpol," she said, "and you should arrest him."

"Thank you, Mrs. Rodriguez," I said. "Who was it and how do you know?"

"I found black hairs in Mrs. Winterpol's bed. And before Mr. Winterpol was killed I saw a tall man with black hair leave by the front door when I came in the back door. Then the same man came yesterday to get some of Mr. Winterpol's things from the bathroom. He spoke Spanish and said he was Mrs. Winterpol's lawyer, her abogado."

"Do you know the man's name?"

"Daniel Martinez."

"How do you know his name?"

"He told me. And Mrs. Winterpol told me his name when she said he would come to the house."

"What makes you think Mr. Martinez killed Mr. Winterpol?" I asked. Mrs. Rodriguez spit out a breath, as though exasperated that the answer wasn't obvious.

"Because Martinez was in love with Mrs. Winterpol and wanted Mr. Winterpol out of the way."

"Why didn't you tell us this when we interviewed you right after Mr. Winterpol was killed?" I asked.

"Mr. Winterpol told me not to talk to anyone about the man. Mr. Winterpol said he was going to take care of it and I should forget all about what I saw."

"But you didn't forget about it, Mrs. Rodriguez," I said. "So after Mr. Winterpol was killed, why didn't you think you should tell us about this other man?"

"Mr. Winterpol deserved respect, even if he was dead. People should not know he was a *cornudo*. I don't know the English. People shouldn't know his wife was with another man. And besides, I didn't know who the man was."

"Thank you, Mrs. Rodriguez," I said. "Could you come to my desk while I type up what you said and have you sign it? It would help us get justice for Mr. Winterpol."

"Yes," she said, "but can we keep it a secret that I told you? I want to keep my job with Mrs. Winterpol even if she is a very bad woman. And I don't want Mr. Martinez to find out about me."

"Nobody has to know except the judge who issues the arrest warrant," I said, "and I will tell him to keep it a secret too." This was true in the short run but deceptive in the long run. If we went to trial against Dan Martinez then Mrs. Rodriguez would have to testify. And the defense attorney would have the right to cross-examine her. Daniel Martinez and Candy Winterpol would eventually know exactly what Mrs. Rodriguez said and so would everyone else. It didn't look good for long-term employment at the Winterpol house.

I typed what she told me into the computer, trying to make the facts as convincing as possible and to make her inferences not sound like the plot of a telenovela. It would be enough, I hoped, to get an arrest warrant for Martinez. I printed two copies, clearly and carefully read her statement to Mrs. Rodriguez, had her sign both copies, and gave her one to keep.

I wrote up an affidavit establishing probability that Martinez killed Winterpol and took it to Judge Ralston to get an arrest warrant. The affidavit described Winterpol's murder, said that Martinez was found at the scene, and that Paloma Rodriguez swore to evidence that Martinez was having an affair with Mrs. Winterpol. It also said that Martinez had not been convincing about why he was at the Winterpol house shortly after Winterpol was assaulted. The judge was eager for us to make progress and he signed the warrant.

Deputy Adam Nelson and I went to the Martinez house early the next morning with the warrant. Dan Martinez was just going out the door in bike-racing clothes when we accosted him.

"You've got to be kidding," he said. "On what evidence?"

"You don't need to bring anything with you," I said, "just your driver's license."

"Can I tell my mother where I'm going?"

"If you can tell her from here." He turned around in the front door and called back into the house.

"Mom, Detective Breuninger is arresting me for Ken's murder. I don't think he'll be able to keep me long so please don't worry. I need to hand you my keys, my wallet, and my cell phone."

I corrected him. "If all that is on your person it comes with you. You can hand those things to me. Do you have anything else in your pockets, a weapon or anything sharp?"

"No," he said, "not even change."

"I need to frisk you. Put your hands up and away from your body."

"Detective Breuninger, this is absurd," Mrs. Martinez said from the doorway. "Can I see the warrant?" I showed her the warrant while Deputy Nelson frisked Dan. Dan asked his mother to call some girl and tell her he wouldn't be riding with her that day. He didn't say her name and he told his mother the girl's number was in the contact list on his PC.

Nelson had the back door of the car open and Martinez sat in the car without protest. I'm sure he wanted to get out of there before the neighbors saw him. Also, if he was cooperative and already in the car I might not bother to handcuff him, which I didn't. I was tempted to switch on the flashing lights and the siren but there was no traffic and no emergency. Our dispatcher would get inquiries and complaints about the ruckus and the sheriff would ask me what the heck I thought I was doing.

Off we went. We arrest a lot of people who have been arrested before. People with drug and alcohol problems, mental problems, health problems. People who smell like they slept in a dump. My problem with Dan Martinez was different. He was looking for any error I made along the way that could spring him from jail or get the charges dropped. But I knew how to do this by the book.

Martinez wasn't too worried about being convicted and going to prison. He was thinking, maybe a little too confidently, that when this got to court, or long before that, he would walk free for one reason or another. He was a lawyer and would find a way out.

What Martinez was worried about, and what was my lever, was that being arrested would cripple any legal career he might want to return to. Why hire an attorney who has been arrested when you can hire one who has not?

Beyond having an arrest record that might not be expunged was an even bigger, more immediate, and more permanent concern for Dan Martinez. If he didn't think of it soon on his own I would remind him: The press would be delighted to report his arrest. All his friends and relatives would read about it. A simple online search on his name would bring up tomorrow's article in *The Bulletin*, now and forever for the rest of his life. The story would never die.

Right on cue he asked, "Is there going to be any press at the jail when you take me in?" Mr. Cool was worried.

"There might be," I said.

"Can you take me in some back entrance and not tell them I am there?" He was trying to sound reasonable, as though he were negotiating with opposing counsel.

"Maybe we could give you a second to say something to the press on the way in. About how you are innocent. Or you could tell them about all the other people you've accused of murder. I'm sure the press would like the full list and all those people would enjoy seeing their name in the paper alongside yours. They might come to thank you personally."

He could see his reputation, his career, and his relationships with dozens of people, including the girl he was going to go bike riding with, slipping away in the next half hour.

"What would I have to agree to keep my name out of the press?" he asked, "And what would I have to say to make this whole arrest go away?" Music to my ears.

"What arrest?" I asked. "I have a warrant but I haven't arrested you yet. You came along voluntarily. I thought I'd arrest you as we drove up to the jail. Handcuffs, perp walk, the whole show. I'll call KTVZ and tell them to meet us there with a camera crew."

"What do you want?"

"Everything," I said, "no holding back. First you tell me what you've been trying to hide and then you tell me everything relevant you can think of. You answer my questions. And you don't just repeat all that bullshit you gave me on the CD."

"It's not bullshit," he said. "I don't know who murdered Ken. I really don't. And all the people on the CD had a reason to kill him. The only thing that isn't on the CD is what Wade what's-his-name told me before he died in the car he rolled. Ken hired him to drive some people out of a house Ken wanted to buy. Maybe Wade thought he should get paid more and Ken didn't agree with him. Wade was certainly crazy enough to slam Ken with a poker."

"Here you go again, Mr. Martinez, trying to muddy the waters further. Let's start with who you are protecting and why. What makes you think they need protection?"

Silence from the back seat.

"I'll give you until we get to Knott Road," I said. We were coming up on the High Desert Museum and Knott Road was about two minutes away. I could feel Deputy Nelson step a little harder on the accelerator. I enjoyed having Martinez sweat.

The dispatcher's voice came over the radio. She was calling me specifically. Judge Ralston had withdrawn the arrest warrant. I blew out my cheeks with annoyance. "How did that happen?" I asked.

"There's no information on that," said the dispatcher. "The judge simply canceled the warrant. That's all I know."

I shook my head. "Well," I said to Martinez, "This is your lucky day. Your mother called the judge, didn't she?"

"I don't know," said Martinez. "But she probably knows him."

Nelson looked over at me. "Do we have to take him home?" he asked. I was thinking that we did. What a bust.

"Tell you what," Martinez said. "Drop me off at the West Side Bike shop and we'll call it good. It's a lot closer than home." If I disliked Martinez before I detested him now. He narrowly escapes being arrested and less than thirty seconds later he's thinking about how he's going meet his girlfriend and go bike riding. You have to be young, smart, and very used to having life go your way to have your mind work like that.

"Okay," I said.

"And could you hand me my cell phone?" There was no opening in the screen between the seats so I rolled down both my window and his and handed him his phone outside the car. He called the girl and explained in an offhand manner that the whole arrest thing had been a misunderstanding, now all cleared up, but the sheriff had taken him to Bend without his car or his bike and would she mind meeting him at the bike shop and giving him a ride to the trailhead. Of course the girl said yes.

And then, in his few minutes remaining in the cruiser, Martinez lit into me.

CHAPTER 20

Rough Trails

(Dan)

"Listen, Detective," I said, "I want you to solve this case. I want you to find the real killer. Your trying to arrest me is not a sign of progress. What about all the investors, large and small, whose lives Ken ruined? What about all the vendors he hasn't paid? What about all his old criminal connections in Burns? What about his first wife and her boyfriend? No, for lack of any better idea, you try arresting me. I'm the least likely suspect. I had no grudge with Ken Winterpol. I had nothing to gain from his death. I am a law-abiding citizen, happy with the world."

Breuninger looked straight at the windshield the whole time I spoke. I was about to add "or happy with the world until we crossed paths this morning." Then he answered me.

"So as long as we are being so frank with each other, what were you doing at the Winterpol house the day of the murder?" I had to give the detective credit. It was a question I didn't want to answer.

"Mr. Winterpol loaned money to a brewpub I'm invested in. We had a matter to discuss." Both my sentences were true statements. But Ken Winterpol would have been very surprised if I'd knocked on his back door at that hour and asked him to refrain from hogging tables at Vandevert Brewing.

"Was he expecting you?" asked Breuninger.

"Here we go again," I said. "If you truly think I'm a suspect you get a warrant that will stick and I'll get a criminal attorney and we'll go from there. Otherwise I'm not answering any questions." I doubted he'd ever get a second warrant for my arrest. I bid him a cheery goodbye at the bike shop. He gave me a wave and a scowl.

"What happened?" Amy asked me after I put my rented bike on her bike rack and sat myself in her passenger seat.

"The sheriff's detective is trying to solve Ken Winterpol's murder. He thinks I know things I am not telling them. He tried to arrest me in order to force the information out of me. But the warrant was shaky and the judge canceled it, prompted, I'm pretty sure, by a call from my mother."

"Your mother called me only a minute before you did. She didn't even mention your getting arrested. She only said you probably wouldn't be able to ride today."

"So you didn't know I was with the sheriff until I called you?" We were driving out Skyliners Road to the bike trails.

"First I heard of it was from you," she said. "So what did he try to arrest you for?"

"Well, technically, he never got as far as arresting me. But he had a warrant and he was taking me to the jail in Bend to arrest me there for the murder of Ken Winterpol."

"The man who may be my father?"

"The very same, I'm afraid."

"So this detective arrested you even though he doesn't think you did it?"

"Afraid so," I said. "On top of thinking I know something, the detective is very unhappy with me. On my own time, not for Oxton, I'm helping prepare a defense for Candy Winterpol, Ken Winterpol's wife, in case she is charged with murdering her husband. She has her own attorney and all I'm doing is finding people who hated Ken enough to kill him. I'm sorry to say this about a man who may be your father, but he made a lot of enemies. I gave the detective a CD with all the information I'd found so far. It means a great deal of work for him tracking down all those possibilities. So he's mad at me and he thinks I'm hiding something."

"But he can't just arrest you because he's mad at you, can he? He's got to have something to base the arrest on."

"Nobody saw who actually killed Ken Winterpol. I was the one who found Ken on his back deck. I was the one who called 911. There's no proof I didn't do it."

"Oh my God," said Amy. "What were you doing at his house?" I didn't want to lie to Amy. But I wasn't about to say I had hoped to climb into bed with Candy. If and when I got to know Amy better I would tell her about Candy.

"Ken loaned money to my friends' brewpub where I am a minor investor. We had to discuss something." Amy didn't ask me what I needed to discuss with Ken so I didn't have to compound the lie. But she considered what I had told her at length before she spoke.

"I'm sorry," said Amy. "I am not ready for this. I don't like being in a car with a man who was just arrested for murder. And, for that matter, suspected of killing a man who may have been my father."

"Amy," I pleaded. "It isn't like that. It's all legal maneuvering."

"Wait a minute," she said. "Am I a suspect? According to you I am supposed to inherit big bucks from this man. Are you setting me up to be one more possible killer?"

"I would never do that to you," I said. "And besides, you had no idea who your father was. You had no way of knowing what was in his will."

Amy stared out the windshield for a moment. "Well," she said, "there is one thing I know for certain. We're not going riding today." She pulled over to the side of the road, made sure no cars were coming, and turned around back toward Bend. "Damn," she said. "I thought you were a perfectly nice normal guy. Now I just want you out of my car. I want to put you out here and have you ride back to Bend on your own."

I felt unfairly treated and I was angry. I began marshalling arguments to justify what I had done and what I had said. But my thoughts were overcome by a deep sadness. Amy's displeasure with me seemed insurmountable. We didn't know each other well enough to argue. Once Amy let me out of that car we might never talk again. I searched in vain for something I could say or do.

Amy shot a quick look over at me and looked back at the road. "My God," she said, "you're crying." My eyes did feel a little wet. "What are you crying about?"

I dried my face on the sleeve of my sweatshirt. We weren't far from the bike shop and I'd soon be getting out. I composed myself as well as I could and spoke in an even tone. "I thought we were beginning a good friendship. But it seems I've pretty much ruined the chance of that happening."

"Do you think?" she asked. "I don't need you and I don't need any mythical million dollars." She was young, I thought. Anyone older would have endured real pain for a million dollars. When had I changed, I wondered, from youthful pride to a practical appreciation for money?

"How are you going to get home?" she asked with a hard edge to her voice.

"I don't know. I'll call my mother and see if she's coming into Bend today. If not, I'll take a bus."

"There's a bus?" she asked.

"I think so. I don't know where it leaves from or what the schedule is."

"I'll take you to the bus station after you drop the bike off," she said, "if there is one."

I checked my phone. There was a bus station on Fourth Street, near Juniper. But the next bus did not leave until late afternoon.

"I'll drive you home," she said, as though she wanted to be done with me and be sure at the same time that no one could say she had been rash, or unfair, or irresponsible, or out of control with anger. I thought I would act the same way if the situation were reversed. In that case I would call it being a gentleman.

"That would be great," I said. "I'm sorry you are not getting a bike ride in this morning." I knew how important every minute of training was to both of us.

"I'll just swim longer this evening," she said, "and maybe a short run."

The bike shop was surprised to see me back so fast. I'd already paid for a half-day rental and I wasn't going to get that money back. A teenager checked out the bike carefully for damage and I got out of there as fast as possible.

"I appreciate your doing this," I told Amy. She didn't scowl or act cold. She just didn't speak. I wanted desperately to talk with her but was afraid she would raise her guard at anything I said.

"Do you mind if I call my mother?" I asked. "I should tell her I am not going to jail." Amy waved her hand in a be-my-guest gesture that would have been gracious if her hand were lower and more open—and more impatient if her hand were higher and more dismissive. I called my mother and said I was on my way home a free man. In response to her question I said Amy was driving me.

"Bring her in," she said, "I'd like to meet her." I said I would ask her. We hung up.

"Would you mind coming in to meet my mother while you're down here?"

"Did she ask you?" said Amy. I said yes.

"You ask for too much," she said. I looked off into the forest as we drove down to Upriver from Lava Butte. The ponderosas had been growing for eighty years since the land was logged and, though the trunks were tall and thick they were not as majestic as the ponderosas near Sisters and Black Butte. The pondos here wouldn't get that big in my lifetime.

"Okay," said Amy, "I will come in and meet your mother. Briefly. Since she asked."

"Thank you," I said. My tone was polite and sincere but did not reflect the gratitude I actually felt.

When we went through the gate I asked Amy if she had ever seen the cowboy on Mount Bachelor. "There's a big snowfield on the side of the mountain that faces this way. Can you see the image of a cowboy with chaps on his legs and a hat on his head? He is bending to one side and holding a coiled rope over his head."

"I see it," she said.

"It usually lasts into August. As the summer goes on it takes more imagination to recognize him."

Amy parked in front of the house and we walked up to the front door. My mother had left it ajar and we walked in. The entryway and living room reflected my father's Spanish taste and, except for the rough wooden ceilings, looked nothing like the exterior. The plaster walls were rich browns and yellows. One small wall was deep blue. The doorways were rounded at the top and the mirror over the fireplace was framed in light-colored metal with patterns hammered into it. The shelves in the living room, not wooden but recessed into the plaster, held vases, colored glasses, colorfully painted plates, and sculptures both realist and abstract.

Mom came out of the kitchen. She wore a blue golf shirt and black golf slacks. I introduced Amy to her and vice versa.

"Call me Elizabeth," she said. "I'm sorry if I bothered you with my call this morning. It was all a misunderstanding."

"Oh, I know," said Amy, as though she no longer had a worry in the world about my near arrest.

"And now we've interrupted your training," said Mom. "I know how important that is. I just play golf and do a little skiing now but I played water polo in college. We practiced night and day."

"Where was that?" Amy asked.

"UC Santa Barbara," said Mom.

"I went to UCB," said Amy, suddenly and truly happy. "My sport was rowing. I got a scholarship."

The two women were off and running without me. They learned more about each other in the next five minutes than I would have learned about Amy in hours. I was not part of the conversation at all. I was getting a little peeved about it when I realized their rapidly building enthusiasm for each other was the best thing I could have hoped for. If they got to know each other then Amy would be much more likely to trust me again.

"You'll need some lunch before you go to work," my mother said. "I just made my best tuna salad this morning. Please stay and have some with us. If you need something special for training, Dan has all kinds of powders and shakes and supplements. I don't think any of them look very good."

"Tuna salad would be lovely," said Amy.

We sat under an umbrella on the deck and looked out over a field of long grass and, beyond it, to a fairway where, on the other side, an undulating row of pine trees marked the far bank of the Deschutes. I had tuna salad too, though it wasn't enough for me and wasn't part of my plan. Amy and my mother sustained a lively conversation with minimal participation from me. The biomedical company Amy worked for was venture-backed and my mother knew some of the investors from her banking days.

"When my own mother was in poor health," said Mom, "it would have helped a lot to have a product like yours. I was always after her over whether she had taken her medicine. She tried to be good but she didn't like it and sometimes she couldn't remember whether she had taken it or not. If every time a pill got to her stomach she got a record of it and I got a signal we would have argued less and both our lives would have been easier."

"I've got an even better idea," I said. "Every time a pub pours a glass of beer they drop a little chip in it. When the chip hits your stomach it charges your credit card and sends a report to your friends. If you've had too many they won't let you drive."

Both women looked annoyed, hoping I would keep my clever thoughts to myself.

"You could play beer-pitcher roulette. Whoever winds up drinking the chip gets to pay for the pitcher." That was it, I thought. I'd better be quiet. After a short silence the two women resumed their conversation.

"It's too bad I didn't meet Mr. Martinez today," said Amy. "And you don't know where he is?" This was not a happy topic and I thought my mother would abruptly change the subject. But apparently she liked Amy well enough to answer.

"Oh, he is off on some jaunt," said Mom. "He had a fellowship to an artist's colony once and we didn't hear from him for two months. We knew where he was and we could have called him but he never telephoned or even wrote us a note. I've decided it is just the price you pay for being married to an artist. He's never done anything foolish."

The word "foolish," I thought, covered a lot of ground. It meant he'd never risked his life. He'd never done anything illegal. And he'd never taken up with some other woman. I hoped he never had. But how could my mother be so sure? Well, in front of Amy, and I suppose other people, my mother had to act as though she was sure.

I didn't think my father would be unfaithful but I was biased. It would be painful to imagine he was.

Then it suddenly came to me where my father was now. I still didn't know where he'd gone when he first left us. But I knew where he was now and my mother must have known too. Detective Breuninger had better not come back and ask us again.

Five years ago Dad had been invited to an "encampment" deep in the California redwoods called The Clearing. The Clearing belonged to a men's club in San Francisco. One of Dad's friends from high school had invited Dad to be his guest for three weeks at the place. My father loved it. There were plays, live music, lectures, art exhibits, and an endless variety of interesting men to talk with. Dad made pencil drawings of his stay there and I'd leafed through them once. The tree trunks were gigantic and fitted among them, up and down hills, were wooden buildings, no two alike, where the men slept. There was a drawing of some gigantic show on a hillside with costumes and sets that would have done Wagner proud. My father drew picture after picture of men sitting around smoky campfires with drinks in one hand and cigars in the other. My mother said it took two washings to get the smoke out of his clothes.

That was where my father was now. That was why my mother wasn't worried about him. That was why he said he wouldn't be in touch with me for a while. There was a rule about not using cell phones at The Clearing. Cell phones wouldn't even work unless you hiked up to the top of a hill. Well, I wasn't going to call Breuninger and tell him where my father was. I was going to pretend I still didn't know.

CHAPTER 21

Explorations

(Dan)

Amy got up from lunch to go to work. As we walked through the kitchen I saw the mail my mother had left on the counter. There was an envelope from the DNA testing company. I opened it and read the instructions as Amy and my mother parted enthusiastically. The two almost embraced. I think the one hitch in their budding relationship was it was only going to develop further if I continued to see Amy.

"I'm so glad you two got to meet each other," I said. We left my mother at the front door while I walked Amy to her car. "Thank you for understanding today, and thank you for driving. I think my mother likes you a lot."

"And I like her," said Amy.

"The DNA kit came today. Can you take a second to spit some saliva in this tube?"

"Oh, of course," she said. "This is great."

The kit looked like a plastic test tube with a big hinged lid on it. Two good spits filled it up to the mark and she handed it back to me.

"It will probably say I'm a tuna fish."

"It's been thirty minutes since you ate. That's supposed to be enough."

"We're riding tomorrow," she said. "And I'm not slowing down for you."

"You got it," I said. I sure wanted to kiss her goodbye but she got into her car too quickly. I fantasized that a kiss had crossed her mind too.

"You better hang on to that one," my mother said when I went back in the house.

"I'll do my best," I said. I didn't talk about where Dad was. Mom and I both needed to be able to say we had no idea.

"Thank you for calling Judge Ralston," I said. "What did he say?"

"He agreed to take another look at the sheriff's affidavit for the warrant. That seemed all I could ask for. He was doing his job."

"It makes me wonder why the judge thought the affidavit was strong enough for a warrant in the first place."

"I'm sorry to have this thought because I like Judge Ralston," said Mom, "but the name 'Martinez' may have made it easier to issue the warrant. That was until I told him which Martinez it was."

"But 'Martinez' could only be part of what happened," I said. "If the facts had been weak, the judge wouldn't have issued a warrant for bin Laden. If the facts were strong enough he would have issued a warrant for the governor himself. The facts must have been on the borderline and I'm just wondering what those facts, or supposed facts, were."

"Could they issue a new warrant?" my mother asked.

"If they got more compelling information, then yes," I said. "But I didn't kill the man and I don't see how they even got enough facts for a warrant the first time."

We did the dishes together. It didn't take long.

"Does Amy have any brothers or sisters?" Mom asked. I had never asked Amy so I said I didn't know. I could tell my mother was thinking of Amy as a potential member of the family. But she didn't dare ask too many questions for fear of jinxing it. I wasn't sure myself where Amy and I were going. But one thing I was sure of. My sexual dalliances with Candy were over. I couldn't be falling in love with Amy while still screwing another woman for recreation. Candy knew as well as I did that we had no future together. Our little vacation from commitments, as exciting as it was, would have to end.

I packaged up the saliva sample and retrieved Ken's razor, toothbrush, deodorant and back brush to send them all, carefully labeled, to the DNA testing company. I videotaped myself packing up Ken's things. Then I sent the remains of the testing kit to Linda at the Saint Cecelia School. I made it to the post office just before the mail went out for the day.

Having missed my planned trail ride, I rode my bike over the top of Ann's Butte, raced along some forest roads, and came back the way I'd gone, covered with dust. I left most of my dirty clothes in the garage and went in for a shower. A hot shower would have felt good but I'd started taking cold showers to condition myself for the swim at Elk Lake. Showers were not fun.

Clean, dry, and warming up I had a minute to wonder again what new evidence had allowed Breuninger to suddenly get a warrant for my arrest. It must have been, I thought, Paloma Rodriguez. She must have glimpsed me fleeing the Winterpol house after my tryst with Candy, then recognized me yesterday. It was a leap from my being in the sack with Candy, of which Paloma couldn't be sure, to my killing Ken. It was a leap, but it was apparently enough for Breuninger to get a warrant.

Over the next two weeks Amy and I allocated more of our training time to swimming. It was odd, preparing for a race where we didn't expect to do very well and didn't really care. In the September triathlon we would strive to do well in three different races, back to back, instead of doing exceptionally well in one. The Elk Lake swim in August would pit us against people who trained for swimming and nothing else.

Amy and I often saw each other at Juniper. I wished we could talk more but we were in separate lanes and our heads were mostly face down in the water. Also, I think, we didn't want our fellow swimmers to notice how interested we were in each other.

On a Sunday when we were both taking a break from training we decided to go look at the Upriver Triathlon course we would swim, bike, and run in September. It started with a 1,500-meter swim in another lake, not far from Elk Lake. The thirty-kilometer bike ride started uphill from the lake but was mostly downhill through the forest all the way to the Deschutes River. The run went eleven kilometers uphill alongside the river and into Upriver Ranch itself.

We drove to the shore of the lake where the race would begin. The beach faced north where snow shined brightly on Mount Bachelor and South Sister. To the east was the ridge we would ride over before beginning the long descent to the river. It was going to be a steep climb and, from what we had heard, parts of the trail were very rough, what bikers called "technical." Technical sometimes meant "to avoid breaking your neck, pick up your bike and carry it." We walked about a mile along the trail and part way up the rise. Before the triathlon we were going to come back and ride this trail a few times to familiarize ourselves with it. It was too far away to ride frequently.

Looking back from the trail we saw two lakes in the forest below us. The sky was bright blue and the air was clear. We were happy, off exploring together. As Amy and I stood there I wanted very badly to kiss her. I thought she might feel the same. It seemed right. If I put my arm around her shoulder I thought it might seem too coercive, even possessive. We were equals. I touched her lightly just above the small of her back. My intent was clear but the choice was entirely hers. She turned and looked up at me. I bent down and kissed her gently on the lips, pulling her lightly toward me. She wrapped both arms around me, firmly but with far less force than her strength could supply. God, it was wonderful.

We stood kissing for only a little while. It was delicious to pause here and enjoy how momentous our embrace was for both of us. I loved being with Amy. We were working hard together on goals we agreed upon. All of my emotions let me think I had found the girl I wanted be with forever. And it seemed to me, count my blessings, that she might feel the same way about me. We slowly drew apart, as if missing each other's touch would make us appreciate it even more.

"Well, that was nice," Amy said. "And now," she said with a laugh, "back to work."

It had been nice. Amy was right. And our kiss held the promise of both love and sex. But Amy had decided, I guessed, that it wasn't quite time yet for either of those things. Who was I to disagree? Anticipation made me appreciate even more how wonderful the future would be.

We walked down the trail to the car and drove a long way around the ridge to where the road cut across the descending part of bike route. The bike trail was steep coming down to this point and leveled out where it crossed an enormous parking lot. The parking lot, built for snowmobilers, would be a rest stop during the race and a good opportunity to pass bikers who might have slowed us down earlier. From here the trail going down to the river was not as steep and we could pick up some speed if we had the energy.

We drove out of the parking lot and followed the road another long way around to where the bike ride would end by the river. We parked the car in a picnic area and got out to explore the start of the running. We didn't get far before the mosquito assault began.

"We should leave this for another day," said Amy, and I agreed. We ran back to the car and swatted at our arms and legs while I started the engine and drove out. No wonder there was nobody setting up a picnic. When we got away from the river we opened the windows to let the remaining mosquitoes out of the car.

"The mosquitoes won't be so bad in September," I said.

"We need to run this trail a few times before then. With a gallon or two of DEET."

I drove Amy to the edge of Bend where she had left her car. I had volunteered my 4-Runner for our exploring. It had four-wheel drive and, I foresaw but did not mention, whichever car we took would come back coated in dust and need to be washed. A minor touch of gallantry on my part, I thought—not as obvious as putting your coat down in a puddle so the queen's shoes would not get wet.

"Thanks for driving," she said. She leaned across the front seats and gave me a kiss on the cheek. Then she was gone. Fair enough. I wouldn't be knocking on Candy's door anymore for anything other than billable time.

After dinner Mom and I played nine holes of golf. She pulled a cart and I pulled one too. I would have preferred to carry but I couldn't use my muscles any more than necessary on anything other than training. I was fitter than I had ever been before but it did not show up in my golf score. Mitch had told me I could play golf for fun but I was not allowed to practice or make any effort to get better at it. I had to stay focused on the tri.

I birdied the third hole with a fortunate putt. I had a good drive on the sixth hole but then went over the green and wound up with a bogey. Still, there was no one on the course but Mom and me. The shadows were long and the air was still. We hardly talked about anything except the quality of our shots and the quality of our luck. Mom won the nine by two strokes.

My father's absence was beginning to grate on me. He had a right to be where he was, at The Clearing having a good time. I would not have summoned him back if I could have. If he were here I didn't know what practical difference it would make to me. But I was worn down by the investigations into Winterpol's death—Breuninger's investigation and my own half-baked one. I couldn't say I was worn down by my triathlon training but all the exercise did use up energy I might have had to deal with other things. I wasn't sure where my relationship with Amy was going and I didn't want her to get away from me through some stupid mistake. I missed the part of my life that was my father. I missed the assurance that my parents' home was complete.

On the day of the Elk Lake Swim Amy rode to the race in a van with other swimmers from Bend. I drove to Elk Lake on my own and met the Juniper group there. The water temperature was sixty-eight degrees, a serious adjustment after swimming in a pool that was eighty-two. I wasn't the only one who had been taking cold showers. Most of the Juniper group, and most swimmers overall, were only going to wear a swimsuit and a latex swim cap. But Amy and I wanted to get used to wearing wetsuits in a race. We estimated the water would be even colder at the triathlon in September. The suits would keep us warmer and more buoyant so we'd use up less energy swimming. In the Elk Lake race, the judges would dock our times by ten percent to offset the supposed wetsuit advantage. In the triathlon it was assumed you'd lose time getting the wetsuit off while transitioning from swimming to biking. So the judges would not adjust our times in September.

The 1,500-meter race at Elk Lake would start in the water at

11:45 a.m., behind a line marked by buoys. The course was triangular, going out into the lake, rounding two buoys, and coming back to the starting point on shore. Starting in the water favored wetsuits because our bodies could warm up the suits before we started swimming. Our wetsuits were sleeveless and went down to the middle of our calves. Full-length wetsuits, built for scuba diving, would have been warmer but, when we ran the triathlon, they would have taken even more time to peel off before bicycling.

Everybody swimming the 1,500 meters would start together. Each of our times would be clocked at the end, and we'd be sorted by age and gender after the results were in. At the starting line we arranged ourselves according to how we estimated we were likely to do and how willing we were to battle other swimmers at the start. Unless you were a top contender you probably didn't want to be in the front. You would be kicked by the swimmers who pulled out ahead of you and run over by faster swimmers coming from behind. I placed myself three rows back and off-center to the left. I wanted to keep out of the crush going around the first buoy on the course. Amy was about five rows behind me in a group of other women. I knelt to get water into the top of the suit as well as the bottom, and blew bubbles in the water. If I didn't rehearse this I knew I would recoil the moment I put my face down in the cold dark water.

We all expected sharp elbows, accidental kicks, and body-to-body collisions. If someone swam over us then we might even find ourselves under water, trying to recover momentum and get to the surface for air. I'd heard races could be brutal and I wanted to see what that meant. I was going to err toward being considerate of my fellow swimmers. I wasn't so desperate to win that I wanted to injure someone. But if the race became more physical than I expected I would give as good as I got. The rugby player in me would come out fighting.

We all tensed for the start and the gun went off. For a second or two there was nowhere to go. The guy ahead of me was still standing up, waiting for the swimmer in the first row to get out of the way. I felt a push from behind and my first reaction in the race was to push backward rather than forward. Then there was space and I dove toward what seemed like a too-small spot of water. I swam eight strokes without breathing or looking up. I bumped into bodies all around me. Blows of varying force landed on my head, shoulders, and back. When I went to take my first breath I opened my mouth to a confusion of spray and water that would not let me breathe. I did a little better on my next stroke, spitting out water and getting some air. I overcame a hint of panic as I wondered how long it would take to get a normal breath.

I was still wondering when I got a good hard kick to my temple and felt my goggles slip off my head. Without goggles my race would be over. I pawed my hand up beside my head and grabbed the goggles. I needed two hands to put them on again so I treaded water while I reassembled my gear. People slammed into me and one even took time to call me an unflattering name as he went by. I got the goggles on, pressed them tight to my face, and started swimming, following the crowd. At least now the other swimmers were more spread out. I got into a rhythm that I knew was too fast. After twenty strokes I backed off to more or less the pace I'd practiced for 1,500 meters in the pool. I was still breathing too hard but that would even out. For the first time I looked up to see where I was, still very much with the pack but with some swimmers substantially out in front. I aimed a little closer to the first buoy and put my head down to swim strong, smooth, and steady—the way I had practiced.

From there on in the race was mostly pure swimming. When we rounded the buoys I swam just outside the bulk of the other swimmers, not the shortest route but I saved more energy for actually swimming. A hundred yards from the beach I gave it all the energy I had left. I saw one guy I picked to overtake before we reached the finish. When I accelerated he sprinted as well. With supreme effort I couldn't gain on him for the longest time. But with ten yards to go I suddenly pulled ahead. He must have run out of gas. I finished ahead of him but didn't turn to look. I didn't want to gloat.

I walked up the beach to clear space for the people behind me. A few women had finished the race ahead of me and more were starting to come out of the water with men still outnumbering them. When more people were standing on the beach than were in the water Amy had still not arrived. Finally I saw her rise out of the water and stumble slowly ahead, as though she were exhausted. I rushed down to help her, careful not to touch her until she had reached dry land. She leaned against me but when I went to put my arm around her shoulder she flinched.

"Not the shoulder," she gasped, "grab my waist." She put her nearest arm around my neck and we walked up the beach together.

CHAPTER 22

Women

(Candy)

I saw a story in a magazine about a race scheduled for August at Elk Lake, up in the mountains. There was a picture, not a very good one, of last year's swimmers on the beach getting ready to start. Mount Bachelor, capped by a ragged shroud of snow, rose above the far end of the lake. There were big red buoys out in the water. What struck me most were the swimmers, still vertical, some on the sand and some halfway into the water. Their swim caps were bright green, blue, red, and purple. Some bodies were black in their wetsuits. The exposed skin of others varied from white to pink to tan. In a painting I could move those swimmers and their colors around to suit me. So I decided to go see this year's swim for myself.

There was no parking close to the lake. And I didn't want to cram the Porsche into a narrow spot where someone could ding it. I walked so far that I got to the beach just in time for the start. I brought a camera to help me remember what I saw. I got only a few pictures before the race began. I stayed to see the swimmers come out of the water. I drank in the day, the sun getting brighter, light winds ruffling the lake, and kayakers out on the water watching the race. Three parallel contrails stretched from north to south across the sky, like chalk lines on a running track. There was a big orange banner stretched between poles stuck in the sand that said, in blue lettering, OREGON OPEN WATER. I would decide later to leave that banner in my painting or take it out.

The swim was a triangular course that came back to the beach. When the first swimmer approached I walked down to take photos.

The swimmers, men and women, all looked fit and strong, though some of them were heavy. The spectators, however, were all shapes and sizes. They hadn't given a thought to what they wore.

One tall swimmer stopped when he reached the beach and looked back at the others still in the water. When he took his swim cap off I could see it was Dan Martinez. A few minutes later he walked down to the water's edge to meet a girl who was slowly walking out. She was clutching her shoulder and didn't want Dan to touch her. He bent a little to talk to her and they walked up the beach together. She had a small waist and well-proportioned hips and legs. But her shoulders were muscular. They went to one of the little pavilions on the beach and talked to a man who looked like a race official. Then they picked up plastic bags that apparently belonged to them and toweled off. They pulled light sweatshirts out of the bags and put them on. Dan's was black and orange and said LEWIS AND CLARK PIONEERS. Hers was yellow with blue lettering I couldn't read.

I watched them together, in some ways like casual friends and in some ways like an old married couple. I decided he was infatuated with her. And she loved him but didn't trust him, or maybe didn't trust herself.

I didn't make myself obvious but I stood where Dan would see me, if he ever took his eyes off the girl. When he spotted me he said something to her and they started in my direction, Dan smiled and gave me a wave. He introduced us in a friendly but proper manner.

"How do you do?" said Amy, offering her hand. "I'm sorry for the loss of your husband."

I recognized her, wet hair and all. It was the girl who sat across the table from Ken at a picnic he gave for people in an apartment building he'd just bought in Bend. He invited me to meet him there. I wouldn't have gone except that it was such an odd thing for him to do, to do anything extra, especially so frivolous, for his tenants. That girl had been on my mind ever since. Was Ken out looking for my replacement? She was younger than I was, but no prettier. Maybe she came from some bigshot family in Portland that had lost all their money.

"Thank you," I said, taking Amy's hand and shaking it lightly. I could see Amy wince and try to hide the pain. "Is this the girl who looks like a Winterpol?" I asked Dan.

"Yes," he said. I pulled my sunglasses off and looked at Amy critically. "Turn," I said. Amy turned her head. "Other way," I said. Amy turned again. Whatever smile she had at the start of the examination had now evaporated.

"You're right," I said to Dan, still looking at Amy. "I hope you are a nicer person than Ken was." I looked away. I resented this girl. Young and full of energy. She believed she could have whatever she wanted in life if she just worked at it. For starters she was going to have Dan. I could see it coming.

"Are you taking up photography?" Dan asked me.

"The photos are just to help me remember details when I paint."

"It certainly is a beautiful place," said Dan innocuously. I was always disappointed that Dan was not an artist like his father.

"Have you decided where you're going to live?" he asked.

"I'll want a condo with a studio in Portland. And something in Upriver or Bend to get away from the rain, maybe the house I have and maybe something different. And I may travel a lot."

"I hope you get exactly what makes you happy," said Amy. Her wish was generous and sincere. I was beginning to hate her.

"I'm going to get some ice for your shoulder," Dan said to her and he walked away.

"Marry him," I said. Amy's jaw dropped.

"Well," the girl said, "we're not anywhere near that. We're only friends."

"You will be near that soon enough," I said. "And when he asks you, you say yes."

"I know you mean well," said Amy, so polite. "But I think you're a little out of line here."

"Listen, sweetheart," I said with a mix of affection and disdain I couldn't fine-tune, "I know life and I know Dan Martinez. He's still unformed but he is going to make some girl a great husband. You can put the finishing touches on him."

"He's older than I am. He knows more than I do."

"You're a woman. It will come naturally to you. Do it. Marry him. Or you will regret it the rest of your life."

Little Amy looked at me hard, like a woman older than she was. "Thank you," she said, leaving me to guess how much of that "thank you" was gratitude and how much was dismissal. She left without a further goodbye. She didn't believe me, I knew, but she would remember what I told her.

CHAPTER 23

Gains and Losses

(Amy)

I swam Elk Lake for my first taste of competitive open water swimming. Some woman kicked me on purpose and I had to swim the last leg with one arm. It caused me to ease up on my training for two weeks afterward. Dan had talked me into the swim and I thought it was a good idea. Maybe it was after all. A slice of the real world.

After the race we talked to race officials about what happened. All the racers had numbers painted on their arms and I gave the officials the number of the woman who kicked me. One looked down a list for the name and rolled his eyes at another official. "Olivia," was all he said. The other official seemed to know who he was talking about and shook his head. They said they would ask other swimmers who finished near Olivia whether they had seen her kick me. That seemed as much as we could do.

Another taste of the real world was meeting Candy Winterpol after the race. She was taking pictures and Dan introduced us. I was intimidated as soon as I knew who she was. I owed her the respect and consideration that I owed any woman older than me and then much more because her husband had just died. At the same time she clearly was not a soft-hearted woman. Dan and I were connected to her in so many ways it was hard to sort out. She had been Dan's father's student. She'd gotten Dan to help reduce suspicion of her possible role in her husband's death. Now Dan was helping her with her husband's estate. He was so mixed up with the Winterpols that he had been arrested.

The idea that I might get a chunk of her husband's estate did not seem to trouble Candy at all. While she looked me over I thought for sure she would tell Dan I looked nothing like her husband's family and I was some kind of fraud. I couldn't believe it when she said Dan was right, that I did look like a Winterpol. I would have stumbled back in surprise except I was tired from the swim and my shoulder was starting to ache.

After Dan left us Candy said, out of the blue, that I should marry him. I hardly knew him! She was crazier and crazier. I said I was nowhere near thinking about that and neither was Dan. She insisted and I left her as quickly as I could. I wouldn't be surprised if she did murder her husband.

I met Dan coming back with a plastic bag of ice and I held it on my shoulder, under my sweatshirt, with my opposite hand. We went to get lunch and Dan filled up paper plates with bratwurst and salads for both of us. There was no place to sit at tables and I couldn't sit on a log and hold up my plate with my bad arm. So we put our towels on the ground and sat on them, near some people from Juniper we recognized but didn't really know. All of us were pleased at having swum the race. We felt a common bond in spite of some of us never having exchanged a single word prior to today. Someone asked if I'd strained my shoulder and Dan explained what happened. He said how impressed he was that the judges took it seriously and seemed willing to do something about it. Getting kicked was a hazard of the sport. It was only when it was intentional that it was wrong. From the judges' reaction, he said, it seemed like the woman who kicked me was known for unsportsmanlike conduct.

"I wish you hadn't told all those people," I said to Dan. "I don't want to play the victim."

"I understand," he said. It was about the only thing he could say. We weren't connected enough for him to say it wouldn't happen again. We got up to walk back to his car.

"Candy is certainly an unusual person," I said to Dan. "I felt like a student's art project being examined by a professor."

"She doesn't mean to be hostile," he said. "She's an artist. She walks the road less traveled."

"It didn't seem to bother her that I might get half her husband's estate. She had no trouble saying I looked like a relative."

"My father told Candy over and over, 'Face the truth,'" said Dan. "I didn't understand how that applied to art but I guess she got the lesson. My prediction is she will let half the estate go without thinking about it. Then in five or ten years she will realize what she's done and sue to get it back. She won't have a prayer of succeeding but she will try anyway."

I guess he regretted what he'd said. "I'm sorry," he went on. "I'm being cynical. I hope it won't turn out that way. And I hope that if she wanted to sue then I, with my father's help, could talk her out of it."

"She told me I should marry you," I said. "I told her I hardly knew you and that I had no intention of marrying anyone until I'd lived life on my own for a while. She insisted. She's kind of a nut."

"She's different," said Dan. "You never know whether what she says is a spontaneous idea or the result of some subtle calculation." We walked a quarter mile in silence. It was a long way to the parking lot.

"Candy doesn't know you," said Dan, "and she doesn't really care what is in your best interest. She told you to marry me for my sake."

"I hope you're not going to take her word for it," I said. "You don't know me any better than I know you."

"You're right," he said. "She may have said it just to upset us, to rock the boat in a way. She's certainly had an effect."

"Well," I said, "we should ignore her. We have plenty of other things to think about."

"Yes," he said. "Let's forget it ever happened."

"Let's focus on the tri," I said.

We didn't talk very much during the ride to Bend. We were a little tired from the race. And Candy had gotten us to think about things we were not ready to think about. Dan carried my gym bag into the apartment for me and met one of my roommates, the yoga instructor. No kiss. We said goodbye like two classmates, nothing more.

"There's a vibe between the two of you," said the yoga instructor after Dan left. Her and her damned third eye. I'd heard enough for that day. I took four Advil and went to bed.

CHAPTER 24

Parentage

(Dan)

After Amy was injured at Elk Lake I had to go back to training by myself for a while. I missed her and I talked to her every evening on the phone. She was doing all the training she could, mostly in her legs. She could run on a treadmill but not on the ground, and certainly not on a trail, because it jostled her shoulder too much. She rode an exercise bike but believed that pedaling was secondary to wrestling the bike through turns, over bumps and over jumps. Her shoulder wouldn't let her do that. It certainly wouldn't let her swim. Though she was frustrated she was philosophical about it. Getting injured was almost inevitable in training. It was part of the sport.

Amy was also working more hours without extra pay and she was studying more of the technology behind what Greenwood Biomedical did. She sure didn't sit around feeling sorry for herself. We both looked at the results of the Elk Lake Swim when they came online. The web site listed the finishing times by age group with the last names and first initials. Among the women age twenty to thirty and thirty to forty, there was no finisher who's first initial was O. Olivia, whoever she was, had been disqualified.

"There is justice in the world," I said.

"And more good people than bad," said Amy. She didn't sound like Ken Winterpol's daughter to me.

Over the phone I told Mitch where my training was. I said my bike partner was out of commission and I'd been allocating extra time to swimming for the past three weeks. It was time to focus on running. Since the running leg of the tri was going to end in Upriver

I could easily train on the same trail I would run in the race. I said I would ride my bike down to the slough where the run would start, run the River Trail to Upriver, then drive back to pick up the bike. The bike portion would not be ideal training because most of the ride would be on a gravel road with no jumps, bumps, or pumps. But I could practice getting the most out of each rotation of the pedals and I would start each run with some of the fatigue I would feel in the race. I would learn to pace my running over this particular course. Parts of the trail were steeper than others. There were turns, stones, and roots that I hoped would become second nature to me. I slipped a stopwatch into my pocket every time I made the run so I could track my progress and try different strategies.

I did this ride-and-run combination every other day for two weeks in spite of discovering some disadvantages. There wasn't much traffic on the gravel road but what cars there were threw up great clouds of dust. If one car followed another, the second driver might not see me. I had to wrench the bike off the road for a few yards of impromptu bushwhacking. The second problem was people on the running trail. The path climbed a steep hill with tight turns alongside Benham Falls, which was popular with tourists in spite of the distance they had to drive to get there. People milled about and gazed at the falls. It only took one or two gawkers to block the trail. Some wanted me to stop and take their picture. I tried to run very early in the morning to avoid them.

The third problem with running this trail was the mosquitoes. With a big hat and mosquito repellant I fended off some and learned to tolerate the rest. I'd gotten light fishing clothes with long sleeves and pants to protect my arms and legs but mosquito bites in various stages of coming and going dotted my face. I used up half a bottle of Benadryl trying to fight the itching.

I kept up with swimming, biking, and weight training. But I couldn't train all day. I was getting worse at golf. My muscles were always too tired or too stiff for a good golf swing. I couldn't putt. I watched some baseball on TV. I took naps. That August I read the first four books in the Aubrey/Maturin series. Patrick O'Brian's descriptions of sailing to exotic places, fighting battles, and studying nature gave my mind a break from thinking about exercise and nutrition.

Not much mail came to the house for me. What there was Mom put on the computer keyboard in my room. When a big envelope arrived from the DNA lab I let it sit there for five minutes while I put my running clothes in the laundry and took a shower. I had to search through pages of boilerplate before I got to the data. The results were embedded in generic language that slowed down my understanding. Who was Person 1 and who were Persons 2 and 3? What were samples A, B, and C? The report said 25 percent DNA match between people but the two people could be a grandparent and a grandchild, an aunt or uncle and a niece or nephew, or it could apply to half siblings. The lab had no way of knowing which person was older and which was younger, or whether they were the same generation or different generations. Nonetheless, I was able to piece together what the test results meant. I checked them thoroughly a second time. The test told me something I had not expected. I called Amy.

"Linda is your aunt," I told her. "But Ken is not your father."

"So they are not really brother and sister?"

"They are brother and sister all right," I said. "Linda is your aunt and Ken is your uncle."

"What?"

"They have an older brother. Linda told me. I don't even know his name. He hasn't talked to the other two in years. But I think Linda knows where he is."

"So no million dollars?" Amy asked. "It's a good thing I didn't spend it already."

"Now all those guys who were after your fortune will stop bothering you."

"They were getting to be a pain," she said.

"Linda should be able to put us in touch with her brother or at least give us some clues toward finding out about your mother."

"I'm not sure I want to meet my biological father. He is the one who skipped out on my mother and left me alone in the world."

"Linda will understand that. She is not a big fan of this brother either. I expect she won't tell him. And you won't have to meet him if you don't want to. But I think we have to tell Linda something. She took the test and she knows the results are coming."

"You're right," said Amy. "But please ask her not to tell her brother about me."

Sister Catherine, when I called the Saint Cecelia School, agreed not to tell her older brother about Amy. She confirmed that shortly after their mother died, her older brother Richard had departed Burns and left his two younger siblings, Linda and Ken, to fend for themselves and cope with their alcoholic father. Richard had moved to Prineville, where he still was, over a hundred miles from Burns and about thirty-five miles from Bend. He had a family there and a wife who had inherited four hundred acres in alfalfa and potatoes. He was a deacon in a church and had served on the city council. He hadn't talked to either of his siblings for years and hadn't come to Ken's funeral, though Linda had left a voicemail at his home about it. He must have known Ken was murdered. It was in all the local papers.

I told Linda what year Amy was born and Linda said her older brother was already married with children at that time. So the man who was now a pillar of Prineville had been an adulterer and had seduced a girl under eighteen. Linda agreed it looked like Richard sent Amy's mother off to have the baby in Colorado. When Vickie died and the baby was adopted, Richard decided he was off the hook. If his impregnation of Vickie Coate became public even now, Richard's reputation in the small community of Prineville would suffer, quite possibly along with his marriage and his hold on the four hundred acres. I did an online search while I was talking with Linda and came up with a couple named Coate, still in Prineville, who might well be related to Amy's mother.

When I told Amy her biological father lived in Prineville and there was a couple in Prineville listed as Paul and Margery Coate, she didn't answer for a minute. I told her I thought she was close to meeting her mother's family. "Do you want to call them or would you like me to?"

"I will call them. I have to rev myself up to do it. I called all the

181

Coates in Colorado a few years ago and kept hitting dead ends. Don't worry, though. I cannot not call them. But I'm certainly not calling this Richard guy, no matter what happens."

Amy called me back a quarter hour later. "I talked with Margery Coate. I talked as slowly and calmly as I could. I told her when I was born and that my mother's name was Vickie Coate. I said I was living in Bend and I wanted to meet her and see if we were related. The first question she asked was where my mother was now. I didn't want to tell her but I had to say my mother had died giving birth to me. She didn't answer me for a while and I waited. She didn't know whether to believe me, of course, and I'm sure she'd always hoped her daughter would come home. She said I could come and meet her, even though I'm sure she was nervous about it. I'm going tomorrow morning. So, Dan, would you come with me?"

I said I would be happy to and I picked Amy up at eight for the drive to Prineville. When we turned east at Powell Butte the sun flooded the car and warmed our skin. The day was going to be a scorcher. On the plateau above Prineville I turned left to show Amy something I thought was amazing, especially in a small town off by itself on the edge of the Eastern Oregon desert. Half a mile off the highway was an enormous rectangular building three or four stories high with no windows and only a small office on one side of it. The building was longer than three football fields. Thousands of people could have worked in a factory that big. But no one was going in or out. No trucks were loading or unloading. There were only about twenty-five parking places out in front.

"You know what that is?" I asked. "Facebook. That's where Sean works. The building is full of computers and disk drives just spinning away, storing millions of Facebook pages and sending them out over the Internet when people ask for them."

"Why is it here?" asked Amy.

"Cheap land and cheap electricity. And, I think, and it is just my guess, if you're a terrorist looking to blow it up, you're really going to stand out in Prineville."

"The Coates don't have Facebook pages," said Amy. "I looked."

"Sorry," I said. "Minor detour. Let's go see them." It was easy to find the address on a side street only a block off Route 26. It was a simple one-story house on a quarter acre. It had a one car garage and a canopy over the driveway that sheltered a red Toyota pickup truck. The lawn was patchy in places but it had been mowed and there was a neatly kept bed of flowers along the front of the house. We stepped up to a small concrete stoop and rang the doorbell. The woman who answered the door was about five foot five with short gray hair. She wore turquoise blue slacks and an ironed white shirt that fitted her shoulders well and wasn't tucked in at the waist. She looked Amy quickly up and down.

"I'm Amy, how do you do?" After a slight hesitation the woman took Amy's hand.

"I'm Margery Coate," said the woman. She wasn't exactly unfriendly but she said, "Pleased to meet you" more from reflex than from any apparent true feeling.

"And this is my friend, Daniel Martinez," Amy said. I tried to look as short, relaxed, and non-threatening as I could. I smiled, stuck out my hand, and said hello.

"Hello," the woman said. "Well, come on in and meet Paul." The air conditioning came on when I pulled the door shut behind me and we found ourselves in the living room. We'd let warm air into the house. The room was paneled in vertical lengths of pine with triangular cupboards in two corners and small framed paintings on the walls. The rug was beige. The couch and two stuffed chairs were covered in a dark plaid. The furniture was neat and well cared for.

Paul was a wiry man, taller than his wife, with thinning gray hair. He didn't smile but he shook our hands politely and said "How do you do" to both of us. Margery asked us to sit down and we sat on the couch facing the two of them in the chairs.

"I know we all have our doubts about this," said Amy, "but I think we are all going to be happy together or disappointed together. In any case, thank you for being willing to see me. Let me start by showing you my birth certificate. It gives the date I was born and it says my mother was Vickie Coate." Amy gave them time to look at it. It was an original with an official seal embossed into it. "Could your Vickie have had a baby on that date?"

"She left home six months before that," said Margery. "If she was pregnant we didn't know it. She was a good girl, a good student with lots of friends. We never thought she would get pregnant. Or that she would leave home like that."

"Did she leave a note?" asked Amy.

"It said she was sorry to leave us but not to worry. She would be back in a year." A sad expression flickered on Margery's face and she suppressed it.

"You don't look like Vickie," said Paul. "You don't look like a Coate."

"We could do DNA tests," said Amy. "Then we'd know for sure."

"Tell me," asked Paul. "How did you pick us to call?"

"I went to the funeral of my landlord in Bend. His sister and I agreed we looked very much like each other," said Amy. "She agreed to DNA testing and it turned out the man was my uncle and she was my aunt. They had another brother who moved to Prineville. So I thought my mother might be from Prineville. The only people in Prineville named Coate are the two of you."

"So you called us," said Paul.

"And, lo and behold, you had a daughter named Vickie!" said Amy. Margery suddenly gasped and all of us looked at her.

"The way you said that," Margery said, "the expression on your face. It was just like Vickie." She broke out in tears. Her husband stood up, walked behind her chair and put his hands on her shoulders. Her crying was silent but she began to shudder. Tears came to Paul's eyes too but I thought he was a long way from convinced.

"Who is the father?" he asked. Amy didn't answer so I spoke up.

"Are you sure you want to know?" I asked. "He still lives in Prineville and, from what his sister told me, is a respected citizen with a family. He may be someone you know, even a friend."

"I was sure when Vickie left," said Paul, "that some man had talked her into it. I've never forgiven him, and I want to know who he was."

I checked that Amy wasn't giving me a look.

"Richard Winterpol," I said. Paul's face hardened.

"We know him," said Paul, looking over our heads at the wall behind us. "Never had anything against him. But all these years he's known what happened to Vickie and he never told us. Never told us we had a granddaughter." He gathered himself and addressed me directly. "All these years I've thought about what I would do to the man who took Vickie. Now that it's real I'm going to have to decide."

"You have the power to cost him all the respect he has in the community," I said, "cost him the respect of his children. Possibly break up his marriage."

"I know his wife, Cary Winterpol," said Margery, still with tears in her eyes. "She's a lovely woman. All this would make her so sad. I don't know whether that's right."

"You'll probably want to take some time before you do anything," said Amy. "We should do a DNA test to make sure I am your granddaughter. Then you can decide what to do."

"Are you going to tell Winterpol?" Paul asked Amy.

"No, I am not," said Amy. "We've told my aunt, his sister. She says she won't tell him. I think whether he finds out will be up to you."

"We'll have the lab send you a DNA test kit," I said. "It's very easy and you send it back to the lab. You'll have the results in less than a month."

Amy asked if she could see a photo of Vickie. Margery pulled an album out of a cupboard by the kitchen door. I stood up so the two women could sit side by side on the couch.

"Paul," I said, "I need to get a carport like yours, with a tarp over a metal frame. Could you show me yours and tell me what I need to look for?" We went outside and I asked what I thought were good questions about what made a good carport. I didn't mention that Upriver would never let us put a tarp-covered carport outside our house. I needed to get Paul out of the house so Amy could say something important to Margery. We had discussed it on the way over. It was delicate. If Margery had any reason to think that Paul wasn't Vickie's father then she definitely wouldn't want to compare Paul's DNA to Vickie's daughter. We should only send one test kit and Margery should be the one to use it. Poor Margery was going to think she had been through a tornado by the time we left.

As a result of my subterfuge with Paul I am now sort of an

authority on tarp-covered carports. Our man-to-man discussion also got Paul to relax a bit. We moved on to fishing, an inexhaustible subject, and spent about half an hour out in the sun, glancing from time to time over the rooftops at the dry mountains and rimrock that framed the town. I felt I could call Paul on the phone in the future and he would be glad to hear from me.

"What did Margery say?" I asked when Amy and I were in the car headed back to Bend.

"Her mouth dropped open," said Amy. "And then she laughed. She said she watched soap operas all the time but her life was not like that. That sort of thing was for other people. I think I went down in her estimation a little for asking the question. Then we moved on. She obviously loved her daughter very much. Margery thought she knew Vickie and then Vickie just left. It was the saddest thing in her life. She kept looking at me. For traces of her daughter, I suppose. We both cried but we were committed to plunge ahead. She's going to make copies of the photos for me and I promised to pay her back."

"So what did you learn about your mother?"

"She was a good student and never gave her parents any trouble. She was taller than I am and she played basketball. She was going to go to become a teacher. She had high-school friends that still live in Prineville today. We decided Margery wouldn't tell them about me until we get the DNA results and she and Paul decide what to do about Richard. But I hope someday I'll meet my mother's friends."

"Margery and Paul have a lot to sort through," I said.

"And so do I," said Amy. "I'm the product of a statutory rape. So many people—Margery, Paul, and Vickie—would have had better lives if I'd never been born."

"And many people are better off because you were," I said.

"My parents," she said, which I took to mean the family that had brought her up. Amy gazed out the window and I chose not to interrupt her thoughts. My mind wandered to Richard Winterpol and how disrupted his life would be if the Coates chose to reveal what he had done to Vickie. Paul and Margery Coate were good people, caught between seeing justice done and not wishing to inflict harm on anyone. The opposite of Ken Winterpol. If Ken had known about Richard's spurned daughter he would have destroyed his brother, or at least threatened to. My hands suddenly clenched the steering wheel and my head lurched forward. Of course. Ken did know. He had seen Amy's resemblance to his family. And that was what the DNA test in Ken's gun cabinet was for.

"Did Ken ever ask you for a DNA sample?" I asked Amy.

"No," she said, "never mentioned it." She looked across the car at me trying to guess what I might be thinking. "But he may have gotten a sample. He did something strange at the party he threw at our apartment building. He brought me a lemonade in a plastic cup. When I was done he put a plastic cup—either his or mine—in a bag that he took with him when he left. I guess it was mine. So he could have gotten my DNA."

"I saw a DNA test he had done on a man and a woman. I don't know who they were. But the test may have shown you were his niece. And therefore Richard's daughter. He may have threatened Richard with that knowledge."

"Why would he do that?"

"I think he hated Richard. Richard abandoned Ken and Linda when their mother died and their father became a drunk. When you appeared Ken saw a chance to destroy Richard's straight and proper life."

"If Ken had already exposed Richard, the Coates would know about it." Amy was thinking like a detective, or maybe a lawyer, the way I'd been trying to think about Ken's murder for almost two months.

"Maybe he just threatened Richard," I said. "Made him fret. That sounds more like Ken."

"Do you think Richard killed Ken to prevent the story from getting out?" asked Amy.

"It's possible," I said. "In any case, we just found one more suspect in Ken's murder." With any luck, Richard would not be able to account for his whereabouts on the morning Ken was attacked. Or maybe Richard hired someone else to kill Ken. I called Detective Breuninger from the car and left him a voicemail, as succinct as I could make it, filling him in on DNA tests, Amy, the Coates, and Richard Winterpol.

My joy in adding to the list of suspects didn't last very long. How far would Richard go to cover up the Vickie Coate story? I didn't know the man. Would he kill or threaten Amy or the Coates? I decided I had to give Richard a call and warn him off. I would tell him who I was so he wouldn't panic into some rash act. But I didn't want the call logged into my cell-phone records. On our way back into town I stopped the car at a gas station to use a pay phone. I got Richard's number from information and called him. Fortunately, he answered. I wasn't going to leave a message.

"Hello," I said, "My name is Daniel Martinez and I am the attorney settling the estate of Kenneth Winterpol. May I speak to Richard Winterpol?"

"I'm Richard Winterpol," said the man. "How can I help you?" He sounded businesslike, even upbeat.

"Well, it appears that your brother uncovered some DNA information linking you to a Vickie Coate and her daughter. Did he share that with you?"

"No, Ken never mentioned it," said Richard. He might have been lying or been telling the truth. But there was a tension in the man's voice that wasn't there before.

"I thought I should let you know because this information might be embarrassing."

"Embarrassing to whom?" said Richard. "Are you trying to threaten me with some trumped-up story?"

"Not at all," I said. "Nobody plans to make the findings public. But I thought you should know the information hasn't gotten lost."

There was a pause while Richard considered what I'd told him. Then he said, slowly and carefully, "I don't know what *information* you're talking about. But I'll sue you five ways from Sunday if you spread lies."

"Fair enough," I said. "I just want to make sure no harm comes to Vickie Coate's parents or her child."

"Listen, Mr. Whatever-Your-Name-Is," said Richard. "Your

insinuations are absurd and you are opening yourself up for a lawsuit. I'd be careful if I were you."

"I think we understand each other," I said. He hung up. But he'd gotten the message. I thought the Coates and Amy were safe now, at least as safe as I could make them. And Richard would have some richly deserved restless nights.

I dropped Amy at her apartment. This was a rest day for both of us. I had lunch at home, ordered the DNA test kits for the Coates and a new one for Amy, read the paper, and then went to the golf course. I felt pretty upbeat. Things were coming together.

I was matched up with two fortyish guys who had come out from Bend for the afternoon. They enjoyed hearing about my triathlon training. When they heard I was an attorney they started complaining about the attorney they had. The law firm was doing what they asked, they said, but it never suggested anything creative. They said the lawyers weren't really bringing anything to the party. They told me I should open my own law firm. I thanked them for the thought but said I wasn't anywhere near ready for that. I knew from past experience, though I didn't say it, that golfers often generate great enthusiasm for people they meet on the course, only to forget them completely the next day. Nonetheless I gave them one of my old Oxton cards and wrote Greg Lyman's name on the back with Greg's direct number. It was a bright afternoon, with a big white thunderhead rising over Newberry Crater, beautiful to look at but too far away to threaten us. We all played well.

CHAPTER 25

Shameless

(Amy)

On our next Friday off from training, Dan suggested I come look at the last mile of the triathlon, near the finish line in Upriver Ranch. We would meet at his house and he would drive us over to look at the course. He mentioned that Friday was his mother's day to play golf and she would be gone until late afternoon. I knew what he was thinking and I expected he knew that I knew. But we didn't talk about it. We had reached a silent understanding and we didn't want to spoil it. We were celebrating that we knew each other that well, trusted each other that much, that we were committed to being with each other. That we knew we were in love. Discussing a meeting of our bodies the way we would schedule a trail ride would make our affection commonplace, a mere practical bargain of desires. So we talked about the last few miles of the foot-race, where the small hills were, and where we might miss the trail even though it would be well-marked on race day. We picked a spot to meet after the race.

Then he wanted to show me the practice area he'd built in the backwoods of Upriver. He'd started with a narrow elk trail and cut branches out of the way while leaving some of the logs that had fallen across the path. Then he'd shoveled parts of the trail into dips and bumps to practice jumping. I rode his bike out there and he rode a street bike he'd had in high school. We rode the little course slowly, just to see it, not to practice. We stood side by side at the end of it, straddling our bikes, and kissed. We embraced as well as we could. The bikes got in the way and we almost tipped over. That was funny. The bikes, the clothes, the rough ground, the possibility of being seen all got in the way of what we wanted. We rode back to Dan's house.

He offered me a choice of water or Gatorade when we got there. Mr. Suave. We stood in the living room, looking out over a meadow toward the golf course and Mount Bachelor beyond. He put his glass of water down and wrapped his arm around my waist. I put down my glass and turned to him, putting my arms around his neck. We bent toward each other and kissed, a long fixed kiss as though we were sealing a bond between us. It felt so good to hold him to me. I slid one leg up the side of his leg a few inches. What a slut. Then, in a show of modesty I would soon abandon, I slid my foot back down to the floor.

"Let me show you my room," he said. We managed to navigate the furniture side by side with our arms still wrapped around each other. When we got to his room we sat on the single bed and un-laced our running shoes. We embraced again when we stood up. Then we got undressed.

"This is like changing in the locker room," I said.

"It's good we've practiced," he said. With all our training we'd gotten in and out of clothes all the time. We faced each other naked. We embraced, barely touching, and then pressed tightly together. It felt like everything right in the world. He licked my breasts until I let out a little sigh. In another minute I pulled away and sat on the bed again, leaning back with my chest thrust out. I looked at his swollen penis and reached my hand toward it. Then I looked up at him.

"Do you have...?"

"At the ready," he said, and pulled open the drawer in the bed-side table. He lifted out a foil envelope, tore it open, and pulled out a condom. He unrolled it partway and put it on. I laughed.

"Can I admit something?" I asked.

"Of course," he said.

"I have one in my jeans pocket."

"We are careful people," he said and he was right. He knew I was almost certainly on the pill, though I had never mentioned it. Oral contraceptives helped women get in racing shape faster and extend their endurance.

"Actually I have two," I said. I burst out laughing.

"And," he said, "you are an optimist."

"I thought we might lose one."

"I think we're covered," he said.

He pulled me gently up from the bed and threw back the covers with one hand. I sat down again, slid further onto the bed and laid back. Dan climbed onto the bed between my legs and lay lightly pressing his chest onto mine. We kissed and I aimed him into me. We began our hip motions slowly and picked up the tempo together as we went along. Our muscles had not needed hours of training to know what to do. As I grew more excited I wanted more and more to wrap myself around him, to press him to me and never let him go. I climaxed before he did. It felt as though I had discovered the purpose of life and had, in fact, accomplished it. He was still hard and energetic enough to bring me more orgasms. Then he urged himself forward and I squeezed him as tight as I could. He burst forth in a flood that seemed to satisfy every wish and prayer within us both.

We lay together happily, his arm around my shoulder, my leg draped over his.

"I am deeply and profoundly in love with you," said Dan.

"I feel the same," I said. "Being with you feels like the only thing in the world that really matters."

"Do you think we're breaking training?" he asked.

"Why even think about that right now?" I said.

"I don't know what my coach would say," he said, "but I know what one runner said about sex."

"It's better for you than raw eggs?" I asked.

"He said that sex makes people happy. And happy people don't win races."

"So we're going to have to get unhappy in order to do well?"

"He didn't say that," said Dan. "But we're going to have to keep the sex down to two or three times a day."

"You're going to need a whole team of girlfriends for that."

"Even one girlfriend can be a lot of work."

"Some are worth it," I said.

The doorbell rang and we snuggled closer together. Dan pulled the covers over us. We settled down to ignore whoever it was. The doorbell rang again and we quietly giggled. The person knocked on the narrow window next to the door. Then we heard nothing for a while. We could have held each other like that for a long time, perhaps gone to sleep. Then we heard a key turn somewhere. Dan whispered that someone had found the key hidden in the barbecue on the back porch. He was obviously worried. I imagined that some-one mixed up in Ken Winterpol's murder could be coming for him.

Dan put his Jockeys back on and picked up a fat red fire extin-guisher sitting in a corner on the floor. He started to slowly open the door.

"Wait," I whispered, "let's go out the window." Escape seemed a much more sensible idea than confrontation. Dan locked the bedroom door and gathered up his clothes. I dressed like a rocket, skipping my bra and shoes, and Dan gently opened the window. He swung his feet out and made the short jump to the ground. He turned around to help me or catch me or something. "Just stand back," I said, and jumped. He motioned me toward the corner of the house away from the back door and then stepped the other way, fire extinguisher in hand, to peek in a living room window and see who was inside. I was afraid for him as he carefully poked his head around the window frame and looked in.

"Amy, come back," he called, the fire extinguisher now hanging from one hand. "It's my father." Then he walked in the door to the house, yelling in an excited voice, "Dad! Welcome home!"

Standing by the corner of the house in a t-shirt with no bra and no shoes, my fear shifted from attack by a murderer to fear of meeting Mr. Martinez looking the way I did. My hair and my clothes were rumpled. Dan was still in his underwear. Mr. Martinez would know in a moment what Dan and I had been doing. Well, I said to myself, any girl who thinks she can run a triathlon ought to be able to handle this.

I walked in the door. Dan was embracing an older man in a gray plaid sports jacket. "We thought you were a burglar," Dan said. They broke apart and the man, who looked very distinguished, gave me a friendly smile. "Amy," said Dan, "this is my father, Leon Martinez. Dad, this is Amy. And I am deeply in love with her."

"Amy," Mr. Martinez said, walking toward me rapidly with his hand extended. "I am very delighted to meet you." What a gentleman he was. What gentlemen they both were. Ninety-nine things could have happened that would have increased my embarrassment. They acted the only way they could have that didn't. I shook Mr. Martinez's hand firmly.

"How do you do, Mr. Martinez?" I said. "Dan has missed you. I worried about you before I ever met you. I'm glad to see you here and looking well."

"If you are special to Dan," said Mr. Martinez, "you are special to me. I look forward to knowing you better. But, if you don't mind, I've had a long journey. I'm going to go rest and read the mail." He gave me another smile, picked up a suitcase, and walked away down the hall. The minute he was gone I put my hands over my face and cringed. I'd put up a brave show but I was still mortified.

"I'm very proud of you," said Dan. He moved to embrace me but I backed away. "You acted as if you were at a debutante ball."

"Well at least I wasn't in my underwear," I said. I had to giggle. "Now you'll have to crawl back in the window. I hope the neighbors don't see you." When he had unlocked the bedroom door from the inside I went in and found my bra. "I have to get to work," I said. "Shut the door so I can finish dressing." I thought how strange it was, the proprieties I insisted on after we'd pressed our naked bodies together not twenty minutes earlier. We kissed in the front hall and Dan walked me to my car. We weren't going to kiss or embrace out by the street, though we wanted to. Shaking hands would be ridiculous. So we smiled and nodded and said goodbye. He watched me drive off. I was in love with Dan and I thought his family was wonderful. Maybe, in time, Candy would turn out to be right.

CHAPTER 26

The Prodigal Father

(Leon)

Dan knocked on the bedroom door and I said "Come in." I was propped up against the pillows at the head of the bed reading the mail.

"Amy is a very pretty girl," I said.

"Yes she is," Dan said, "and a wonderful person."

"If she is the one," I said, "No dejes para mañana. ..." Meaning, Dan shouldn't wait to make a commitment.

"Gracias, zapatero," he said, telling me politely to mind my own business.

"So Dad," he asked, "where have you been and what have you been doing all this time?"

"I will tell you and your mother all about that over dinner," I said. "But you and I need to have a discussion we could not have over the phone. What's happening with Ken Winterpol's murder?"

"The only person they've arrested so far is me," said Dan. "They didn't have enough evidence to arrest me, much less convict me, and the judge backed off on the warrant. Mom called him."

"God bless your mother," I said.

"All my life," said Dan. "Anyhow, they thought I knew something and they wanted to scare it out of me. In the meantime I've found so many people with a motive to kill Ken I don't think they could bring a case against Candy or anybody else without an eyewitness."

"And where is your mother?"

"Today's her golf day, remember? She may still be at lunch in the clubhouse. We could call her."

"No, we can wait," I said. "Let her enjoy her golf. Here is what I need to tell you. I've come to a decision. I will not say what I saw the morning of Ken Winterpol's death, though I am astounded at it. I will never see you as I once did. But if I am not loyal to my son then I don't know who I am. I need you to move out of the house. But you can rest assured that I will never say I watched you murder Ken Winterpol."

Dan looked as though all the blood in his body had drained to his feet. He stumbled to the one chair in the bedroom and sat down heavily.

"Dad, what are you talking about? I didn't kill Ken Winterpol. When I got there he was already collapsed on the deck."

"I saw the whole thing," I said. I was saddened that Dan would lie to me, murdering Ken Winterpol aside. "I went for a walk on the golf course that morning and I was across from the Winterpol's house. You were arguing with Winterpol. When he turned to go back in the house you picked up something from the fireplace and swung as hard as you could."

"And then the person that you saw took the poker he hit Ken with over to the fountain in the back yard and dropped it in, right?"

"Yes, but you looked down at Ken for a minute first. And you wiped whatever you hit him with on your shirttail while you were walking over to the fountain. After you dropped the fire tool in the fountain you walked away. I saw it plain as day."

"That's very important, Dad," Dan said. "You should tell the sheriff what you saw and describe the man you saw as well as you can." My son was glaring at me. I was surprised at his reaction.

"Are you trying to play some sort of lawyer's game with me?" I asked.

"What was the man wearing?" he asked.

"You had your khaki pants on and your dark blue jacket."

"That wasn't me, Dad. I was on my way back from running that morning. I had on running shorts and an Oregon sweatshirt. Candy can tell you that. So can the cops and the EMTs."

My whole body flinched. I managed to sit in one place on the bed, seemingly calm. I had steeled myself for weeks to have this conversation with my son. Was he elaborating on his lie? Or had I trusted my old eyes more than my heart and my head? I had so carefully considered the implications of what I believed Dan had done. But, in trying to bravely face the truth as I supposed it, I had deluded myself. A line which I always thought was funny and humble, came back to me as a withering critique: *When everything seems to be set to show me off as intelligent, the fool I always keep hidden takes over all that I say.* Neruda had it right.

The expression on Dan's face, the attitude of his body, and his whole presence convinced me of his honesty. His direct denial of killing Ken made me despair at my own lack of faith in him.

"Ken was already injured when I got there, Dad. Candy came out and helped me carry him inside. Did you see that part?"

"No, I didn't," I said. "I must have left before that happened."

"So all the time you were away, you thought I was the one who killed Ken?"

"I don't know how I believed that, son, but I did. I thought I was facing a hard truth but I see I was being stupid."

"And did you tell Mom I was the one who hit Ken?"

"No," I said. "She would have been so unhappy." Dan thought I was an idiot. I could see that. Losing his respect was a harsh blow.

"I'm very sorry to have ever thought what I did," I said. Dan slumped in the chair and seemed to be thinking.

"You have to tell Breuninger, the sheriff's detective, what you saw. I'll call him tomorrow and line up an attorney to be with you when you talk. I found a bunch of people who had a motive to kill Ken—people Ken had cheated in business, vendors he hadn't paid, old drug dealers he'd turned on, government officials he'd bribed. I'm still finding more. I wish I knew what all of them looked like. I've never actually seen any of them. Maybe one of them will look like the man you saw."

"You look like the man I saw," I said. "Isn't there a chance this detective will arrest you?"

"Probably not," Dan said. "The detective saw what I was wearing when he showed up at Candy's house. And furthermore, with all the other people who might have killed Ken the detective knows he'll never be able to convict me. I thought with all the possibilities I uncovered they might never convict anyone. But with what you saw, they might be able to."

"Can we agree you won't tell your mother I thought you were the man who killed Ken?"

"Agreed," Dan said, and he left to find an attorney to sit with me while I talked with the detective.

I heaved a great sigh of relief and thanked God for the way things had turned out. I was deeply, deeply relieved to be in my own house, in the room I shared with Elizabeth, and knowing I had a fine son who loved me. I fell asleep on top of the covers fully clothed. Elizabeth found me and woke me up.

The three of us cooked a celebratory dinner at home that night. Norwegian paella. It was my mother's recipe except the fish in it was cod. Elizabeth and I had wine while Dan nursed a beer from his friend's brewery. I thought with all his exercising he should eat more but he said he couldn't afford to stuff himself. He said we shouldn't talk about Ken or Candy until after I'd had a session with the detective. Dan and his mother had been curious for weeks about where I was and what I had been doing so I told them about my stay with Gabriel and Maria Isabel in San Francisco.

"Gabriel and Maria," I said, "have a small house in what used to be a workingman's neighborhood. It's on a hill overlooking the Mission District in San Francisco. Out my bedroom window I could see the Bay Bridge and the Golden Gate. The part of the Mission immediately below the house was far enough from downtown that it was only starting to be gentrified. It was still a poorer neighborhood with many immigrants from El Salvador and Nicaragua.

"Twenty-fourth Street in the Mission District looked like a street in Madrid. The signs were in Spanish and there were tall leafy trees shading the street. But it was still in America. In four blocks there were two Chinese restaurants and an Irish bar.

"Every day I walked down the hill from Gabriel's house to visit the Mission. The walls of the buildings were decorated with murals, like Mexican murals, though they had evolved a long way from Diego Rivera. They mixed in old Spanish, Mexican, and Aztec images with ideas from modern cartoons. One that amused me was painted around two windows. Between the windows were the heads of two round-faced sweet-looking young women, both brunettes but not necessarily Latina. The artist scattered roses beneath them and above them were two birds with fierce expressions. The Mexican muralists would have used parrots or eagles but this artist chose bluebirds. In a wavy band below the heads, and in fat round purple and pink letters, was a motto in English: *Once a Mission girl always a Mission girl.*

"Another mural I liked was on the second story above an auto-repair shop. It was a street scene where painted people leaned out of painted windows, mixed in with the real windows. Two men played conga drums and three people, two women and a man, paraded in carnival costumes. A crowd of people marched toward the street to join the party.

"So I have been thinking of painting a mural on the dining room wall here. I have been thinking about it, how to work in the doorways, the light switches, and even the thermostat."

"What's your subject?" Dan asked.

"There's a song that Gabriel plays called 'Oh Happy Life.' So that's the idea and the title of the mural, if it has a title. It will be the story of the three of us, not portraits but places we've lived and the things we've done. At the right Dan will be striding off on his own path."

"Headed for the kitchen," said Dan, "sounds happy."

"If you work slowly enough," said Elizabeth, "Amy may be in the picture with the rest of us."

"Oh, Mom" said Dan, "don't jump ahead like that." He was laughing but he clearly didn't want that discussion to go any further. He excused himself and went off to wash dishes while Elizabeth and I remained at the table. What a kind and generous son we had raised.

While Elizabeth and I drank our coffee I asked her how Amy came into the picture. I'd told her earlier how I'd met Amy, emphasizing how impressed I was with her and minimizing the circumstances in which we met. Nonetheless I did get Elizabeth to chuckle about it.

"She moved to Bend in June and works for a biotech company," said Elizabeth. "She's training for the same triathlon Dan is. She came to lunch a few weeks ago and I liked her immediately. I told Dan he should hang on to her."

"She looks like she could be related to Ken Winterpol," I said. "Is that part of the story?"

"She's his niece. She just found out. She was adopted and there was no record of her real father. It turns out her father is Ken's older brother and he lives in Prineville. He seduced a teenage girl and the girl died in childbirth. Amy thinks she's found her mother's parents in Prineville. Dan is arranging all the DNA tests."

"Well, I hope she's a nicer person than Ken was," I said.

"She certainly seems to be."

CHAPTER 27

Benham Falls

(Dan)

I went out at six the next morning to run the River Trail that would form the last leg of the triathlon. I was going to practice running a little slower on the parts of the trail where it would be impossible to pass anyone and pick up the pace after I went through a good passing spot. At that early hour I should have the path to myself. After the run I'd ride my bike from our house down to the starting place to pick up the car.

When I pulled into the Upriver Shell station to get gas I saw yet another gray truck. I was getting tired of taking pictures of gray trucks and was tempted to skip this one. There was a gas nozzle plugged into the truck but the driver had gone into the convenience store to get something. I parked my 4-Runner behind the truck and gave my credit card to the attendant.

While the guy was sliding my card into the pump I got out my cell phone and took a picture of the truck with the license plate in the middle of the frame. When I went to take another photo from the side I saw a logo painted on the door and the name of a business, Little River Masonry. Robbie Thoreson had a gray truck. I'd never thought of that.

Inside the store a tall brown-haired girl stood behind the counter, a little on the hefty side but with a beautiful face and piercing eyes. Every time I saw her I'd thought she should be able to get a better job. Robbie was at the counter paying for a burrito wrapped in foil and a big bottle of soda. He didn't look happy to see me.

"Robbie," I said. "How are you? Did you get the check from Winterpol's estate?" The girl watched us as I walked up to him and we shook hands, I with enthusiasm and Robbie with reluctance. He had a big hand that he held up to mine, closing his fingers only slightly. I knew this might be the last time we would still be friends. He might have sensed it as well.

"Yeah, I got the check. Thanks," he said. Then he smiled and acted friendly. He gripped my hand and pumped it. He could have crushed it. We walked out of the store together and over to Robbie's truck. I wanted to talk with him where no one else would hear us.

"Robbie," I said, "you need to get yourself an attorney, a criminal attorney."

"What do you mean?" he said.

"Ken Winterpol's murder. Evidence is adding up. It's starting to point to you." Robbie's face went white and his eyes opened wide. But he wasn't an athlete, a competitor, for nothing.

"Bullshit," Robbie said. "I had nothing to do with it. Ken had lots of enemies."

"Bringing up Ken's enemies would be part of a good defense. I can help you with that part."

"What," said Robbie, "do you want to be my lawyer?"

"No," I said. "I'm not even the right kind of lawyer. But with a good lawyer you might walk away from this scot-free. Or at least things would go easier."

"This is baloney," said Robbie. "You're the one the detective picked up. I heard about that. They haven't even talked to me."

"They don't have all the evidence yet," I said. "Now is your opportunity to get ahead of this. Get a lawyer."

"Get lost, man," said Robbie. He climbed into his truck and started the engine. He didn't look at me again before he drove away. Poor Robbie. When he calmed down he might have enough sense to call me. I hoped he didn't think he could bluff his way through this. Or maybe he'd try to run. I'd done my best for Robbie, or I'd done all I could think of at the time.

I picked up my gas receipt from where the attendant had stuck it in the door handle and I drove out. As soon as I was out of the gas station I called Breuninger's cell. I could hear conversation and a clatter of dishes in the background when he answered. It could have been any diner in the state of Oregon but something about the sounds made me picture the Red Rooster in La Pine. I could see Breuninger there with a deputy or two.

"I found the man who killed Ken Winterpol," I said. "I promise this is not one more suspect for you to look at. Unfortunately he's a friend of mine. His name is Robbie Thoreson. He was in Candy Winterpol's class at Bend High. Even dated her. I just left him at the Shell station in Upriver. I saw the gray truck I told you was parked by the bridge the morning Ken was killed. It's Robbie's truck. I'll message you a picture of it with the license plate."

"You mean it looks like the same truck," said Breuninger. "This is all you've got and you're telling me he's the killer? You're out of your mind."

"Winterpol owed Robbie money for the big fountain in the back yard and wouldn't pay it. The name of Robbie's company, Little River Masonry, was on the list of companies Ken was behind in paying. Winterpol wouldn't pay Robbie because he said Robbie built the fountain wrong. There's a painting of the fountain in Mrs. Winterpol's studio upstairs. Except it doesn't match the fountain. I thought Candy had taken artistic license. But that wasn't it. She painted the fountain to show what Robbie should build. But he built something different. He blew it."

"This is fascinating," said Breuninger. He didn't sound fascinated. "A few days ago you were telling me Richard Winterpol killed his brother."

"Richard had reason. He was a suspect. But Robbie Thoreson is the one who actually killed Ken. Remember the footprints in the grass from the back porch to the fountain and back? The ones that could only have been made the morning of the frost? Robbie and Ken walked out to look at the fountain and walked back to the porch again. Ken would have no reason to do that with anybody but Robbie."

"So they had a dispute," said Breuninger. "As you have demonstrated ad nauseam, there were a lot of people who had disputes with Winterpol."

"How many of them were tall young men with dark hair? My

father got home yesterday. Do you know why he left so quickly and didn't tell us where he was? He was walking on the golf course that morning and saw a tall man with dark hair hit Ken Winterpol. He thought it was me and he disappeared so he wouldn't have to say so."

"You sure you want to tell me this?" asked Breuninger.

"Yes," I said. "My father didn't see me. He saw a different tall man with dark hair. He saw Robbie Thoreson."

"How convenient," said Breuninger.

"Yes," I said, "and what was the new evidence that suddenly led you to arrest me? Wasn't it that the Winterpol's housekeeper told you that she saw me leaving the house under, let's say, dubious circumstances. That was a week or two before Ken died? I bet she volunteered this long after the sheriff's department had first interviewed her. Am I right?"

"Let's say maybe you are," said Breuninger.

"The point is when Paloma saw someone leaving the house she may have only seen him from the back. She saw a tall young man with dark hair. She thought it was Robbie Thoreson. She'd certainly seen him around when he was working on the fountain."

"So why didn't she tell us that when we first interviewed her?"

"I don't know. Maybe she didn't think Robbie had seen her. Maybe you didn't ask her the right question. Maybe she didn't want to get mixed up with the law. Or maybe, and this is what I think happened, she told Ken that Robbie had been in the house with Mrs. Winterpol and Ken told her to keep it to herself. He would take care of it. She was still following Ken's advice when you interviewed her, even though he was dead."

"Maybe," said Breuninger.

"Then when I came to the house later Paloma decided it was me she had seen fleeing the house before Ken died. It was too much for Paloma. She came to tell you what she knew."

"So Winterpol had a grudge against this Thoreson," said Breuninger. "But he didn't kill Thoreson. Thoreson killed him. It's a stretch but we'll talk to him. And I want to talk with your father."

"As soon as I can line up an attorney for him. I'll call you this afternoon."

"I hope you haven't found a new and more complicated way to waste my time," said Breuninger.

"I'm not trying to waste your time. I know I've found the answer. One more thing, though. You should probably look for a gun while you are talking to Robbie. Remember Ken had a revolver in his desk drawer in Lake Oswego? But you never found one in the Upriver house, did you?"

"Go on."

"I'll bet Ken had a revolver with him when he went to meet Robbie on the back porch. In a jacket pocket or tucked into his belt. Maybe he pulled the gun out to scare Robbie off. Keep him away from Candy. After Robbie bopped Ken on the head Robbie took the gun. He might still have it."

"Maybe," said Breuninger. "So where does this guy live?"

"If he's not in the phone book under Thoreson his business has got to be. It's called Little River Masonry. When we were in high school he lived on Bear Creek Road."

"Okay," said Breuninger. "We'll look into it."

"I'll send you the photo I took of his truck with the license plate."

Breuninger didn't say "thank you." I turned off the paved highway onto the dirt road that led to the River Trail. Then I pulled over and messaged the photo I had taken of Robbie's truck to Breuninger. That was a lot to accomplish already and the sun was barely up. Candy was off the hook. My father was off the hook. So was I. I felt badly for Robbie, though. I didn't think he had set out to kill Ken. Just confront him, maybe threaten him. Somehow things got out of hand. Robbie wasn't that bright to begin with. We had been teammates, even friends. We had other friends in common. Now I had turned on him. His life as a free man, trying to make his way in the world as best he could, was over. He would probably be in jail for a long, long time. He wasn't fundamentally a bad guy. Still, I told myself, Robbie had brought it on himself.

And I did have reason to celebrate. The district attorney might or might not be able to convict Robbie. But the DA would never be able to charge Candy or me or my father when so much evidence pointed to Robbie. I had accomplished the goal I had set for myself. We didn't have to look over our shoulders anymore.

It was a sparkling morning and I was looking forward to my run. I drove down the gravel road kicking up dust and getting the car filthy as usual. I turned into the picnic area by the river where we would drop our bikes during the race and start to run. I parked beside two ponderosas where the shade would last all morning, took a swig of Gatorade, and locked the car. I hid the keys under the edge of a log and leaned against the car to stretch.

I heard someone else turn off the road and looked over to see who would come here at this early hour. It would be a fisherman, an early tourist, or someone like me starting a run or a bike ride. It was a truck surrounded by a dirty cloud. But it was a gray truck and it was Robbie's. He had followed me all the way here and I never saw him behind me in the dust. He came straight in my direction and stopped abruptly next to my car. He jumped out and looked over his door at me.

"I need to talk to you," he said. He had one hand on the top of the door and the other arm straight down out of sight.

"Robbie," I said with a smile and a surprised look on my face, "you could have called me. Why come all the way out here?" I was hoping he'd ask me to help him find a lawyer. But he seemed too angry, too determined, to be thinking that rationally.

"Well, I want to show you something," he said. "Could you come here a sec?" There's something pitiably obvious about a not-too-bright man trying to be clever. There was no way I was getting one step closer to Robbie.

"Could you just tell me what this is about?" I said. "I need to start my run." He stepped out from behind the car door with the one hand held down behind him. He began to walk toward me. The time for talking was over. I spun around and ran through the brush toward the trail. I'd taken five steps when I heard a bullet go past me with a sound like a whip cracking. I sprinted up the trail, bent over like a fullback with the ball. Robbie had either fired a warning shot or he had fired for real and missed me. I ran for my life. I hadn't warmed up and hadn't been training for sprints. My legs wouldn't wake up. After twenty seconds I felt out of breath. I kept going as fast as panic could drive me. The trail curved through a pine forest with open spaces between the trees. I blessed the trees and the curves, anything to prevent Robbie from getting a good clean shot. No fancy stuff, I told myself, just run.

My body and my training told me to slow down to a pace I could sustain. But fear and reason told me to sprint. I didn't look behind me. No matter what I saw, what could I do about it? I hadn't thought that playing amateur detective would lead to Robbie trying to kill me. My life was so much simpler a short time ago.

The trail came back to the river and began to rise. There were rapids in the river and I could hear the falls up ahead. Benham Falls were not a straight drop, like more picturesque falls in the Cascades. The falls consisted of broad rapids and narrow chutes choked with white water. The water bounded off the walls on the way down and sprang up into the air, forced up by huge rocks and ledges hidden under the surface. The trail climbed steeply beside the falls, twisting around trees and approaching the edge of the cliff to provide views of the crashing water. I was recovering my breath and getting into a pace that felt close to familiar. I was thinking I must be putting distance between me and Robbie. I hadn't heard any more shots.

Then my foot slipped on a root, jammed on a rock, and went out from under me. I fell forward. I caught myself on the ground and stood up. A stabbing pain rose from my ankle. This was going to set back my training. Also, and this was my second thought not my first, it would allow Robbie to catch me if he hadn't given up. I looked down the hill and caught glimpses of him through the trees. He was looking at the trail, not at me, and he was holding a revolver backwards with his hand wrapped around the middle of it. I supposed it was easier to carry that way. I thought he would reach me in about a minute. I hobbled behind a tree where he wouldn't see me as he approached.

I thought if I stayed there, or edged back around the tree as he went past, he might keep going and never see me. But if he did see me I'd be doomed. He could turn and shoot me at his leisure. The best plan, desperate as it was, would be to lunge at him, pushing off with my good leg, and bump him over the cliff edge down into the river. It was that or wait to be shot. I stood as tall and straight as I could behind the tree, rehearsing my moves in my mind, and being interrupted every few seconds, by a plea from somewhere else in my brain, to think of a better plan.

Robbie came huffing up the trail. His breathing was labored but steady. He had found his pace. When he came abreast of me I leapt out at him with a practiced rugby tackle. I slammed him hard and ignored the pain in my ankle while I kept driving him toward the water. Bumping him would not be enough. I knew we would go into the falls together. He still had the gun backwards in his hand and he tried to hit me on the head with it. He didn't have the right leverage for a good hard blow and the handle of the gun only hurt a little. I buried my shoulder further into his stomach and continued to push. We stepped, almost ran, toward the top of a steep embankment and somersaulted together over the edge.

In midair, Robbie hit me again with the gun, this time on the back. It didn't hurt that much. I prayed he wouldn't get the gun pointed at me. I could feel him trying to bring his hands together behind my back so he could turn the gun around. But we hit the water hard and the currents threw us around until we quickly lost any sense of direction. My legs whipped around out of control. My arms were still wrapped tightly around Robbie, my hands clenching each other. I pressed my head into him in hopes that his body would shield me from being knocked unconscious by a rock. I didn't try to reach the surface. Keeping us both underwater worked to my advantage. Robbie, still breathing hard from running up the hill, would run out of breath before I did. In fighting to reach the top of the water he wouldn't even try to protect himself from the rocks. Eventually he would suck a mouthful of water into his lungs and drown. If I could just hold on until the river brought us to calmer water he would be dead or be so flat-out exhausted I could subdue him.

I wasn't sure either of us would make it. My body wanted to panic and it was trying to talk my brain into panicking too. I kept thinking no matter how bad it was for me, it was worse for Robbie.

The current stopped its violent lunging when we reached the rapids. Robbie wasn't moving and I kicked myself up to the light. I gasped for breath, breathing as rapidly and deeply as I could. There were rocks and white water all around me. I pointed my legs downstream, lay on my back, and swept my arms to slow myself down, still pushing air in and out like a calliope gone wild. After dodging a run of big rocks and getting pushed under water twice I floated into a big pool where the bank on the left came down to the river. I pulled for the shore. The current weakened as I got closer. Finally I sat in shallow water, gathering my strength and watching the river. In a standing wave that came out from behind a rock I saw Robbie go by, barely under the water and looking peaceful, as though he had paused in a side stroke to look at me. One arm was stretched beside his head, reaching upstream. His other arm rested along his body, reaching toward his hip. His legs stretched out, relaxed and together, as though he were gathering them for a perfect kick.

I had an impulse to try to save him, to swim after him, pull him to shore, and give him CPR. We had known each other most of our lives. He was basically a good person who had made mistakes. Wasn't trying to rescue Robbie the right thing to do, no matter how unlikely it was that I could reach him, much less save him?

But surely Robbie was dead already, or if not technically brain-dead, he soon would be. And I was beat. It would be a futile gesture to go back in that river and I would probably die myself. Beyond that, what was justice? Robbie had tried to kill me. I let my chance to save Robbie go by.

I sat there in the shallow water longer than my recovery dictated, glad to have escaped death. I stood up slowly and shuffled out of the river. My ankle was tender but not as bad as I'd thought it would be. I walked to my car, leaning on a stick to take weight off my injury. Then I called Breuninger to tell him what happened. He said I should wait there and he would come. The sun slowly dried out my clothes and I did some stretching and exercising while I waited. My ankle was getting better but I wasn't about to run on it.

I wanted to call Amy to tell her I was fine. But she had no reason to think I wasn't fine. So I didn't call Amy. I called Candy.

CHAPTER 28

The Color Black

(Candy)

Dan told me that he and Robbie Thoreson had gotten into a fight and Robbie drowned at Benham Falls. I asked Dan how he was so sure Robbie killed Ken and he took me through all the things that pointed to it—the non-payment for the fountain, the gray truck, the footsteps on the lawn. And the idea that Paloma may have told Ken—rightly or wrongly—that Robbie was having an affair with me. I didn't like that part and I didn't confirm or deny it. Dan is such a Boy Scout that he didn't ask me. Anyhow, the clincher was that Robbie had tried to shoot Dan with a gun that looked like the one Ken had at Lake Oswego. It was presumably the one the sheriff could never find at the Upriver house. Robbie had taken it when he clobbered Ken.

Breuninger came to my house the afternoon Robbie died. Dan arranged for Tod Morgan to be there too. I said up front that I had known Robbie in high school and that knowing him from before was part of the reason we hired him to build the fountain. I said he had built it wrong and showed the detective the painting in my studio of what it was supposed to look like, with a flat rock at the top and the water streaming out beneath the rock like a spring. Robbie built it with a little pool at the top, kind of a puddle, with the water bubbling up in the middle of it. Ken wouldn't pay him and I guessed that Robbie came to demand payment. I said I supposed they got into a dispute and Robbie hit him. But I said I was only supposing.

Breuninger asked me straight out whether I was having an affair with Robbie.

"What are you thinking?" I blurted out. Then Morgan told the detective I wasn't going to answer any more questions like that and he asked whether the detective thought Robbie killed Ken.

"It certainly looks like it," said Breuninger, "but let me ask you, Mrs. Winterpol, would you be satisfied with that conclusion?" I was surprised by the question. I thought the law worked to find the truth, to dispense justice as well as it could. But Breuninger sounded like his company fixed furnaces and followed up with a survey.

"Well," I said, "it's hard to think the Robbie I knew in high school would kill anybody. But people change. I certainly couldn't say it was impossible. And I certainly don't have anybody else I think did it."

"So if we stopped looking for other suspects that would be okay with you?" Now he was sounding political. I could see where he was going. If the sheriff and the district attorney announced they were closing the investigation they didn't want the victim's widow protesting their decision in the press.

"That would be okay with me," I said. "If you think Robbie Thoreson killed Ken then I do as well. And I want to be done with this whole thing. I want to grieve for my husband and move on."

Dan came over to my house multiple times after that to discuss progress on Ken's estate. What I wanted was to take him upstairs and get his clothes off. And he knew that. But he had his girlfriend now and there wasn't room for me. Little Amykins would never need to know about Dan's fling and I'm sure Dan figured it that way too. He knew his course and he stuck to it. He didn't play around with amorous glances in my direction and hints at maybe yes and maybe no. And Amy trusted him. I admire people like that but I don't think I envy them. Life has only so many opportunities for happiness and you better grab the ones that come along.

One thing Dan asked me to do before the estate was settled, and he said it was legal to do this, was to sell off Ken's interest in the Vandevert Brewing Company. Dan introduced me to Sean Wray, a friend of his who wanted to buy out Ken's loan. Sean worked for Facebook and had plenty of money. At Oxton's recommendation, I suggested a price and Sean took it. After the sale Oxton became the brewpub's attorney. Another feather in Dan's cap.

Pete Slesnick, one of the brewpub owners, was about to marry a girl who worked for him named Ginny and they invited me to the wedding. That was nice and friendly of him, the way people still do business in Bend. I don't think that would ever happen in Portland.

Dan, Amy, and I went to the outdoor wedding at the High Desert Museum and Amy sat in the middle of us during the ceremony. The reception and sit-down dinner inside the museum were served by the best caterer in Central Oregon, owned by a husband and wife who had been high school sweethearts and built their business up from nothing. Beer, wine, and a full bar. Ginny wore a strapless white sweetheart wedding gown that she filled to the brim. The dress had a three-foot train that came off so she could dance. She and Sean looked extremely happy. It was a nicer wedding, with more people, than my own—better than any wedding my parents would ever have been invited to.

Dan and Amy wanted to leave early because the triathlon hadn't happened yet and they were still in training. But Dan arranged for me to get a ride home from Frank, Pete's partner and the brewmaster. I made it worth his while.

I gave Paloma a raise and a serious talk. I didn't care what she'd seen or hadn't seen, what she'd thought and hadn't thought. If she ever breathed a word to the sheriff or anyone else about what went on in my house then she would be out of a job and her mother would be out of the country. Paloma was a legal resident but her mother wasn't. I'm sure she wished she'd never told me about her mother. It will help Paloma remember to keep her mouth shut.

I am painting as much as ever. My agent says she is sorry about Ken's death but it's been a big boost for my career. People love a good story to go with the art. My name keeps showing up in the news. My agent keeps asking me for new developments to put on Facebook and Twitter. When there isn't anything she makes something up, some comment I supposedly made. She told me to make my paintings more somber for a while, with suggestions of violence if possible. I showed some to Leon and he said they were awful, so far from my best work. He suggested I do a series of explorations and experiments as we did when he tutored me.

"See what you can do with black," he said, "or more black than you are used to, like Juan Miró." He said it might satisfy my agent and expand my range at the same time. It's working. The paintings are better and I'm more interested in painting them.

The first week in November I am going to an artist's colony in Chile, where summer will be starting. It's next to the Andes so it's a little like here. I'll see some new landscapes and challenge myself to paint them. Once I am down there I am going to offer to pay Leon's way to come join me. This is something I can do for him that he would really like. Elizabeth can come too if she wants.

If I stay down there I'll miss the ski season at Bachelor. But I can afford to fly north for a week or two to wherever the snow is good in Utah, Colorado, or Idaho. People that Ken and I met skiing have already invited me to come stay with them. It will be a short ski season for me because I'm expecting a baby in March. I decided to keep the child because I think the experience will deepen my art. I can afford people to help me take care of it. The child is Robbie's or Ken's. It started too early to be Dan's. I hope it's Robbie's. Robbie was better looking.

Too bad about Robbie dying but, really, it worked out for the best. I will never have to worry about what he might say, not that I couldn't have handled it. I thought that if Robbie told people we planned Ken's death together they would not believe him. Why would I be interested in Robbie after all I had with Ken? What future could Robbie have thought he would have with me? What interest could I have in a slow-witted, unambitious man? How deranged would I be to imagine Robbie could get the best of a clever man like Ken?

Robbie did almost ruin everything. He came to the back door when Ken was in the kitchen and demanded payment for the work he had done building the fountain. That was the plan. I had told Ken that Robbie hadn't built the fountain right and we shouldn't pay him. I stood behind the door from the living room and heard the argument out on the deck. When Robbie started to back down I opened the door and asked Ken what was going on. Ken turned around to answer me and Robbie hit him from behind with the poker.

When Robbie saw that Ken was still breathing he should have hit him again. Instead he ran off like a coward. I went back to the living room and waited for Ken to die. Then, unexpectedly, Dan arrived and helped me get Ken into the kitchen. I didn't really want to implicate Dan. I didn't know what to do. So I played the little wife, overwhelmed with shock and grief, as any normal wife would be. Dan tried to act all lawyerly and professional with the sheriff. That was the good luck I had that day. My lawyer was telling me not to speak. Dan got me a real lawyer and then spent days finding other people who might have killed Ken.

It was just the right time for Ken to disappear. I liked living in luxury—nice houses, nice clothes, trips to the best resorts. But Ken spent money to impress people, to have access to them. I wanted money for new sights and new experiences. Sometimes what we wanted overlapped but that was happening less and less. I wanted more freedom.

Ken didn't die because he hit me. His beatings gave me leverage. Beating me didn't fit with the image he wanted to have of himself—a strong man making his way in society. What man, confident of his masculinity, beats a woman? What country club would admit a man knowing the man beat his wife? What organization would want him on their board? What leading citizen would want to be seen with him? Beat me, Ken, I thought, and I own you. One call to the police and all your dreams unravel.

I didn't think Ken would kill me, even if he found out about Robbie and me. But there was the possibility. He would hire some poor stooge to do it. But rather than kill me for my transgressions he would more likely make me pay in some other way. Like collecting a debt—if one way of inflicting pain didn't work, he would keep trying. He might hurt Leon or Elizabeth, or maybe Dan. They were the only people in the world I would lift a finger to protect.

My looks are going to go. They haven't gone yet but they will. And Ken was already starting to get as bored with me as I was with him. He didn't even know it yet. There was a lot of money I would have as a widow that I would not have as a divorcee. I realized, I think, that I could be happier with Ken's money than with Ken.

When we hired Robbie to build the fountain I wasn't thinking about killing Ken. I just thought Robbie might be useful. Then everything came together. You don't know how a painting is going to turn out when you start it. You have ideas and you add to them. The next brushstroke in my life hit me like an inspiration. It was bold. It was black. It was the death of Ken Winterpol.

I would like to keep Dan around. But he is besotted with that big-shouldered girl. Nothing has ever gone wrong in her life and nothing ever will. As for me, I have the house to myself and plenty of money. I will never depend on anyone else again.

The Race

(Dan)

My last three weeks before the race would be different. The physical training would get easier. I would save the energy and endurance I needed for the race. It was called tapering. The mental problem was, and it was almost every racer's problem, I wanted to do exactly the opposite, to train harder, to keep building on the earlier training.

Tapering gave me too much time to think. I wished I could have kept Robbie from shooting me without killing him. If I just hadn't sprained my ankle I could have outrun him. Robbie would be in a courtroom instead of a grave. I should have trained better or harder. It was an illogical way to think but I kept coming back to it.

After I called Breuninger from the river it only took the sheriff's department a few hours to find Robbie. He washed to shore in a slow stretch of the Deschutes a mile below Benham. His body was beat up and it wasn't clear at first whether he'd died from injuries or drowning. The autopsy said drowning but he might have died from injuries if he hadn't drowned first.

Breuninger accepted my version of what happened at Benham Falls, at least provisionally, and they didn't charge me with anything. The DA didn't want to close the investigation until they found the gun that Robbie had when we fell in the river together. The divers said they couldn't search for the gun unless the water master dropped the volume of water going over the falls. The water master didn't want to reduce the flow until the farmers downstream were done irrigating for the year. A judge decided that finding the gun in August versus finding it in October wasn't important enough to justify hurting the farmers. I'm sure they'll find it, though they haven't found the bullet Robbie fired at me and maybe they never will.

Oxton decided to open an office in Central Oregon and they offered to accelerate me on the partner track if I would set up the office in Bend. We agreed I'd start two weeks after the triathlon was over. I had brought a lot of business to the firm without even working there and convinced Greg I could bring in more. We even got the business of the guys I met on the golf course. Greg offered to pay me more than I'd been making before, though it would be cheaper to live in Bend than in Portland.

I stayed away from Candy. She didn't call me and that was fine. My father said she needed to get past some difficulty with her art. He hoped he helped her. Candy always seemed to get help when she needed it.

With all the time I wasn't spending training I thought about Amy. We agreed to keep our romance at a simmer until we were done with the race. We had both invested too much time in the off-road to let love, as important as it was, distract us. We didn't discuss what would become of our bond after the race. It was too important a subject, at least to me, to touch lightly on without an openness to our deepest wishes and reservations. Pairing myself with Amy seemed like the best idea I'd ever had. Was she ready for that kind of commitment? Was it even fair to ask her? She was twenty-three with many roads open to her. There was so much I wanted to talk about with her. I couldn't wait for the race to be over.

The thing about tapering was you cut back on the amount of training you did but you still went to the highest level of intensity. So our workouts became shorter. Because the race would end in Upriver I ran the last four miles of the race course every other day. I got to the top speed I would use in the race and the top heart rate I expected to reach. I'd started wearing a heart-rate monitor only a month before. Mitch said not to get too attached to the numbers it reported. It was more important to know how my body felt during the race. Still, the heart rate was one more piece of information and it would help keep me from pushing too hard.

In swim practice I concentrated on the start of the race where

I'd want to go fast to get out ahead and where I wouldn't always be able to take a breath when I wanted to. I practiced dolphin kicks and swimming underwater. My whole swim workout was under a thousand meters.

The bike course broke naturally into three segments. Amy and I did one of them, up and down, for each training session. This made us more familiar with the course and it honed our responses to the twists and turns of the rough trails.

We kissed at the end of our first ride and moved into an embrace. I wanted Amy and I wanted her to know it. I could tell she felt a similar urge for me.

"Would you like to join me in my carriage?" I asked.

"You're such a romantic, Dan," she said. "We are both sweaty and covered with dust and you want to make love in the back seat of a Toyota when anybody could show up at any moment. No thank you. You're sexy but you're not that sexy."

"I was thinking," I said. "We still have days off from training. Why don't I get us a nice hotel room Saturday night? We could spend the night together."

"A lovely idea," said Amy, "but now is not the time to let love distract us. Just think about all the sex we're going to have when the race is over."

"That'll make me run faster," I said. But Amy was right. We'd worked too hard on our training to let it slip. Love, sex, and any thoughts about our future were going to have to wait.

The day of the race we met at the finish line in Upriver to catch the bus that took the racers to the starting line by the lake. We loaded our bicycles and our small bags of supplies into a truck that would take them up there as well. We'd have about forty-five minutes by the lake before the race started to put our bikes in racks where we could find them after swimming, get our race numbers painted on our arms, and get to the water's edge for the start of the swim.

A man in a yellow vest stood up in the front of the bus once we got going. "I'm here to wish you well in the race and remind everyone about some of the rules. This is for your own good so listen up. No moaning or groaning or smart remarks. Which brings me to the first rule. You need to treat your competitors, the officials, volunteers and spectators with fairness, respect and courtesy. No abusive language or conduct. Let's all behave ourselves and have fun. That means, by the way, that if you're going to change clothes in the transitions you find a way to keep covered up. I know you all have gorgeous bodies but public nudity is a rule violation." The man who was speaking was big, in his fifties with a balding head and a big barrel chest. If he'd ever been a racer he'd been a Clydesdale.

"Remember you can't get assistance from anyone other than a race official. If your bike breaks down and a spectator or another racer helps you, you'll be disqualified. You cannot abandon your bike and just walk," he went on. "Bring your bike with you."

I'd been studying the rules for months. Everyone had, or should have. I gazed lazily out the window. I stopped listening until he said something that didn't sound like more rules.

"Don't Drown. Don't Crash. Don't Walk. And remember what the elite triathlete did when he met a talking frog during a tough training run." The man paused while our eyes and minds came back to him.

"The frog said to the man, 'If you kiss me I will turn into a beautiful princess.' The triathlete picked up the frog and put it in his pocket.

"After a while the frog shouted from the pocket. 'If you kiss me I will turn into a beautiful princess and I will be your girlfriend for a year.' The athlete considered this for a moment but left the frog in his pocket.

"In another mile the frog shouted out again. 'If you kiss me I will be your beautiful girlfriend and we'll make mad passionate love whenever you want. Take me out of this stupid pocket.'

"The triathlete, who was just about to increase his pace, looked down toward the frog, 'I am training too hard to have a girlfriend,' he said. "But a talking frog could be fun.'"

That hit home with all of us. We'd let training rule our lives. Amy smiled without looking over at me. There were some on the bus, though, who were so wrapped up in themselves that they missed the story altogether.

Amy and I stowed our bikes next to each other and recited detailed descriptions of where we'd put them. Coming up from swimming, anxious to get on with the race, we might lose whole minutes trying to spot our own bikes in the sea of other bikes and people. We got our race numbers painted on our arms. Mine was seventeen. Amy's was fifty-three.

I thought I swam well. My start was strong but under control. My stroke was steady. No one passed me after the first buoy and I even passed a few other guys before the second one. I had told myself I wouldn't put too much stock in getting ahead. Mitch kept telling me to run my own race. But I was still pleased to be outdoing some others.

When I practiced swim-to-bike transitions on my parents' lawn I must have looked insane. I came out of the house in my tri-suit, the one-piece shorts and top I would wear for the whole race. I got into my wetsuit—a crazy thing to do on dry land on a hot day. I soaked the wetsuit inside and out with a hose. Then I started a stopwatch, got out of the wetsuit as fast as I could and did everything I would have to do in the actual race—put on my bike shoes, strap on my heart rate monitor, and wrap a belt around me with Band-Aids and snacks in it. I ran my bike to an imaginary starting line, leapt on it, clipped in my shoes, and rode off twenty yards, stopping abruptly at the same tree every time to check my stopwatch. I did this over and over. After I got past making mistakes, I thought I was going through the transition as fast as humanly possible. But I kept practicing and took another ten seconds off my time. It wasn't aerobic or even strenuous. So I kept practicing during the three weeks before the race and took another five seconds off.

When we came out of the lake I remembered where my bike was and got through the transition without a hitch. As soon as the bike started rolling I drank some water from a bottle strapped to my bike. I ripped the end off a GU packet and squeezed some calories and caffeine into my mouth. I had five more packets for the rest of the race.

I had barely gone two hundred yards along the bike route when some guy passed me. He had number thirty-nine painted on his arm. Maybe biking was his strong suit and his swimming was not as good as mine. Either that or he was doing a terrible job of pacing himself. If pacing was his problem I'd probably see him again, gasping along the trail. But being passed had an effect on me. After a quarter mile my heart rate was higher than it should have been. I was pushing too hard. I could feel it in my body as well as see it on the monitor. I backed off a little. I had to keep focusing on my pace to slow my heart rate and line up my effort with what I was used to.

When the trail started uphill I had the course to myself for a while. Amy and I had ridden up this hill five times. I kept calm while climbing at the pace I was familiar with. Halfway up the hill I heard another racer behind me. This was discouraging and I focused harder on keeping the pace I knew I could sustain. I kept waiting for the words "on your left" before he passed me but the words didn't come. The guy was right behind me. The rules said he should either stay seven meters behind my front wheel or pass me within fifteen seconds. Technically he should be penalized for not doing that. His position was illegal because, at least on an even road, the air currents I generated would let him keep up with me using less effort. It was called drafting. But the trail was uneven enough and our speed was slow enough that I didn't think drafting was an issue. Still, it was annoying to have that guy there, and wonder when and whether he was going to pass me. He was in fact, getting an advantage from my setting the pace. He didn't have to think about that. He just had to follow me. I was tempted to speed up and slow down just to throw him off. But that would waste energy. And Mitch's reminder came back to me again: "Run your own race." The guy behind me fell back as we went past the aid station at the top of the hill. There were race officials there who would have penalized him. I could see now he was a big guy in an orange shirt.

A woman in the aid station handed me a paper cup of water and I drained it. I took advantage of the level spot to push two more GUs into my mouth.

I hated the thought that Mr. Orange would be thundering down the trail behind me on the next leg. But my training and Amy's tutelage kicked in. After a few turns on the downhill the guy couldn't keep up. I was better at this part than he was. I actually had fun carving the turns and jumping down the rocky parts. I anticipated the moves ahead and flowed down the course, braking to a crawl only ahead of the switchbacks.

In the middle of the downhill leg was an enormous snowmobile parking lot where I could ride fast and straight with only one hand on the handlebars. I was feeling good. My heart rate was about where it should be. I took long pulls from the water bottle I had with Hammergel in it. That would give me energy to finish the biking and start the run. I could swallow another GU or two while running. I passed one guy in the parking lot who was fixing a flat tire. It was an expensive bike and I thought he must have new tires on it.

That could be me, I thought. I stifled the fleeting joy of having one more competitor behind me. I saw no one on the second downhill leg of the bike section. The field was spreading out. A quarter mile before the next transition I got ready for the run by standing up on the bike to stretch my legs. Then I dropped into a low gear and pedaled faster than I otherwise would. My legs would still feel like lead when I started the run but they would feel better and get in the groove quicker if I got them ready.

The transition to the run was in the dirt parking lot by the river where Robbie had taken a shot at me. The memory was only a momentary distraction. I put on the brakes and pedaled at what seemed a glacial pace to the bike rack. Racers could get a penalty for not slowing down when they entered the transition area. I took off my helmet and strapped it to the bike. I drained the bottle of Hammergel and left it on the bike, along with my bike shoes, still clipped in to the pedals. From now on my liquids would have to come from the aid stations. There was a plastic rug where our running shoes were laid out by race number. There was even a bench to sit on.

Starting up the trail did remind me of Robbie's pursuit and my desperate attempt to sprint from a cold start. This time I was warmed up and held my pace back until my legs could adapt themselves from the bike and get into a rhythm. My eyes focused on all the uneven spots on the trail, on the roots and rocks. No sprained ankle this time around.

Two hundred yards past the place where Robbie and I tumbled into the river I saw a runner ahead of me. It was a thrill to think I'd caught up to someone. Still gaining on him, I realized it was number thirty-nine, the guy who had passed me on the bike right after the swim. He had lasted pretty well but he was starting to give out. He hadn't paced himself as well as I had. We were coming to a place where a wooden bridge went over the Deschutes and there was plenty of room to pass. I timed it perfectly. "On your left," I said loudly, trying not to sound too self-satisfied.

The rest of the dirt trail into Upriver was wider, flatter, and less bumpy. The very last part would be on paved streets and bike paths. We could all increase our speed a little if we had the energy. But it was important not to increase speed too much. We had precious little energy left. At the same time, motivation and concentration were as important as ever. Our bodies were hurting. Certainly my hips were hurting in places they had never hurt before. This was the time to think about how long we would have to live with the results of this race. Any lessening of effort would haunt us for years. The last half mile I felt I could do more and I accelerated slightly. I was risking a breakdown but it paid off. I kept my pace until the end.

The second I stepped on the finish line I checked my time and slowed to a walk. Finally coming to an end felt weird. My body sent me worried signals: *You should be running! What's wrong? What's changed? What's happened?* It was like the chief engineer on a steamer wondering why the captain suddenly wants to stop in the middle of the ocean. My legs were afraid to relax for fear they would be asked to rev back up again. It didn't take long, though, for my breathing to slow and my heart rate to come down. After a few minutes of walking around my legs stopped aching. My hips still hurt. It might take a few minutes or it might take weeks for that pain to stop. I wouldn't let it worry me now.

Other racers were ambling around the area reserved for them, slowly cooling down, drinking Gatorade or chocolate milk and nibbling on sports bars. There was an unspoken bond among us. We felt, I think, that we knew each other in a very deep way, even though we might have very little in common outside of the race. I even felt a warm regard for number thirty-nine when he stumbled in. He had made a mistake but he had finished. The last few miles must have been torture for him.

I asked what the winning time was and shifted my brain into arithmetic mode. I had finished twenty-one minutes behind the leader. I had beaten my twenty-five minute goal with four minutes to spare. I'd always known it was an arbitrary goal, based only on an estimate of how well I might do. But if I hadn't run my best possible race I would never have beaten the goal.

My body needed water. It needed carbohydrates. I drank plain water and chomped through a bagel with mounds of peanut butter on it. I ate as I walked around with a sort of stupid grin on my face, finally having time to get curious about my fellow racers. I counted ten guys who had finished ahead of me. The winner was a guy from Canada I had never heard of before. I wished an Oregonian had won it but a winner coming all the way from Alberta raised our estimation of the competition and, indirectly, our estimation of ourselves. Racer thirty-nine, the fellow who passed me on the bike and I had passed on the run, was from Texas. He'd come to Bend a week before the race to get used to the altitude. He said his heart and lungs might have adapted but his brain had not. It was a good learning experience, he said. He'd only raced on smaller hills at lower altitude, often when it was baking hot. The more temperate air in this race had led him to overestimate his endurance. It wasn't an excuse. It was simply an analysis of where he could have done better. If there was something I could have done better I was blind to it at this moment. I would think of possibilities later, though I might start imagining them. I needed to talk with Mitch.

Amy came in twenty-five minutes behind me and only fifteen minutes behind the first woman. I was happy for her and jealous at the same time. I had trained longer for this race than she had. Yet her time was closer to that of the leading woman than mine was to that of the leading man. She had outperformed me.

All the energy Amy and I had left went into smiles and high fives. We had accomplished something important. We had worked on it together and encouraged each other. I wanted to put her up on a podium and tell everyone how well she had done. I told so many people from Juniper about her time she told me to stop. I was embarrassing her.

The race people brought our bikes and our plastic bags to the finish line. Amy packed up her car to drive back to Bend. I was sad to see her go but we could not embrace for very long in front of all those other people. What I really wanted was to take a shower and collapse into bed.

Amy and I would see each other again that evening. We would meet other racers at a Bend brewpub that had a big beautiful lawn. We would slowly sip our beers and watch the sun set over the Cascades.

I didn't want to sit on my bike for another second so I walked it home.

"How was the race?" my mother asked.

"I did well," I said. "Amy did very well too."

"Do you want anything to eat?" she asked.

"Later," I said. "I'm to go lie down for a while." I took my shower, got into bed, read one page of O'Brian's *The Wine-Dark Sea*, and fell asleep.

In my dreams, Amy and I were married.

Acknowledgments and Sources

My heartfelt thanks to three very smart people—Tom Parker, Deon Stonehouse, and Jim Thomsen—whose excellent recommendations on earlier versions of *Suspects* have made this a better book. Many thanks also to my early readers, Pat Phillips, Barb Tate, and John Charles Tippet for their excellent improvements.

For insights into triathlon training, craft brewing, and the effects of blows to the head I am very much indebted to Mike Lynch, Bob Bruce, Tom Neuhold-Huber, Dr. Kent Preston, Denise Del Cole, Dr. Taraneh Razavi, and the many excellent brew pubs in Central Oregon. Still, any erroneous representations are my fault alone.

Above all I am grateful to Joan Haynes, my wife of forty-three years, without whose encouragement there would be no book.

The ingestible sensor technology ascribed to the book's fictional Greenwood Biomedical company derives from products developed by Proteus Digital Health (www.proteus.com).

The following books were essential to the writing of *Suspects*.

Abernathy, Jon. *Bend Beer: A History of Brewing in Central Oregon*. Mount Pleasant, SC: The History Press 2014

Beevor, Antony. *The Battle for Spain*. London, England: Penguin 2001

Bergman, Paul, and Bergman, Sara J. *The Criminal Law Handbook*. Berkeley, CA: Nolo 2013

Coffman, Ron. *Diary of a Northwest Cop*. Bend, OR 2013

Finch, Michael. *Triathlon Training*. Champaign, IL: Human Kinetics 2004

Friel, Joe. *The Triathletes Training Bible, Third Edition*. Boulder, CO: Velopress 2009

Haynes, Ted and McNellis, Grace. *Vandevert: The Hundred Year History of a Central Oregon Ranch*. Menlo Park, CA: The Robleda Company 2011

Lopes, Brian and McCormack, Lee. *Mastering Mountain Bike Skills, Second Edition*. Champaign, IL: Human Kinetics 2010

Paperno, Jill. *Representing the Accused*. Eagen, MN: Thomson Reuters/Aspatore 2012

Plantinga, Adam. *400 Things Cops Know*. Fresno, CA: Quill Driver Books 2014

Slosberg, Pete. *Beer for Pete's Sake*. Boulder, CO: Siris Books 1998

About the Author

Ted Haynes graduated from Dartmouth College and the Graduate School of Business at Stanford. He has studied writing with Nancy Packer and Hillary Jordan at Stanford and with Tom Parker and Donna Levin at UC Berkeley. He serves on the board of the Waterston Desert Writing Prize and is a member of Mystery Writers of America, the Pacific Northwest Booksellers Association, and the Central Oregon Writers Guild. He lives in Central Oregon in the summer and on the San Francisco peninsula in the winter. See www.tedhaynes.com for more.

CPSIA information can be obtained
at www.ICGtesting.com
Printed in the USA
LVOW12s1714090517
533889LV00001B/95/P